THE WORK OF ARSEN DARNAY

Publishers Weekly called THE KARMA AFFAIR "An intriguing novel."

Library Journal called it "Brilliant . . . fascinating . . . a gem of a book!"

And now Ace Science Fiction is proud to present the latest novel by the man they're talking about—a chilling tale of a man who wanted only to be free, in a world where that was just too dangerous to be allowed:

THE PURGATORY ZONE

Other Ace Science Fiction titles by Arsen Darnay:

The Siege of Faltara

The Karma Affair

The Splendid Freedom

THE
PURGATORY
ZONE

ARSEN DARNAY

SF
ace books

A Division of Charter Communications Inc.
A GROSSET & DUNLAP COMPANY
51 Madison Avenue
New York, New York 10010

The Purgatory Zone copyright © 1981 by Arsen Darnay

An ACE Book

First Ace Printing: July 1981
Published Simultaneously in Canada

2 4 6 8 0 9 7 5 3 1
Manufactured in the United States of America

THE PURGATORY ZONE

THE TIME VAN

1

The people of Zen Richelem knew that Shannon was a hard-core retrograde from the very first, the day of his arrival.

He came one morning in the spring, arriving at the station by bus. He was the only passenger alighting at the station's stop that morning. As the bus pulled away, it revealed him standing beside a duffel bag. The bag turned out later to be half full of books. He was a slender man in his early twenties dressed in cotton shirt, khaki slacks. He had dark hair, a narrow face, and hard empty eyes that spoke of retrogression. Those seeing his arrival mingled their thoughts and reached out collectively to welcome him to Richelem, but they encountered the brittle-bouncy barrier of his mind instead, a zone of stiffness and resistance, and the people knew the truth about him ever after. Shannon stared after the bus for a moment. Then he turned to look at Richelem with an expression that combined distaste with boredom. Finally and with a shrug, he lifted his bag and approached the encavation.

Benny Franks said after dinner that Ravi Shannon was a

heavy case, not your ordinary retrograde. "He will end up in the Time Van one of these days," he said, "and I don't exactly look forward to that day; it will be nip and tuck at best, and chances are that we will lose him. He is one of the worst cases I've seen." Those who heard Benny's comment shushed him and cried For Shame. But Benny turned out to be right in the end, although three years passed before the matter came to a head.

Shannon did not distinguish himself in any way during that period, either in positive or negative ways. He was taciturn and on occasion aggressive, but no more so than other retrogrades who had been sent to Richelem for therapy. Like so many other retrogrades, he was obsessed with the past and spent inordinate amounts of time in studies, by himself. He read and reread the books he had brought with him, mostly ancient volumes of history. He was a diligent worker, a worker with a knack for things mechanical.   Then at one of that station's periodic festivities, he became aware of Lilly Waterburg—and she of him. They had met before, of course, but nothing had ignited. This time their chemistries reacted, and a love affair bloomed out of that collision of personalities. In due time, and despite Waterburg's gentle resistance, Shannon petitioned the station's council requesting permission to marry.

With the exception of Shannon, everyone at the station knew or could predict that Shannon's petition would be denied. And having watched him courting Lillian, the people expected trouble at last. The trouble came one evening in summer, the evening set aside for the July meeting of the Richelem council.

Early that morning, Shannon and Lilly and a group of others had been sent out to pull maintenance on a tilling, seeding, and harvesting machine that Richelem had dubbed "Colossus" for its size. Colossus had been sent to the station as part of a program to test new agricultural implements in what was still known as the Arizona "desert" in those days.

Colossus was a giant millipede of a machine, a veritable reptile of steel and glass and plastic with a hundred-meter frontage. Colossus was too large, unwieldly, and not very efficient at that—although everyone admired the photosynthesizing cell-mass built into the ungainly device by way of musculature and motive power. Colossus needed constant maintenance—which gave those who worked in labs and in administration jobs a chance of tinkering like engineers.

Shannon liked these maintenance details. He had been trained for the transportation sector and professed a love for it. Before his sudden transfer to agriculture, he had been a navigator of jumbo jets on a random route between Asian settlements. He liked machines. He liked to putter. Like so many retrogrades, he felt a greater kinship with the inanimate than the animate world. He always volunteered for maintenance detail—and especially when Lilly came up in the rotation. He was in love with her. He sought to be alone with her as much as possible. He tried to talk her into having sex with him out in the fields and orchards—but, of course, she never yielded, not in the fields nor yet inside the Richelem encavement. She loved him sincerely in the man-woman mode, but she could never yield to him, not while he was retrograde. But he never tired of trying, and field trips were full of opportunity.

He went out this day in a surly humor. Riding on the flat-bed airlift lorry, his legs dangling, seated beside Lillian, he said nothing all the way out. He brooded about the evening ahead. The station council was scheduled to meet that evening and had promised to give a decision on his marriage petition. The decision was predictable and so was Shannon's reaction. Only Lilly Waterburg persisted in a stubborn hope that her man would suddenly shed the attitudes of many years and quietly accept a two- or three-year postponement. Quietly and cheerfully. She did not deceive herself, but in those days she was practicing one of the primary virtues—faith, hope, and charity. Her thing was hope.

Out in the field at last, Shannon threw himself into the

work as if bent on distracting himself. He disappeared into the bowels of Colossus, emerging only at rare intervals, sweaty and greasy. He still said nothing to anyone, but his hard and empty eyes sought out and rested on Lilly Waterburg for long moments at a time. She felt his gaze, but she did not respond to him. She knew quite well what he was thinking. Ravi Shannon faced yet another ordeal this day, but this one he would have to face alone.

After the work was done that evening, and the party prepared for the return—people were loading tools and empty lubricant drums on the flatbed airlift lorry—Shannon pulled Lillian aside and asked her to walk with him instead of riding. She agreed to this. The party got underway. All the others settled around the edges of the truck, the engine came on, the lorry lifted, the jet began to hiss, and they were off, moving slowly. Shannon and Lilly walked behind, side by side. Shannon still would not talk, but his thoughts were gathering on his face like thunderclouds. Soon the lorry moved out of view ahead, down into the valley. The people riding on its rim sang last week's compositions; between songs they laughed and joked.

Tall fields of maize alternated here with freshly plowed land on either side of the path Lilly and Shannon followed. Artificial rain misted over the plowed fields from levitating pipe grids (another new invention Richelem was testing). Down in the center of the valley stood the station, a community of four thousand souls. Richelem was a massive structure, a flattish, earth-covered dome; its hexagonal skylights were the color of bright copper that evening, reflecting the setting sun. In the far distance to the east a line of hazy mountains marched across the horizon. High above them looped the irridescent outline of the Phoenix-Albuquerque skyway, presently nothing but a tracery of ions.

Shannon broke his long and stubborn silence at last.

"Well," he said, sounding on edge, "what will you do if they say no to us tonight?"

Lilly walked along; she did not answer. She was slender

and dark like Shannon, but she had big, pool-like eyes. She was looking at the distant sky. She gazed at the faint, pale shadows of gathering Teilhardian phantasma—the traces of a dozen communities dotting the valley—and she tried to read the meaning of these twilight patterns. She tried to find a confirmation for her hopes, but the phantasma were pale and shadowy tonight. They did not sparkle with the anticipation of fire that sometimes predicted new conversions.

"Tell me," Shannon said. "What *will* you do?"

She looked at him now and saw the sharp focus of anxiety in his eyes. Then she looked away again.

"I will go right on living, Ravi," she said. "Just like you will. There isn't anything we can *do*. You always want to *do* something. We'll just have to wait. They won't give an unconditional 'no.' They never do."

"We could run away," he said.

She looked at him with genuine astonishment. Then she laughed. Her laughter tinkled sweet and clear, like a glass bell. Her white teeth gleamed. She reached over and touched Shannon's arm; she touched and stroked his arm.

"Oh, Ravi," she said. "What a thought. Where would we go? No matter where we went—even if they approved our going—why—our records would follow. If our council thinks that we should wait, every other council will think the same way."

Shannon made a disgusted sound. "I don't mean another station. And I don't mean another work assignment, either. I mean *away*. Clear the hell away. I want to disappear. Go south, go to Brazil. Anywhere. We could live by ourselves. We might find others. In the jungle. Somewhere."

Shannon meant those vast tracts of land in South America under ecological quarantine for a century or more—wild places where the tentacles of civilization were not allowed to reach. Shannon often talked about the wilds, musingly, with a faraway look in his eyes.

Lillian laughed. "You know that that's impossible."

"Why?" he asked. *"Why!?"*

"Honey," she said, "this is the Kibbutz Zone. People don't *do* things like that—except in Youth Camp novels. And it's a crime to settle in the quarantines."

Shannon's face darkened, and the muscles of his cheeks grew stiff. He suffered the age-old frustrations of the retrograde. Those of the community able to penetrate the brittle-bouncy barriers he held around his mind sometimes experienced the power of his inner rages—and inside Shannon they sometimes encountered what the lore called 'wailing and gnashing of teeth.' Shannon's mind was like that now, choked by a feeling of impotence. But he controlled the feeling.

"All right," he said, sounding brisk and tight. "What about another time zone?"

"You mean—you're not serious, are you? You mean the Time Van?"

"That's right," he said. "The van is back in Catosward. Just in time," he added. He smiled without a trace of genuine mirth. "As if they knew," he said. "If they say 'no' tonight, we take a jeep and drive to Gatosward. Tonight. Right away. We both pick the same time zone. We go across. And to hell with all these people. You love me and I love you. So to hell with their permission."

Lilly did not answer. She walked along, eyes in the sky, practicing the virtue, hope. The lore asserted that genuine hope was hope at a time when everything looked hopeless, and everything looked hopeless to Lilly Waterburg just now. He had raised the subject of time Time Van himself—hence the Teilhardian phantasma in the sky showed no trace of near-future conversion . . .

Meanwhile Shannon stared at her; he stared at her profile. She looked serene to him, very calm and very well collected, and hence he felt what he had felt a thousand times before in similar circumstances—a hollow emptiness in his guts, a tightness in his throat, the urge to scream and shout and break things.

"Come on," he said, barely controlling himself, "say something, Lilly. Goddamit, say something."

"You make it very hard," she said.

"Why?" he cried, incensed. "Because I don't take this bullshit lying down? Because I agitate? Because . . . because I'm a retrograde. That's it, isn't it?"

She gave him a shy look; then she averted her eyes.

"I've never minded that," she said.

"Come *on*," he cried. "You do too mind. If I were like the rest of you, if I were forever tripping out on some strange stuff up in the sky, your worries would be over. I'd be sweet and pliable like everyone else. If they yelled squat, I'd squat. If they yelled dance, I'd dance. You wouldn't have to worry about me. You'd never be embarrassed about me."

"I've never been embarrassed," she said. "That's unfair. There is nothing wrong with retrogrades. Some of the greatest people used to be retrogrades."

"Used to be," he said. "*Used* to be."

"It's just a matter of time," she said. Hopefully.

"Time," he cried. "Listen, Lilly. I'm nearly twenty-seven. It should've happened ten years ago. Earlier."

Shannon meant his Maturity Trip in outer space aboard the *Saffire* at age sixteen. He had failed that and earlier tests, but he did not know that consciously. Awareness of the test itself would have destroyed its effect, of course, and having failed he did not know. He thought that the difference between a normal human and a retrograde was something physiological, the response to a certain drug, a matter of genetic endowment.

He recalled the last day of his trip just now. It was a jumble of images—flickers of which Lillian sensed. He recalled standing by the observation port on his last afternoon in Space, gazing down at the earth, having just drunk the milky drug. He remembered staring down at the greenish-whitish world below, waiting, waiting. The other youngsters all around him oohed and aahed in ecstasy. But Ravi Shannon hadn't seen a goddamned thing, not a goddamned thing. No visions, no colors, no Teilhardian phantasma whatsoever. He had had a splitting headache. Sick to his stomach. Wanting to puke.

Lilly touched his arm again. She felt the wash of his emotions as a faint but nonetheless real pain.

"Don't," she said. "Please don't start in on that again. The more you rail, the angrier you'll get. And the angrier you get, the harder it'll be for you—later."

"What if I don't care?" he asked, his tone all edge, all challenge. "What if I like being a retrograde?"

"You *do*!" she said. "You don't want to be like us. You like to stand there, all alone, defying the whole world."

"That's not it." He gestured wildly with his arm. He shook his head. He seemed to search his mind for the right phrase, the right way to express what he felt about himself and the world he had been born into—without being asked to do so, no sir, never asked—as he so often asserted. Here he was. And he didn't like it.

"I—Lilly, you don't understand," he said. "I don't understand you, but you have no idea what I'm really like either. We're like strangers, you and I. I sometimes wonder . . ."

He sometimes wondered how she could love him or how he managed to love her. He forgot for the moment that they weren't always arguing. Love bloomed in magic moments, other moments, when they walked these same paths beneath a sky filled with stars and swarming satellites. Breathless embraces—but short of fulfillment. Just the other day she had taken and kissed his hands, one at a time, gently, murmuring: "Love you, intelligent hand."

"I don't know," he said, remembering those soft, pecked kisses. He stopped. She also stopped, a step ahead of him. "This world," he began, gesturing with his arms. "I've never lived anywhere else, but . . . somehow it isn't right. Everything is too—too goddamned *nice*. There is no conflict. Nothing ever happens. I want—I don't know. Battles. Action."

"You've read too many books," she said. "And you're trying to live in the past."

"The past? Let me tell you something about the past," he

cried. "It was dynamic. It was like nature. Competition.
Strategy. Great things went on. There were movements,
there was struggle. People had a chance to test themselves.
The winners were winners, the losers were losers. God!" he
cried, suddenly carried off by an emotion he had felt so often
before when pondering the wonderous panoramas of the
history of the world, "Lilly, it was beautiful back then.
There were heroes and villains—not these billions of zombies all staring up into the sky by night looking at God knows
what. I don't mean that you're a zombie. You know what I
mean. I may be a retrograde, but at least I have my feelings. I
long for something—I'd like . . . The truth of it is, I don't
really want to be a nicety-nice, sweetness-and-light citizen of
a global culture doing what they tell me, serving the global
Kibbutz, squatting when they say to squat, dancing when
they say to dance. I want to be me. I want to build my own
world."

Lilly listened to all this, thinking of Battles and of Action.
She thought about her own struggle to maintain the fading
hope she felt about this man, this man she loved despite his
retrogression. She though about the tests he longed for so, the
heroes he thought were in the past. She thought about the
past.

"Vileness and crimes," she said.

"What did you say?" he asked.

"I said, vileness and crimes. You've read too many books
and you've got yourself believing that the past was wonderful, romantic, exciting. Nothing but Youth Camp all through
life. But it wasn't like that at all. It was 'vileness and crimes,'
as Bartelson has written. Someday you will see the shapes
yourself, and then you'll understand."

"I'll never see them," he asserted.

"Oh, yes you will," she said.

"Maybe I won't," he said, staring at her with something
like malevolence. "Maybe I'll just go away. If they turn us
down tonight, if you refuse to go with me, then . . . " He
lifted his hands, he tilted his head, he raised his eyebrows.

They stood alone between two fields. Water spurted from levitating grids to either side. The air was odorous. Lilly turned to Shannon, her expression serious. A dark smudge marked her forehead at the point where she had touched her skin in adjusting her glistening black hair.

"Time vans are for the desperate," she said. She was aware that she was trying to influence his decision, which was illegitimate, but she loved him too much for strict obedience. "You're not desperate," she said. "You're just willful and obstinate. All that business about love—it's just a sham. You don't love me, Ravi. I swear to God, you don't. You're in love with Ravi Shannon—and your fantasies. You've never tried," she said, knowing that she skirted on the edge of the forbidden. "Not even once. And I'm starting to think that you never will."

She turned abruptly, her long hair flying, and she marched off, leaving him standing. She began to run after a step or two. Shannon hurried after her. He caught up with her and arrested her by grabbing her arm.

"Lilly. Listen, Lilly."

"What is it?" She had brought herself under control again. Her face was serene, bland and devoid of expression—maddeningly calm from Shannon's perspective. He hated her now as much as he usually loved her. He saw her face as if it were a wall; her eyes had turned opaque. She looked at him now the way strangers did when he complained or groused—trumpeting his retrogression, advertising what he was. An old suspicion rose in him, a suspicion he sometimes voiced.

"It's no use," he said, sounding bitter. "You're just like all the rest. You're over on your side of the barrier, and I'm on my side. You want me to come across to you, but you'll be damned before you cross over to me. You're all the same— you, and Benny, and all my so-called friends. I'll bet that you have assignments from the council or whoever. Somebody took you aside and told you to cure Ravi Shannon. Make him come out of his shell. Make him kneel down before the great

Lord Kibbutz. Make him bow his head, make him join the herd. That's what you are working on, aren't you? Benny has his angle, you've got yours. Benny uses friendship, you use love. Let me tell you something, Lilly. As for love, if you really loved me, you would've let me make love to you a long time ago. Real love. Not just sighs and kisses and promises about some tomorrow that'll never come—not until I buckle down and roll on the ground and do whatever it is you zombies want me to do, which isn't anything I can even guess. But let me tell you this, it won't work, I assure you, I mean to tell . . . ."

He stopped talking.

Lillian had broken through. She had succeeded in overcoming the psychic darkness he spread about himself like a pall. She had begun to smile with all the power of her soul behind her smile. Her hope was now a blazing fire.

Shannon saw her smile. In his mind he called it That smile. A shiver passed over him. Lilly's face radiated, glowed; fine, misty, elusive light shimmered around her head, a nimbus of radiance. Her eyes had become like pools of brilliance—huge, deep, and compelling. The sunset world, the fields, the hiss of moisture, the smell of earth—all this disappeared. Shannon felt as if he whirled. He was dazzled and overcome. Drawn to her as to a magnet, he embraced her, suddenly sobbing and beyond himself. He kissed her greedily, eyes closed, hiding from her shine.

Quickly and expertly she broke away from him at last. She had established her own independence again, her own point of serenity.

"I'll talk to you after the Council Meeting," she said. Like Shannon, she was a little out of breath. "I know they'll make the right decision. For both of us. Trust me."

With that she turned and ran off down the path swiftly, never looking back.

Shannon stood. His skin tingled. Lillian had a special gift of intensity which she rarely used. Shannon had experienced it before. He had seen her like that on two or three earlier

occasions over the last year or so—a dazzling apparition of
energy and light and overpowering love. When she appeared
to him like that, he lost control over himself and his emotions. Now he stood as if entranced, caught by an odd
astonishment.

After a while he broke out of his trance. He shook himself,
shedding a peculiar excitement. Then he set off after Lillian,
down the grass-covered path, toward Zen Richelem, where
everyone was gathering for the evening meal.

2

The people of Zen Richelem were keenly and almost
painfully aware of Shannon's upcoming test that evening.
For that very reason, and by way of compensation, the mood
in the dining hall was almost festive, almost joyous. Jokes
flew from table to table like tossed canaries. Laughter rolled
across the hall. The food steamed richly from the pots. Only
Lillian and Shannon sat inside invisible cocoons of silence.
Her cheeks bright with color, Lillian ate with her eyes down
on the surface of the table; she took no part in the general
merriment. Shannon resembled a dark and slender hardness;
he was like a skinny-black column of stone among the
others—and the rest were blooming poppies swaying in the
breeze.

Shannon left the room as soon as he had bolted down his
food. He went off to brood in the men's dormitory where he
shared a room with Benny Franks. The merriment ceased as
soon as he left the dining room. Silent expectation fell on the
community; all there thought about the evening ahead; all
wondered how Shannon would react; all wondered how they
would perform if Shannon opted for the Time Van. Few ever
ever taken part in such an exercise, and those who had
recalled such times as an ordeal.

Benny expressed the general opinion as chairs began to scrape. "It can't be helped," he said to those around his table. "If he goes into the Van, we must simply hope for the best." Those who heard him nodded. "I'd better go and talk to him," he added. "I think it's only fair to give him a little warning. Even if he decides to go, I'd just as soon that he go calmly. We will have more of a chance to get him back that way."

Once more the people nodded. They knew that warning Shannon had its risks, but Benny could do it gently. He had become Shannon's closest friend over the year. Moreover he was the station's therapist and skilled in such matters. And they agreed with Benny's reasoning.

Shannon was opaque to telepathics, a symptom of his retrogression, but he also felt the mood of tension in Zen Richelem. He stood at the window of his room and stared down at the padded courtyard enclosed by three dormitories and the dining hall. He often stood there after hours watching the people moving back and forth, or playing volleyball, or simply talking in clumps around the yard's periphery. The dome shimmered faintly above; the night-lights were coming on. The people started streaming from the dining hall, and he scanned them as they appeared spying for Lillian. He glimpsed her at last. Walking alone, she disappeared into the women's dormitory without looking up to Shannon's window. Benny came walking out, chatting with Ludwig Riser, his most able chess opponent. The two men came toward Shannon's building and disappeared from view.

Little by little, the courtyard cleared. Benny and Ludwig had come upstairs. Shannon heard them talking in the hall. Then people appeared in the courtyard below. They crossed from the woman's dormitory to the dining hall. They carried baskets full of flowers, and seeing them, Shannon frowned. Somebody would be marrying again, he guessed, and he guessed that it would not be Lillian and him. *No, sir,* he though, *not by a long shot.* Then he experienced a surge of irrational hope. *What if . . .* he thought. *What if . . .*

He began to pace up and down the room, from concave window to the door and back again, passing beds on either side, his bed and Benny's. He heard Benny chatting in the hall, chatting and laughing and chuckling. Benny had a moist, soft, infectious laugh. The laugh reminded him of doctors and of bedside manners. *Benny could charm a god-damned snake. He could make a goddamned boulder laugh. Like Lillian.* Shannon knew why the council had put him in the same room with Benny three years ago. The doctors watched him day and night.

He wished that Benny would stop chortling out there and get his fat ass into the room. Shannon had a question for the doctor: Whose wedding were those people preparing in the dining hall?

He threw himself down on his bed, exceedingly nervous and itchy. Lillian had avoided him out in the fields. She had mesmerized him with her radiance, she had thrown him into a state of emotional paralysis. But she had avoided answering his questions. What a maddening creature she was. He loved her so—and yet he also hated her. If it hadn't been for her, he would have left this time zone a long, long time ago . . .

Another zone . . . A world of real, of pulsing people. With passions and ambitions. Like the old days. He stared up at his books, three rows of books on shelves hung from the wall at the foot of his bed. He stared at them and fell into a gloomy musing about the past, about his books, and about the ways of Kibbutz and of retrogrades.

He had a nice collection of what the others insisted on calling "fossils"—books from the time before the Change, books produced by men and women of the so-called unre-generated era—about that era. The books he had brought with him were a fraction of those that he had read during his Youth Camp days and in the transportation sector—a time when he had consorted freely (if secretly) with other retrog-rades.

Deep down he was certain that his sudden transfer to the Arizona agricultural sector had been ordered because he had made too many of the wrong kinds of friends. Retrogrades were seldom left alone to join, to form communities. Despite lofty disclaimers, the Kibbutz Zone had its own biological imperatives. Retrogrades were harried; they were pecked. Gently but relentlessly, they were nudged toward a choice—to join, to grovel, to conform. Or to leave.

Shannon felt now that such a choice was imminent. Unless, of course . . .

Time passed. Shannon brooded. And people around Zen Richelem listened and waited, wondering about the outcome of tonight's events.

Benny came into Shannon's room at last. He was a huge, fat man. Blondish red hair streamed from his head and cheeks. His mustaches were stiff and bristly and the color of old rust. His green eyes twinkled now. Benny still smiled about a thing that Ludwig had said.

"Well!" he said. He sank down on a chair before a tiny desk on his side of the room. Feet apart, hands on his knees, he took a look at Shannon. He was a gifted telepathic, and as he concentrated on the retrograde, he moved into the "feel" of Shannon's psychic state. Shannon seethed under some pressure now, like a volcano. It was a bad sign, by and large, and Benny regretted coming. He suspected that he might not be able to control the conversation, but now it was too late for retreat. Shannon was bursting with a question.

"Who is getting married?" Shannon asked.

"Married?" Benny said.

"Yeah. I saw people hauling flowers into the dining hall just now."

Benny thought about that for a moment. Lillian had requested that wreaths and garlands be made—just in case that all went well. Shannon might be cheered to learn that, Benny thought, but he had no inclination to discuss Lillian's "Project Hope" just now.

"Clancy," Benny said, picking a likely name. Clancy was engaged to marry a girl from a nearby station.

"Clancy?" Shannon asked.

"Clancy Roberts. He works in communications."

"I don't think I know him."

"Don't you? Oh, you must. He is marrying a girl from John Baldwin. Our people are just helping out, I think."

"How old is Clancy?" Shannon asked.

"Oh," Benny said, "twenty, twenty-one."

Shannon made a face. "Everybody marries," he said bitterly. "Some marry and divorce, like you. Everybody marries except me. Ravi Shannon hasn't got it. He is just a retrograde. When Ravi Shannon needs a little sex, he trots down to the toilet and locks himself in. That's how it is. I'm twenty-seven, Benny. Twenty-seven. I've tried to get married twice before this time. Once in Paris: her name was Claudine. Too young, they said. Once in Vladivostok: her name was Marishka, and she was a retrograde like me. You know what she did when they turned us down? She ran off and went into a Time Van. Good-bye. I asked Vladivostok Central to let me know what zone she'd picked. I wanted to go after her. Do you know what happened?"

Still smiling, Benny shook his head.

"They refused to tell me," Shannon said. He nodded to himself. "When I made a stink about that, they took me out of transportation and stuck me into agriculture. That's how I came to be under your psychiatric care, good doctor. And guess what, Benny? If they approve of Lillian and me tonight, I'll—I'll eat this goddamned rug. So help me God." He pointed to a multi-colored throw rug by his bed.

"I'm through," he said. "I've had it up to here. No more. Sorry folks. Hate to spoil your therapeutic plans. No cure for Ravi Shannon. He is a chronic case. Just put him down the throat of a cannon and shoot him out into funny cosmic space. Good-bye. Good riddance. I don't even know why I'm still here. No. I take that back. I want to spit Janet Brood between the eyes before I zoom off into infinity."

Benny Franks chuckled moistly and shook his head from side to side.

"Ranting and raving," he said. "Ranting and raving. What if they approve tonight? Have you ever thought of that?

What if they told you to get married and gave you a big double across the way?'' Benny gestured across the courtyard. "Settle down to make a baby. What then, Ravi? Would you be happy finally? Would you stop your ranting? Is that all you really want?''

"No,'' Shannon said. "But that'd be a start.'' He stood up, walked to the window, and looked down at the empty courtyard. He wondered why the place was so deserted, unaware that people all across the station waited, waited, and waited. Many of those with advanced abilities followed his conversation with Benny Franks; and many were concerned about the turn that the conversation was taking.

"It would be a start,'' Shannon said. "The next thing after that—I want to get back into transportation again.''

"You could work in transportation right here at Zen Richelem,'' Benny said. "You never applied.''

"Sure. I could drive a cabbage truck.''

"That's transportation.''

"But I'm an airman, Benny. I've been navigating jumbo jets since I was twenty. Sometimes I've filled in as a pilot. I don't want to jockey trucks on fifty-kilometer runs.''

"Okay,'' Benny said. "Let's suppose that you applied for a transfer back to the air service. Let's suppose that they approved. Would you be happy then?''

"What are you getting at?''

"You know exactly what I mean.''

"You mean that I will never be happy?''

"That's right,'' Benny said. "You won't be happy until you are like the rest of us. All of your ranting and raving is just a big complaint about the fact that you're a retrograde.''

The word echoed in the room. Shannon was clearly taken aback. He had been pacing up and down the room, but now he stopped and looked at Benny. People in the community understood Benny's approach. Benny was trying to jar Shannon out of his rigid, angry mood, but judging by the erratic pulses of feeling Shannon sent into the psychic ether, the tactic wasn't working.

"That's the first time you have told me that," Shannon said.

"Nevertheless, it's true."

"It may be true," Shannon said, "but I find it odd that you have never bothered to discuss my 'status' before. Not directly. You're trying to prepare me, aren't you . . . Well, aren't you?"

"Prepare you?" Benny asked. He had been clumsy. The conversation was going awry.

"That's right," Shannon said. "You know damn well how the council will vote. You're trying to let me down easy. Well, you don't have to bother. I'm prepared for the worst."

Shannon's words belied his true feelings. He had entertained a secret hope until this moment, but the truth dawned in him suddenly now, and he felt the certainty of upcoming defeat. The telepathic image of his feelings brought to those who listened the picture of a dark abyss.

Benny shook his head. He had lost control but could not stop. "I don't know how they will vote," he said a little lamely. "I haven't the faintest idea. Nobody told me anything—that's what I mean. But I would be lying to you if I told you that you have much of a chance. You don't. If I were on the council, I would have to vote against you, Ravi. You're dense. You don't want to get the message."

"What message?" Shannon asked. His voice was small, suppressed. He asked his question from a depth of weakness, from the bottom of a gorge of loss and impotence.

Benny went on, suddenly reckless, feeling that Shannon was already past the breaking point.

"The message?" he said. "Look, Ravi. You're living in the very best of times. Ever. And in the best of time zones. We've made the breakthrough here, in the Kibbutz Zone— and nowhere else. We're at peace. War is a distant memory—something we play at as youngsters. No more disease, plenty of food. You work thirty weeks a year, the rest of your time is yours. Most of us do what we like to do. Most of the time. The ecology is fast recovering. And yet you can't be happy. That's the message. You want to marry Lillian, but after you get your fill of sex, you'll just start bickering again. That's the message. The council has to think about her too. Has that occurred to you? You're dense, dense as a rock.''

Shannon stood there for a moment. Then he sat down heavily.

"So it's all decided, isn't it?'' he said. "It's been decided all along. My petition—I shouldn't have bothered. One big charade. I've been pegged all along—since my Maturity Trip. That's the trouble with this perfect world. No god-damned freedom. Not a shred. No room to move, no place for the human spirit. And nothing ever happens, everything is all planned out, well in advance—''

"Wait a minute,'' Benny interrupted. He held up a huge, well-padded snow-white hand. "You've had that sort of freedom; you've had your fill of it. You didn't like your Youth Camp days—war, crimes, politics. You've been there, I've been there, we've all been there. You didn't like the freedom that you had. You stayed out of all the fun and games.''

"How did you know that?'' Shannon asked.

"It's in the record,'' Benny said. "You know exactly what I'm talking about. I've heard you talking about Youth Camp to others—the great hero that you were. Nonsense! Fantasies. You couldn't wait to leave. And now that you are in the adult world, you refuse to put aside that childish stuff. And until you do, a hundred marriages to a hundred Lillians won't help you.''

There was a momentary silence, heavy with the echo of words.

"So that's it,'' Shannon said. "So it's supposed to be my fault. My fault that I'm a retrograde? Is that what you are telling me?''

"Nobody is a retrograde unless he chooses to be one,'' Benny said.

"Chooses!'' Shannon cried. "I've never heard of such a thing! I went up into orbit like everyone else. Did I refuse to go? No, I didn't. I took the drug like everyone else. I stared out of those ports like the others. My eyes were bulging out, that's how hard I stared. I did not refuse to look. I wanted to see. But nothing happened.''

Benny did not respond to this. The transformation of a person from retrogression to the New State was and would remain largely a mystery, and drugs were not the major but the minor part of the process. Shannon had consumed the drug like every other youngster, but he had failed an earlier and more profound test without even knowing that he'd failed. Such was the nature of the experience, and no one who knew about it would ever tell a retrograde. It was something you had to experience rather than hear about.

"Well,'' Shannon said, "what does choice have to do with it?''

Benny sighed moistly. He made as if to speak but broke off and shook his head. He had blown this conversation and meant to say no more.

"What were you going to say?'' Shannon asked.

Benny shook his head again. "There is no point in talking,'' he said. "It's obvious that I'm not getting through to you. And ultimately you don't need me. You have to solve your own problems—and in your own way.''

For a long moment Shannon stood and stared down at the station's bulky therapist. Pulses of panic and of rising rage moved from him outward in the form of flickering images. The muscles of his cheeks had begun to twitch. Benny and the others felt the bursting of a dam. The worst was about to happen.

"All right,'' Shannon said at last. "All right. I knew it all along. All of you—my so-called friends! All you think about is how you can succeed with me. Well, sir, I don't want your goddamned therapy. I'm not sick. Thanks a lot—but I'm a man!'' He hit his own chest with a fist; he hit himself so hard that it hurt, but he felt such a violence within that he barely felt the pain. "I can take care of myself. And you can shove your therapy cross-wise up your ass, my friend. Friend!

God-*damn*! Some friend you are! And she is just like you, that *bitch*." He hit his own chest again in a veritable convulsion of rage. "That goddamned *bitch*! She knew it too, all along! Goddamn her eyes."

He stepped up to his bookcase and began to throw his books down, in bunches, one by one. Books tumbled down on his bed and from there to the floor. Shannon kicked at them. They skidded toward the door. His rage grew. He picked up books and tore them in his fury; paper and canvas ripped. But even these actions failed to satisfy him. He rushed toward the door, but Benny rose quickly to block his way.

"Let me out," Shannon cried.

"Where are you going?"

"Never mind that. Out of my way."

"Calm down," Benny said. "You can't have fits every time you hear the truth about yourself."

The statement demolished the last vestige of Shannon's self-control. "Get out of my way," he shouted. Then he lunged at Benny and shoved him out of his path.

Shannon ran out of the room and clattered down the stairs. He crossed the padded courtyard at a run and rushed through an alley separating the women's dormitory from the married quarters. The alley led to a small, tiled quadrangle enclosed by structures. A fountain played in the the center of the enclosure. The light from two windows in one of the lower buildings touched the troubled water in the fountain's basin, and the water seemed to boil like molten copper.

In the men's dormitory, Benny Franks sighed moistly. He took a handkerchief from his pocket and dabbed beads of moisture from his forehead. Sometimes the best intentions had the worst results, he thought, but there was little value in bewailing one's mistakes.

All around Zen Richelem, groups stirred uneasily.

Lillian sat with others in the dining hall. She was wearing garlands of flowers. Her face was calm and her eyes still radiated hope, but her fingers had stopped working. She stared ahead, unseeing.

Zen Richelem's councilors were meeting in the station's recreation room around a billiard table; they stopped talking when they sensed and then heard Shannon's approach. He burst into the recreation room without knocking and stopped in the frame of the door facing the councillors, his face a mask of rage. He looked at the councillors arranged around the bright green cloth of the billiard table under a low-hanging lamp—four women, and two men. Janet Brood rose slowly. She was the council elder this season, a tall, slender woman in her late fifties.

"Ravi . . . ?" she said.

"I just came to tell you," Shannon said, out of breath, "just came to say you needn't bother." Emotions gripped him to such an extent that he could barely speak. "I'm no longer any of your business." Then he spied a folder in front of Janet. "As for that," he gasped, striding forward and grabbing the folder, "you won't need this any more." He flung the file into the relative darkness of the unlit portion of the recreation room. The folder opened and papers scattered in all directions.

Shannon strode back to the door and turned. His lips worked as he tried to find a parting shot, but he could not think of anything to say. He grabbed the door instead and slammed it behind himself with all his power.

Moments later an engine came to life in the motor pool not far from the dining hall. Then with a mad screech of tires, Shannon drove away, out of Richelem, taking the road to Gatosward.

For awhile the tension in Zen Richelem persisted; then, suddenly, it broke. The worst was over, in a way . . . and the worst would now begin. Telepathic messages came from the council asking all to gather in the station's large auditorium on Richelem's west side. Janet Brood sat down to place emergency calls to various parts of the globe. People

outside Zen Richelem were needed for this exercise of life
and death. Benny left his room and went to the auditorium.
He stopped in the library along the way and picked up a
microfiche version of the Time Zone Catalogue. As Shannon's best friend and therapist, he would begin the briefing as
soon as the Time Van informed the station about the Time
Zone Shannon had picked. Little by little the people
gathered. Lillian was one of the last to arrive. Her face was
white, but her eyes still radiated hope.

3

Shannon drove to Gatosward, and at first he drove as if he
had no more tomorrows. He roared up a hill, down a hill. The
washboard surface of the highway on this side of John
Baldwin's station made his headlights wobble. The engine
labored. Shannon's foot hurt from pressing the gas pedal. His
fists hurt from gripping the wheel so hard. Up another hill he
went, then down a second. John Baldwin appeared to his
right. Young couples, hand in hand, came into his headlights
up ahead. He roared past them. Then came the long, flat run
to Gatosward on a smooth section of highway.

Little by little his emotions cooled, reason returned. He
thought about his actions, wondering if he had acted rightly,
but the more he thought, the more he convinced himself that
he had done the only sensible thing under the circumstances.

Yes, sir, he thought. Benny had let the cat slip from the
bag. No way that the council would ever let him marry, not in
a hundred years, not until he was 'cured' whatever that might
mean. Lillian? She didn't love him. No way. If she had loved
him, she would've let him make love to her out there in the
fields somewhere. Vladivostok Central had sent him to the
boonies to cure him of his retrogression. All a great big sham.
Cure . . . If they had only told him *what* he was to do. But

they never had. And if they would—he wanted no part of
Kibbutz. He came from another mold, thank you.

I should've done it long ago, he thought, thinking of the
Time Van now. *I should have done it after pilot school. Or
later when they shipped me off to agriculture. I shouldn't
have fallen for that bitch and that damned smile of hers.*

Better late than never.

*There is only one kind of freedom here, the freedom to
escape. I should've made use of it, by God.*

He drove through a landscape bright with light. Swarming
satellites crossed the sky like fireflies; stars abided behind
them, seemingly motionless. Like columns supporting the
firmament, two regional skyhooks shot up like spears of light
on the left and right extremities of his view. Curving away to
Shannon's left, the electrostatic skyway phosphoresced at
middle altitude. Next to the road the Silver Ocean ran, a huge
pipeline; it terminated on an artificial island in the Pacific
hundred of kilometers away. Desalted water moved through
the pipe pumped by photosynthesizing muscle cells massed
in glass-domed booster stations between here and
California—the same technology that powered Colossus.

Like a pale ghost, a wide searchlight beam rising up from
Gatosward gestured across the heavens, seeming to beckon.
The light marked—it advertised—the presence of the Time
Van. It had arrived on its recurring visit to the region three
weeks ago.

He reached Gatosward an hour later and drove through the
deserted logistical station passing enormous cubical
warehouses on either side. No one lived in Gatosward. It was
a staging station. The subcontinental tube-train sent one of its
many shafts to the surface there; several overland lines sent
trunks into the station. Highways intersected at Gatosward
and moved on into the four directions of the sky.

Shannon found the Time Van in the center of the station.
He parked his jeep and looked at the van. He had never seen a
Time Van up close before, and the simple, longish trailer

disappointed him. He had thought about the vans a great deal over the years, these gates to freedom, and somehow he had expected a little more, something more memorable. He saw a simple trailer, painted white. Metal steps led up to a door at one end of it. A huge cable fed it power; the cable lay on the ground, placed between wooden blocks. The searchlight squatting next to it reminded Shannon of a seated frog.

He sat for a moment, gripping the wheel. The turned-off engine crackled. He still had time to change his mind, he thought. Once he "broke through" that skin of time separating the Kibbutz Zone from the many other zones, there would be no way to come back. Lillian. Pecked kisses, murmured words. *Love you, intelligent hand. No,* he thought, grim, decided, *now is no time to weaken. Behind me. Onward.* He pushed himself away from the wheel decisively, got out of the jeep, and went up the metal stairs to the Time Van's door.

He entered a cramped and empty lobby. Chafed leather chairs flanked a low table. A stack of brochures leaned precariously on the table. On the walls on either side hung posters depicting time as a lake, as an ocean; he has seen these diagrams as far back as his childhood.

Through a wire-reinforced glass pane above a counter, Shannon looked into a laboratory and saw a dirty cabinet littered with grimy glassware and, at the opposite end, another door. His knock on the window raised a disembodied voice; it issued from a perforated metal disk above his head. "It'll be just a moment," the voice said, and Shannon guessed that it belonged to James P. Schuster. He could read that name on a plate slid between metal grooves under a sign saying TECHNICIAN ON DUTY.

He looked around the shabby and—yes—dirty lobby. He had expected something a little more sophisticated inside this van . . . signs of some arcane technology. Transzonal travel was supposed to be the Kibbutz Zone's greatest achievement. He saw only a dirty lab, a lobby in need of better furniture.

A loose spring sang inside the leather chair as he sat down, reached for a brochure. The cheap booklet purported to explain transzonal travel in layman's language. He began to read.

Time, he was told, could be viewed as water in a deep mountain lake, layer upon layer separated by differences in temperature. Each layer of time contained a separate dimension or zone with its own stream of history. A laminar "skin" separated the zones and prevented passage from one to the other. A transdimensional energy projector focused force-beams in such a way as to disrupt the skin, permitting passage from zone to zone.

This much out of the way, the brochure became a little more sophisticated. It confided that in practice the matter was a good deal more complicated, of course. The lake of time was really an ocean without top or bottom. It was continually in motion, the layers conforming to the shape of waves. The laminar skin between the zones was not really a skin at all but a complex kind of interface with strong "cortical resistivities." The phrase was not explained. Temporal storms and other motions disturbed the layers from time to time, and when that happened things and energies, physical and psychic, could and did pass from one dimension to the other: an odd geological formation, a prophet, flying objects without rhyme or reason, unexplainable fossils, erratic magnetic changes, buried treasures no one had buried, even stars no one had noticed before. The temporal cosmos appeared infinite but behaved as something curled upon itself. It seemed like a lung, breathing in and out, now expanding at a terrifying speed, now contracting. At present time was in expansion, zooming to infinity with a ravishing sway.

Shannon lowered the brochure and stared pensively at the laboratory door, at James P. Schuster's nameplate.

Higher physics were beyond his grasp, even in layman's language. He could not imagine "time" as a kind of substance that, like water, could run over your hand. Skins of time, even if they were really "complex interfaces," sounded absurd. Oh, well. The proof was in the trip itself. If it worked, it *was*—whether you could picture it or not.

He glanced at the back of the brochure briefly; he scanned a section that traced the history of transdimension under a series of dates. Hm. The invention was said to date back to the 1950's! That long ago? More or less simultaneous discoveries in Russia, in India, in Israel . . . the first exploratory trips came in the 1980's. Then came 1992, a crucial date. The ICO was formed that year, the International Coordinating Organ. In those days it was still a secret group of scientists, statesmen, and diplomats with headquarters at an Israeli kibbutz—hence the name of this zone and of the era. 2001: the ICO becomes a world government after the famed Zurich Summit at which seventeen world leaders are told about the existence of alternate worlds. All view TD tapes. Access to the transdimensional technology is opened to everyone in 2005. And by 2009, the first reports of Teilhardian phantasma had begun to circulate . . .

Ninety-seven years ago, Shannon thought, He tossed the brochure back on the table.

He sat for a moment, brooding on what he had read. Suddenly he nodded to himself, struck by an insight.

That's it, he thought. *That's the way they do it.*

He had been thinking about the text of the brochures, that stress on "layman's language." He had never heard transzonal travel explained in technical detail, always and only in layman's language, and the answer was simple. This technology was very carefully guarded by the global authorities. Shannon knew about secrecy from his historical readings. Kibbutz had no secrets anymore beyond this one. And thinking about that, he understood something else.

The Kibbutz Zone was sweetness and light and harmony and all those things for one reason only; all really strong, aggressive and creative men were pushed out of the Kibbutz Zone; they were forced to leave sooner or later. It was like England in ancient days; England sent its dissidents and malcontents to far-off colonies. But nowadays there was this difference: you couldn't come back. And to make sure you didn't, Kibbutz made sure that you left without a shred of useful knowledge about the trandimensional technology.

Shannon sat and waited.

His rage was still there, below the surface, but now it had
frozen into stone, like lava. He played with the thought of
inventing transdimensional travel over there, on the other
side, in the zone of his destination. He imagined launching an
army of *real* people across a huge gash in that skin of time.
He could just see the faces of these zombies when that
raunchy and passionate mob materialized all over the planet
and began swarming. Materialized? Shannon had no idea
how you appeared on the other side, but he guessed that you
materialized.

A defective light fixture hummed maddeningly, underlin-
ing the silence in the waiting room. Encouraged by the
stillness, a big, brown cockroach had left some dark recess
and moved with a dry sound across the floor. It hesitated in
the center fo the lobby; its long, droopy tentacles moved from
side to side. Shivering in sudden disgust, Shannon stamped a
boot on the floor; the roach ran toward the laboratory door
and slipped out of sight in the dark slit beneath it.

"It'll be just a minute," came the voice of James P.
Schuster from the metallic disc overhead.

4

James P. Schuster appeared at last. He was a sharp-faced
man, about Shannon's age, a strangely ratty-looking creature. His white lab coat was stained; he needed a shave. He
raised the window above the counter with a rattling sound,
peered out. "Hi," he said, glimpsing Shannon. "I'm Schuster." Then he reached under the counter and came up with a
heavy, loose-leaf binder. He dropped it on the counter with a
thud.

"I'm sorry to keep you waiting," he said, "but this has
been a busy night. You're my second customer." He beckoned to Shannon. "If you don't mind . . . I have to have
you fill out a form, and I need a sample of your skin. You can

pick your destination while I process that.'' He tapped the thick binder. ''Unless, of course, you've already picked your zone.''

''I have,'' Shannon said.

''Good,'' Schuster said. ''That'll save time. Where are you going?'' He took a glass slide and a small needle-like device from a drawer. Then he dabbed alcohol on a wad of cotton and reached out for Shannon's hand.

''The Purgatory Zone,'' Shannon said. ''I think it's Zone F-39.''

''That's right,'' Schuster said. He jabbed the device into Shannon's finger; the finger burst out but didn't bleed. Schuster placed a bit of tissue on the slide.

''A good choice,'' he said, ''a very good choice.''

''Why do you say that?''

''Well,'' Schuster said, ''it's a sister world, for one thing, and almost next door. In a manner of speaking. We go through a single skin rather than a dozen, and that's always easier. Easier on me. And easier on you, too, once you reach the other side. F-39 is almost like the Kibbutz. Same language, almost the same history. Why'd you pick it?''

''I saw tapes of it on my Maturity Trip,'' Shannon said. ''Even back then, I figured that if I ever went across . . . .''

Schuster nodded. ''it's a popular world,'' he said. ''Lots of people go there. Makes my job easier. Now the woman I just sent across, she wanted to go to D-14. That's a fifteen-layer trip, and let me tell you. It was nip and tuck.''

''Are there dangers?''

''Not on a trip like yours, no. But if you go much above five or six skins—sure. There is always a chance that you'll end up somewhere else or that you'll end up between zones. I always point that out to customers. Going far has its risks. I don't mind—if they don't. So I point it out to them. But I can't take too many of those long trips in a night. Excuse me,'' he said, ''but I've got to put this into the analyzer.'' He lifted the slide with Shannon's skin. ''Meanwhile, I need you to fill out that form.''

Schuster busied himself at the back of the laboratory with a rectangular machine; circular instrument panels crowded its face; it had a keyboard on top. Shannon filled out the form. Then he leafed idly through the heavy binder. The book held resumes of two-hundred-some-odd time zones arranged under tabbed classifications—Primitive, Early Technological, Advanced, and Neo-Primitive. He opened the Advanced section and found F-39. He had read the profile of the Purgatory Zone many times before, but the last time had been three years ago. The profiles were updated once a year at least as conditions changed in the other worlds. He glanced down the sheets, looking for changes.

Purgatory was an Advanced world separated into five hundred some nations. Many diverse cultures competed with one another. The book showed a list of cultures followed by brief capsules of the more dominant among them. Shannon bent his head over the book to look at the fine print about America, the place where he'd be landing.

He read for a moment. Not too many changes had taken place since he had last looked at this section. America was still called the "United States." It had four distinct organizational units. The U.S. had an urban culture, and most of the population lived in cities. "Squattings" surrounded the cities—places where those people lived who could not enter or had been forced out of the cities. Food was raised in so-called "protected agricultural areas." And finally there were so-called "unclaimed lands."

Revolutionary elements—called Mao-Mao's—occupied the unclaimed lands. They harrassed the cities, the squattings, and the agricultural areas from those bases.

Regional defense forces, popularly known as "Raddies" protected the cities and the agrilands. The central government had military forces of its own, but these only fought against foreign nations beyond the borders of the U.S.A.

Shannon had read all this before. No change.

He read the paragraphs under the subheading of "Social Structure."

"In the late 1980's," he read, "the social structure of the

U.S.A. began to crystallize into fairly rigid castes or clans usually designated by initials.''

"Beautiful People (BP's) are the dominant caste—the owners of enterprises and the political/military leaders. The designation 'beautiful people' had once been a pejorative, but the phrase has become 'neutralized' over time.

"Managers, professionals, bureaucrats, offices in military formations are the second caste, the Bodyguards or the BG's. Only a small minority of BG's are actually employed as bodyguards, but the designation spread to include other functionaries whose activities ultimately protect the Beautiful People. This came about after the rural upheavals of the 1990's (see *History*) when Mao-Mao propagandists accused the middle class of being nothing but 'bodyguards' of the rich.''

"The last of the castes is designated by the letters SD. Officially SD's are called 'social dependents', but popularly the letters stand for 'slum dwellers.' SD's are manual and service workers and the unemployed (by far the largest portion). They subsist on the economic surplus and represent a labor pool.

"Mobility between the classes, once common, has become virtually impossible in F-39. Dissidents sometimes leave to become 'squatters' or to join the Mao-Mao's in the unclaimed lands. Young Beautiful People sometimes engage in what is known as 'dipping,' i.e., they take up occupations as BG's or they live among the SD's under assumed identities, but such inter-caste mingling is very rarely permanent. Hereditary entry into castes is becoming the rule, although a few BG's are sometimes raised to BP rank by adoption owing to the Beautiful People's low fertility.''

Interesting. He wondered where he would end up. Were pilots BP's or BG's? Would he serve in the Raddies and battle Mao-Mao's? He thought he might enjoy that.

He closed the book, nodding to himself. The Purgatory Zone would have the challenges he had always missed in this namby-pamby world. But why did people in the Kibbutz call this the "purgatory" zone? It reminded him of purgation—washing . . . ?

He looked up. "How do they pick the names for these zones," he called over to Schuster.

"The guy who finds the world usually names it," Schuster said.

"What does 'purgatory' mean?" Shannon asked.

"Damned if I know," Schuster said. "Something to do with religion, I think."

"Oh," Shannon said. He searched through the resume, looking under the heading "Religion," but he found such a long and bewildering list that he gave up the effort. The Purgatory Zone was nothing if not creative. They had thousands of religions over there. Everything was different. So many differences, so much wonderful variety.

"Almost ready," Schuster called. "When you hear the buzzing sound, push on the door and come on in." He fiddled with a dial, peered at a gauge and nodded. Then he reached out and pushed a button on the wall. Something buzzed by the lock of the laboratory door. Shannon pushed and entered.

"Through there," Schuster said, his eyes still on the analyzer. He pointed to the back door of the lab. "Make yourself comfortable in the barber chair."

Shannon walked the length of the lab and opened the door. He looked into a faintly lit room. A bed stood against a wall, a barber chair in the center. A complicated metallic device with jointed arms was mounted on the wall above the bed and extended out over it; it reminded Shannon of X-ray machines he had seen in the dental sections of medical stations. Was that the transdimensional beam generator? He had expected something more. He looked at the barber chair.

"Why a barber chair?" he asked, standing in the doorway.

Schuster was nodding to himself, apparently pleased with the readings of the analyzer. "What?" he said.

"What's with the barber chair," Shannon said. "Are you going to style my hair . . . for the other side?"

Wiping his hands on a dirty rag, Schuster laughed. "No, no. I have to shave your head. I have to wire you into the transmitter."

"Wire me . . . ?"

"Don't worry about it," Schuster said. He tossed the rag. "Now comes the acid test," he said. "We will find out if F-39 is able to receive you. If not, you may have to pick another world."

"What do you mean?"

"I'll explain it in a minute." Schuster said. He bent over his analyzer again and pushed four buttons on a keyboard at its top. He waited. Then a light went on. "All right," he said. "All clear. I guess you'll go where you want to go. F-39, coming right up." He came into the room and flipped a switch. Harsh light revealed more dirt and grime.

Shannon settled into the chair cringing a little from its greasy surface. He wondered why they let this place get so filthy. Was that supposed to prepare him for conditions "over there"? Schuster approached, and in a moment the scissors he carried began to hack mercilessly at Shannon's hair.

"All right," Schuster said, barbering, "let me explain all this to you. There isn't much to the transmission, but there are a few things you should know. After you are wired up and I leave the room, you'll feel a sharp pain at all your points of attachment. You'll know that the pain is coming because you'll feel a lot of heat just before it hits. Don't worry about it. The pain won't last long. Next you'll feel yourself spinning, and then you'll want to vomit, and soon after that you'll pass out. Don't worry about that either. And don't fight the feeling. Go along with it. When you come out on the other side, you'll be fairly close to this spot. And it'll be night time, just like here. F-39 shouldn't give you a lot of trouble; but remember—you will still be maladapted. Your best bet is to claim that you lost your memory—but what you do is up to you. Don't tell them that you came from over here—and not because we care. They're not going to believe you, and if you insist, they may lock you up for a lunatic. Another thing. You're likely to run into people you know, people you will recognize. Don't worry about them. Some of them might even know you, others won't. You will have to feel your way.''

"Say that again," Shannon said, a little puzzled. "Did you say people I know?"

"Sure. These are parallel worlds."

"But what about . . . Am I going to run into myself?"

"No, sir," Schuster said. His scissors snipped with energy. "I was coming to that. There is nobody like you in the Purgatory Zone, not now. That's why I took a sample of your skin. I sent your genetic patterns over to F-39 in the analyzer—which is just a miniature of that thing.'' Schuster pointed to the metallic construct above the bed. "The readout was negative, so you're not going to meet yourself coming or going.''

"What if the reading had been positive?"

"You would've had to pick yourself another world. We use so much power in that thing, your double would be flung into another zone—and we can't do that. So we always test for that first. Mind you," Schuster, said, pausing in his work, "it's very possible that you'll wake up in a hospital or in a car wreck or something. Your double might just have died—and some people might think that you have risen from the dead. So I'd be careful about that. But one thing you can be sure of—there is no other guy like you over there.''

Most of Shannon's hair lay on the floor now. Schuster snipped a little here, a little there. Then he turned, threw the scissors on a little shelf next to a miniature sink set into the wall, and picked up a mechanical shaver.

"Moving right along," he said. switching on the shaver. Then he began to harvest the remainder of Shannon's hair in wide, buzzing, tingling swipes. Shannon had a pleasant thought. Nobody had ever told him that he might meet people he knew on this side over there in some other zone. He thought. Nobody had ever told him that he might meet people he knew on this side over there in some other zone. He thought about Lillian, of course, and he wondered if Lillian had a double in the Purgatory Zone, a double who might not only like him but who would be more generous in dispensing the favors of her body . . .

The buzzing stopped. Schuster went to his sink and ran some water. He began to whip up lather in a mug. The bristles of the old brush he was using were bent sideways from sitting in the bowl. The smell of the soap puzzled Shannon; it reminded him of something, but now he could not remember what.

"Sorry about this," Schuster said. He slapped the lukewarm soap on Shannon's skull, spreading and whipping it with the lopsided brush. He worked the soap into the skin with vigorous motions. Then he stepped back and nodded his approval, mug and brush in hand, like an artist before a canvas. "We will let that soak in just a bit," he pronounced. Then he took a strop and began to slap a straight-razor against its shiny surface. Presently he approached again, testing the razor's edge against his thumb.

"There is one more thing you need to know," he said. The blade began to scrape, and Schuster concentrated on the first few strokes before he went on. "You may not think so now, but after you've been over there a while, you might want to come back. If that should happen, here is what you do."

Schuster paused again in order to scrape a little more.

"Is that even possible?" Shannon asked. He tried to hold his head still as he spoke.

Schuster transferred a pile of hairy lather from his blade to a napkin. "We don't exactly advertise it," he said, "but the fact is that you can come back. We don't advertise it because the procedure is very tricky and dangerous. The risk will be all yours, and the odds are against you. I don't mind it if you try—if you don't. In sixty-three percent of the cases, we only manage to bring back part of a person, and that means death, of course. But to answer your question, yes, it's possible."

"I don't understand. Are there machines over there?"

Schuster shook his head. "We don't need machines. I'm not a theoretician, but as I understand it, once your energy

patterns have been punched through that skin, you can be
brought back. There are only two requirements. We must be
ready. And you must be in exactly the same spot where we
dropped you. Got that? So when you get over there, try to
mark or memorize the spot.'' He stepped near and resumed
his shaving.

"For some period of time, we monitor that spot every day,
once or twice a day,'' he said, ''If we see you, we try to pull
you back. No guarantees, you understand. We try. That's
all.''

"How long do you keep it up—the monitoring?''

"That all depends,'' Schuster said. "It's a question of
time and energy. Monitoring takes more power than sending
a body, believe it or not, and the more people leave, the
greater the budget. Lately we've been abandoning spots after
two weeks or so, but sometimes we monitor for a little
longer.''

The blade scraped in silence. Schuster finished at last. He
stepped to the small sink and ran water again. He soaked and
then wrung out a small towel and wiped the residues of soap
from Shannon's skull. "Very well,'' he said, ''you're all set.
Now take off all your clothes and lie down on the bed.''

"You mean—strip?''

"All the way. And don't look so worried. You'll arrive
properly attired.'' Schuster smiled. ''You'll even have your
hair back. Don't ask me to explain it. Even if I knew the
mechanism, I couldn't tell you. Transzonal travel isn't travel
as you know it.''

Shannon stripped. He felt very uneasy now. The smell in
the small room bothered him, and his head had begun to
ache. Although it was summer outdoors and comfortably
warm inside the van, he shivered. Goosebumps formed on
his arms and chest, and he felt a little silly. Once on the bed,
he shrank from the approach of ice-cold disks attached to
sheathed wires suspended from the metal framework above
him. Schuster attached the disks to Shannon's skull, throat,
heart, and navel using a cold unguent to paste them in place.

"It feels as if you were about to give me a cardiac check," he said.

"Same general technology."

"And these little things will get me across?"

"Not these," Schuster said. "These just transmit the energy. The beam will bend the barrier, and then you'll slip across."

Schuster now lowered the metal device down over Shannon and pointed a pyramid-shaped attachment at the center of Shannon's forehead. He threw switches on a nearby wall, returned to investigate his work again, adjusted the pyramid somewhat, nodded.

"Well," he said, "you're all set to go." There was a pause. "Needless to say," Schuster said, "all of us in the Kibbutz Zone hate to see you go. But you know that. Nevertheless—good luck. And good-bye."

"Thank you," Shannon said. His voice was thick with sudden emotion, and he nearly changed his mind; he steeled himself against the temptation to back away from all this in the final minute. Then the lights went out, the door closed, and he was alone in the darkness.

THE GATES OF PURGATORY

5

He woke up and heard a rushing sound. He lay on the bare ground. A triple-decker speedway roared with the traffic of a hundred cars to his left. The cars raced at high speed toward and away from an urban complex blazing beneath an orange bubble in the distance. The speedway stood on gigantic columns of cement rising up, up, up like stately trees in a climax forest, and the road itself seemed like a peculiar kind of canopy capping these concrete trunks. The Kibbutz Zone had no such roads.

Shannon sat up and looked down on himself. He wore faded, canvas slacks and a leather jacket decorated with little stars made of metal. His hair was long, longer than he had ever worn it; a band across his forehead kept it in place. He knew that he had slept—but not for long. Hair and clothing were a mystery.

Unpleasant fumes lay thickly in the air. He did not like the smell and experienced a slight nausea. Then he saw movement above him and glanced up just in time to see a paper sack sailing down toward the ground from one of the road's ramps. The sack landed, burst, and scattered empty cans on

the clay ground with a tinny rattle. Almost at once, a skinny
figure in loose trousers and an open jacket emerged from the
dark shadows underneath the speedway. It was a man. The
man hurried forward and squatted down beside the cans. He
took can after can with hasty motions and lifted them to his
lips. Head tilted back, he shook the cans.

Shannon got up and advanced toward the man. He hoped
that the man would understand him. "Hello," he called.
"Hello there." The man continued tilting cans with peculiarly hasty, almost frenetic motions. Done at last, he turned
to Shannon. His washed-out eyes reflected caution, perhaps
fear. Whitish stubble covered his sagging cheeks; his open
mouth revealed gaps in his teeth.

"Excuse me," Shannon said, "but I am lost. Could you
tell me where I am?"

The man rose from his squatting position and retreated a
few steps.

"Get out of here," he said; his voice was hoarse and
raspy. "Go on. Get. This is my turf."

Shannon felt encouraged. He understood the language
perfectly.

"You must excuse me," he said. "I must have passed out.
I must have fainted. I don't seem to remember a thing."

The man retreated a little farther. "Look, wise guy," he
rasped. "I've heard them all, see! Bad luck stories of all
kinds—mother is sick, wife ran off, killed his own kid,
police is after him, lost him memory, diabetic—the whole
smear. I'm not buying, understand? Off you go, speedy-
bye."

Headlights now caught a bottle tossed from a racing car. It
tumbled end to end from the top ramp of the highway. The
man had glimpsed it first. "Don't you do it, kid," he murmured. "Don't you bust on daddy." He folded his hands and
raised them in an act of pleading as he spoke; he grunted with
satisfaction when the bottle landed with a thud on the soft
clay nearby. He pointed with a skinny, trembling index
finger. "That's mine," he rasped. "You clear out of here."

"I don't want your bottle," Shannon said. "All I want to know is where I am."

The man emitted a snort of irritation and moved back another step. He cupped his hands around his mouth. "HEY RUBE!" he bellowed. Then he crouched low. From that crouched position he suddenly threw a broken bottle with a flick of his wrist; the object came at Shannon, jagged edges foremost. Shannon avoided the missile thanks only to a reflexive duck.

As Shannon ducked, he noticed movement all along the speedway's underside. Men were emerging from the shadows under the massive construct—seven, eight, nine men, perhaps more. They were coming carefully. They converged on Shannon. He could clearly see, despite the darkness, that some of the men carried clubs, broken bottles. Their intention was obvious from the crouched and wary postures of their bodies. Shannon looked behind and saw that the way was clear. He had no intention of tangling with a crowd, not so soon after his arrival. He turned and ran from the speedway, across a stubble-covered field.

He ran for some time, across the field. He came to a wooden fence, clambered over it, ran on. He stopped at last on the other side of the field. The men beneath the speedway had not pursued him. He leaned against the wooden fence to catch his breath. He wanted to sort out his impressions. He hadn't had much time for thought and planning since his sudden arrival in the Purgatory Zone.

The speedway was now some distance to his left. It looked like a river of white light streaming in nervous waves away from the city—and a river of red light entering the city. At the point of entry, the river of light spread like an estuary before it merged with the urban hemisphere. The city's dome resembled one half of a gigantic orange illuminated from within. A clump of nearby trees stood out against its luminosity in sharp, black silhouette.

Shannon sniffed the air. He tried to find an explanation for the strangeness that he felt, but whatever the cause of it, it was not the smell. The place where he now rested had begun to noise with crickets. The rich aroma of the soil and of the grasses might just as well have risen up from a plot back "home." Nonetheless, there was a difference here. Shannon felt a kind of tension. It seemed as if taut forces were stretched across this world high up in the starless sky. It seemed as if hot cables sweated metal in the darkness under some tremendous torque.

Well, never mind, he told himself. *What did you expect? This is a different world.*

Even back home in the Kibbutz Zone, he reflected, Asia had had a different feel from Europe, Europe from America. It only made sense that the Purgatory Zone should have a different atmosphere from the Kibbutz Zone . . .

But now what? He guessed that the men beneath the concrete skyway had been renegrades—probably primitive men and inclined to violence when their territory was invaded. In a natural society you had to expect natural behavior, biological behavior. His reception into Purgatory should not seem as an unfavorable sign, an omen. Quite the opposite. Here he was at last, among real people like himself, people with natural urges and instincts . . .

Still, what to do next?

He eyed the distant city dome. He had to make it to the city, he decided, find someone in authority, turn himself in. He would tell them that he had lost his memory. He might give them a hint or two about his skills—point out, for instance, that he thought he was a pilot, that he vaguely recalled an engine failure, a crash, something like that. They'd send him to a medical station, look him over . . . And in due time they'd send him to an air command, perhaps an airborne Raddy squad. Shannon decided that he would like that best of all. He had read a lot about the air wars of the past and guessed that he would make a first rate combat pilot . . .

He stood for a while longer, his back against the fence,

thinking. Then he pushed off, walking across the field, hoping to find a road leading to the domed city in the distance.

After crossing four fenced fields, he came across a simple road at last. It resembled the highway connecting Zen Richelem to Gatosward. A broken yellow line separated the road into two lanes. He set off along the road. He walked in the direction of the city.

An hour later he saw a light ahead. A low building emerged from the darkness on his right hand. Flickering electric letters on its roof spelled the word "EAT". The scriptograms were almost exactly like those used on most continents of the Kibbutz Zone. Box-like columns stood next to the building; hoses with metallic nozzles were attached to them, on the sides. Above these columns loomed a big red sign. "TEXACO." Shannon did not understand the word, but he guessed that this was a fuel station. He hesitated for a moment. He felt a twinge of anxiety and wondered whether he should risk contact here or wait until he could find the authorities in that domed city ahead. The he continued on toward the station, having decided that he might as well. He was curious. And hungry.

A cattle bell jangled above the door as he entered the eatery. The room was empty. A brightly lit panel displayed a list of food and drink above a longish counter. Round stools stood before the counter like a line of mushrooms. A fat woman emerged from a door behind the counter. A soiled towel hung around her center like an apron, and her hair was curled tightly around huge rolls of yellow plastic. She eyed him oddly as he sat down on one of the round stools.

"You sure came quiet-like," she said. "I didn't hear your car. What'll you have?"

Shannon stared up at the panel. He wondered what the numbers meant but didn't think it smart to ask. "How about . . . What is a hot dog?"

"Honey," she said, "If you want a hot dog, say so. Okay?

It's getting a little late for jokes.''

"A hot dog."

"And to drink?''

"How about a cup of chili,'' he said tentatively.

"You're just a funny man, aren't you!'' she said. "You're cracking me up. Ha, ha, ha. Okay? You're funny. So what'll it be?''

"Milk?''

She turned away without a word and set to work.

Shannon had a curiously unpleasant feeling about the woman, her manner, and about this eatery. Grime sheathed the counter-top, fibrous yellow stuffing peered from holes poked into the red plastic covers of the stools; the smell of burned oil lay on the air. *No matter*. He was in a natural society now where people acted out their predilections, and this woman had no predilection for cleanliness or friendliness. *Who am I to critcize? I wanted to escape that cloying uniformity up there. Up there*, he mused. Yes. It seemed to him that the Kibbutz Zone was up, Purgatory down, that he had dropped into this zone from up above.

The woman brought him a lukewarm sausage inside an ice cold bun; and a plastic cup filled with milk. Then she positioned herself behind a box-like device at the end of the counter and glanced toward him from that perspective from time to time as he ate.

The food tasted of preservatives and the milk lacked life. Nonetheless, Shannon consumed what he had ordered. He was still hungry when he finished but didn't want to ask for more, not in this place. He slid off the stool and went over to her.

"How far is it to the city from here?'' he asked.

"To Phoenix? Ten minutes, give or take. Eight by the tollway. That'll be two-forty-eight.''

"I beg your pardon?''

"Two-forty-eight. A hot dog and a glass of milk. Plus tax.''

"I'm afraid I don't understand,'' he said. "I'm not from around here.''

"Fun-nie," she said. "Look, sweetie. I ain't got all night."

Shannon felt hot. "I . . . I really don't understand," he said. "I lost my memory, I don't know where or how, but I honestly don't—"

"George!!" she called sharply. "Hey, George!"

A chair scraped somewhere, and then a large man in an undershirt appeared in the doorway behind the counter. He was balding, muscular, middle-aged. He scratched his armpit and peered forward with an unpleasant expression.

The woman shook a finger at Shannon. "This joker here!" she said. "It seems he lost his memory just when it came time to pay. He had a hot dog and a glass of milk."

The man came forward and placed his hands on top of the box-like device. "That'll be two-forty-eight," he said.

The woman moved off and took up a position behind the counter.

"Two forty-eight *what*?" Shannon asked. Then he stepped back involuntarily, reacting to a sudden expression of totally incomprehensible rage in the man's dark eyes. The man's eyes flickered, narrowed; and he came around the end of the counter with a motion so sharp, determined, and threatening that Shannon turned and fled, crashing through the door. The man called George came in hot pursuit. He roared words Shannon couldn't understand.

Shannon ran down the two-lane road that had brought him to this place. George came behind; he shouted curses and threats. After a while he fell behind, unable to keep up with the younger, thinner Shannon. Shannon ran on alone, angry with himself.

He had forgotten about money—he, of all people, a student of history. They used money in this zone, like in so many other natural societies, but habits from his Kibbutz life had fooled him. It had not even occurred to him that he should pay the—they called it "price." As for money . . . He ran a little farther, then stopped. He searched through his pockets of his faded trousers and his leather jacket. He even checked the pockets of his cotton shirt. James P. Schuster had supplied him with hair and clothing in some mysterious way—but not with money. Hmm. That might turn out to be awkward. He suddenly remembered that in natural societies failure to pay the price could lead to unpleasantness with the authorities. *Ah, Police*. They wore strange uniforms.

He heard the excited barking of a dog and looked back. The headlights of a car had come alive next to the eatery. He also saw, far in the distance, another set of headlights coming in his direction. A shiver passed over him. He was sure that the man called George had called for the police, and the distant lights were those of a police car. He saw then that George himself also came in hot pursuit, this time by car. The headlights of the car next to the eatery bounced over some fields as George drove the vehicle up on the road. Shannon moved. He ran again—off the highway this time and into another field.

He did not get very far. George's car slid to a halt near the spot where Shannon had left the road. A car-door opened and a huge dog leaped out baying in excitement. Shannon turned and faced the beast. He tried to soothe the loudly barking, snarling, lunging creature. Meanwhile George paused in front of the still shining headlights of his car. Carrying an oblong object that Shannon recognized as a gun, George came down the embankment.

"Shut up, Caesar," he called, arriving. "Down, boy. One wrong move, freak," he said to Shannon, "and I'll blow your goddamned head off." He gestured with his weapon. "Walk back to the road. Nice and easy—Shut up, Caesar—Move! And I don't mean maybe." When they reached the road, he directed Shannon to the front of the car. "Put your hands up on the hood. Spread them apart. All right. Now move your feet back. More. Go on, freak, do it. Don't you watch TV? You know what to do. Way back!"

Shannon assumed the posture and understood the intention behind it: it rendered him incapable of violent action. The man called George approached him from behind and began to search his pockets for the money Shannon knew he didn't have. The dog growled nearby its lips pulled back, its teeth exposed.

George was still busy when the whine of tires could be heard and the car that Shannon had glimpsed in the distance drew up and stopped in the opposite lane. Pale, blurred faces stared out through grimy windows.

George then moved abruptly, and his dog began to bark in renewed excitement. "Move along," George shouted; he seemed to be behind his car now, and Shannon heard fear in his voice. The car's occupants paid no attention to this warning. As if flung outward by an explosion, the doors burst open and figures scrambled forward swiftly. Moving like a blurr, a huge, fat man led the attack. He passed behind and brushed hard against Shannon, and Shannon lost his balance and fell. Rising again, he heard a scramble, the sharp discharge of George's weapon, angry curses, dull blows, and the fearful snarl-whine of the dog that somebody had kicked. Shannon looked; he saw four men beating and stabbing George. They drew back presently and left their victim standing against his car. Blood stained George's undershirt. For a moment he stared at the ground with a curious incomprehension; then he sank down on his knees, pitched forward, and his forehead cracked against the pavement.

Shannon stared in shock, not sure how to react. He had seen dead men before, even men killed violently in accidents. He had never seen anyone stabbed to death. It made his skin crawl. The body lay there—dreadfully inert. It was just there. A heap. It would never move again.

The men who had done the killing were also momentarily frozen; they stood looking at their victim. The dog whined somewhere in the field, in darkness. The huge fat man who had led the attack—he stood near Shannon, he had not participated in the stabbing—suddenly moved. He turned, moved up to Shannon, and hit Shannon across the face with the back of a meaty hand. Shannon staggered from the blow.

"Where have you been, you idiot," the fat man cried.

"See what you've made me do? May God have mercy on my soul."

Using three fingers of his right hand, the fat man touched his forehead, navel, left shoulder, and right shoulder in sequence. Then he looked at Shannon and pointed at the idling car in which he had arrived. "Get in that car and let's get out of here." He gestured toward George's car. "Goulash, Clancy, Johnny! You boys bring the other car. Get the gun. Quickly now. And kick that sinner into the ditch. It doesn't pay to advertise."

Shannon stood as if turned to stone. He stared at the fat man and tried to sort out his madly tumbling reactions, tried to calm a kind of rising dread. The fat man was an almost perfect replica of Benny Franks.

"Go on," the fat man cried, addressing Shannon. "I mean *you*. Wake up, Raver, and get into that car."

Shannon's lips trembled. "Benny?" he asked.

"Who *else*. For the sake of Christ, move it."

6

The car zoomed down the deserted road at a breathtaking speed, with pseudo-Benny at the wheel. One man sat up front with him, Shannon in the back. Benny spoke incessantly and loudly glancing back at Shannon. From time to time he hit the wheel with huge, fat fists by way of emphasis. He was upset and agitated.

Shannon watched and listened like a rat held by a constrictor, aware of danger, too numb to act. Benny spoke as to a man with whom he'd been together a few hours ago. And by implication, the man Benny called Raver must have died just before Shannon's arrival in the Purgatory Zone. And Shannon was entangled with a bunch of thugs and murderers against his will in consequence. And he couldn't very well explain to them that he wasn't Raver . . .

He tried to concentrate. He had to make a plan. He tried to think, but Benny drove so recklessly that Shannon couldn't focus.

Benny's double resembled that other Benny except for dress and hair. His fat flesh bulged beneath a tinted undershirt. Oddly oozing letters on its back spelled out a message: TUNE IN TO CHRIST, TURN ON TO SALVATION. His arms issued like smooth trunks from his sleeves; tattoos covered the skin. One showed a naked man suspended from beams arranged in the shape of a cross; a second one depicted an eye inside a triangle; yet another one was the picture of a woman; she stood on top of a globe, her foot about to crush the head of a snake. Benny's shaven face was full yet pale; his darting eyes resembled shattered glass. Short bristles covered his round skull.

"Unbelievable, undependable, freaky," he said. "I tell you to stick close to me, but when I turn around, you disappear. I can't leave you back at the Center. I can't take you out into the boonies either—not without a *leash*. Jesus. I try to tell you what to do, but you don't listen, Raver. You have ears but you don't hear. You have eyes but you don't see. I had a sneaky feeling that you'd try to sneak away and try to get PD's again. I should've chained you to the car—like the rabid dog that you are. You lied to me, Raver. You ain't cured—far from it. And every time we turn around, there's more trouble. The last thing I need is Raddies on my tail. Irresponsible, that's what you are. I put my faith in you, I believed in you, I trusted you, Raver. And what do I get in return? A kick in the balls. You'd sell your own mother to a soap factory for a candy bar, that's the kind you are, and if I weren't such a bleeding heart I'd turn you over to the Feds like one, two, three and let them make a soldier of you or fry your brains or *something*. I swear to God! Well, let me tell you something, Raver. I'll cure you of your PD habit even if it kills you—and I'd be tickled pink if it did, believe you me. I'm not going to fail this time, no way my friend, and you can bank on that . . .

Benny went on, pausing only to glance at Shannon through
his shattered eyes. He drove like crazy. Cars in this time zone
were powerful and had no automatic speed control. The man
in the front seat next to Benny sucked smoke from a thin tube
of tobacco. Dead George's car came some distance behind.

What bad luck, Shannon kept thinking. *What stinking bad
luck.*

He couldn't very well deny that he was Raver without
explaining who he was. He had to claim amnesia—but doing
so suggested that he was Raver. What stinking bad luck! He
had left the Kibbutz Zone to get away from Benny's harping
voice—among other things. He was not about to submit to it
here. And this Benny was both talkative and dangerous . . .

The giant bubble of the city loomed closer and closer.
Benny stopped talking; he let the car coast to a stop. Then he
slapped the dashboard, and the headlights went out. The car
rolled on, travelling slowly. They drove between low shacks
made from bits of timber, metal, cardboard boxes. More and
more shacks appeared, piled in a jumble. They covered the
land all around the bubble. They lay like some kind of
devastation in the huge dome's orange glow. The bubble rose
steeply to the left, a colossal skin of hexagons. Thick fumes
came inside the car. Giant fans in the skin of Phoenix exhaled
the city's poisoned breath. They were driving through the
"Squattings."

Then the pavement ended. The car bounced, swayed, its
springs and frame in agony. A series of hangars stood out
against the bubble on the left; long strips of aluminum con-
cealed their concrete walls; some of these had lost their
adhesion and drooped like pieces of crumpled paper. Wheeling hand over hand, Benny turned toward these structures.
The car entered one of the hangars; the men got out in
darkness. The second car drove in; men lowered a door with a
rumble.

A flashlight in one hand, keys in the other, Benny opened
the trunk of his car. Four huge sacks lay in it side by side, but
they were light and held dried leaves or straw; they rustled as

Benny threw them to his helpers, calling each by name—
Mack, Johnny, Goulash, Clancy. Then his light-beam
searched for Shannon.

"Ah, there you are," he said. "Tell you what, Raver. Just
because you're such a nice guy, I'll let you lead the way.
We'll be behind you. You'd better sound off loud and clear if
you see the fuzz. Or anything. I want to hear you."

Shannon guessed that the time had come. He gathered up
his courage. "I don't know the way," he said.

"What?"

"I don't know the way. I don't remember it. I don't
remember this place. I don't remember *anything*. I think I've
lost my memory."

"You did, did you!" Benny cried. He moved swiftly,
grabbed Shannon by the collar, and lifted Shannon to his
toes. The flashlight beam blinded him, but he saw Benny's
shattered eyes and smelled the residues of alcohol on Benny's breath. Benny stared; then Shannon felt released.

"Mack, Johnny, all of you," Benny said. "Take a look at
Raver and tell me what you see." He handed the flashlight to
the first of the men.

The men approached one by one and stared at Shannon's
face. They handed the flashlight to one another. They withdrew into darkness. Shannon heard them whispering. Presently Benny approached again. He seemed to be shaking his
head.

"You don't remember anything?"

"Nothing," Shannon said.

"What was the first thing you saw when you woke up?"

"The dog. There was this huge dog next to me."

"And then?"

"A man dragged me up to a car. He started looking in my
pockets."

"And then we drove up."

"Yeah," Shannon said. "I sort of guessed that you were
Benny. Other than that, I couldn't remember anything."

"He doesn't sound like Raver," someone said.

"It's Raver, all right," Benny pronounced.

"But he doesn't have Raver's eyes. He doesn't have Raver's voice." He pondered the matter for a moment. "You finally did it, Raver. You've blown your brains to kingdom come." He paused.

"Okay. Let's get the hell out of here." He shook a finger at Shannon. "What I said in the car still goes. You'll have to kick that habit of yours, even if you don't remember it. And if you're putting me on . . . " He left the rest unsaid.

Moving in single file, their way lighted at intervals by brief on-and-off flashes from Benny's light, they walked deep underground in an echoing tunnel. Water gurgled softly; sometimes they heard a slow drip pinging into a puddle. Benny sometimes stopped to listen; then everyone held his breath.

They were entering the city by some illegal route carrying forbidden merchandise. Shannon searched his memories. They had called this "smuggling" in the old days of the Kibbutz Zone. Well, he had always longed for adventure. Now he had it—and to spare. He had to try to get away from these antisocials in a hurry, turn himself in, and then would start that career of his . . . as a combat pilot.

Benny stopped at last beneath a shaft and trained his flashlight on a rusty ladder set into crumbling stonework. Shannon followed the others up. He found himself inside a warehouse filled to the ceiling with old, filthy, broken furniture. Through a row of broken windows high up in one wall, he saw the bubble as it domed over the building like some giant reptile's skin. They were inside Phoenix. Benny's people scattered. They hid the sacks amidst the furniture. Then Benny took Shannon by the arm and led him by way of a dark alley into a busy street. The others followed.

Shannon had never seen a street or neighborhood like this one. It was ancient, wretched, crowded. Identical, multi-story brick buildings lined the street. People hung from the windows. Wild children chased each other down below.

Vendors hawked cheap goods. Couples clung to one another in displays of affection. Thin dogs sniffed offal in the gutters. The sweetish smell of garbage came in wafts. The street rang with noise.

In stark contrast to all this, Shannon saw above the dark and crumbling buildings the distant center of Phoenix. Hundreds of elegant towers—white, pink, silvery, golden—rose like competing flowers toward the apex of the dome. Coiling like silver springs around these towers in intersecting circles gleamed transport ways. Cables linked these towers; spherical gondolas pendulated slowly on the cables moving people.

"Stop gawking, Raver," Benny said. "Move it."

They walked swiftly for some minutes. Benny glanced behind from time to time, his shattered eyes apprehensive as if he feared pursuit. At last they arrived at the destination.

Shannon saw, to his left, a tall, black, iron fence—the leftover of some more stately era. Behind this fence stood another made of wire. Barbed wire topped this second fence. Set back from the street loomed a large mansion with several wings, four little towers, and a stately front with columns, marble steps. A large sign proclaimed this to be THE NEO-CATHOLIC CATHARSIS CHURCH, *Reverend B. Franks, Pastor.*

Benny stopped before a gate. Unlocking it, he entered what must have been a garden once. Now it was a courtyard. A sadly sagging volleyball net hung on laconically leaning poles in its center.

"Do you remember the pad?" Benny asked, pointing to the mansion. Shannon shook his head.

"You're in a bad state, Raver," Benny said. He led the way toward the mansion. "We're going to have to cure that. We're going to have to clean you up. Clancy," he called, turning, "check out the john next to the sanctuary. Search every inch of the place. Knowing Raver, he has PD's hidden all over the damn place, especially in the johns." Clancy moved ahead. "You might not remember your PD's just now," Benny told Shannon, "but when you start sweating

and thrashing, your memory is sure to come back. It had
better come back or we're in heavy trouble with the Feds.''

"What are PD's?" Shannon asked. But Benny just
laughed. They mounted marble steps and stood before a
heavy door. Shannon saw a small sign on the door.

PROJECT DARE
Drug Abuse Rehabilitation Experiment
Bureau of Narcotics Control
DEPARTMENT OF HEALTH AND WELFARE

From a lobby with worn carpet, Shannon glanced into a
littered room. Women sat on the floor and stared at a cathode
ray tube set into a box; colorful images moved on its screen.
They munched yellow flakes from colored sacks oblivious of
a very little child in a crib in the corner. The child stood with
tiny fists balled around the uprights of his cage; its face purple
with rage, it screamed with all its power. A record player
blared a rudely rhythmic piece somewhere.

A wide stairway rose up ahead, its carpet also worn. "This
way," Benny said. He went up the stairs and stopped on the
upper landing. His huge chest heaved with heavy breathing.
He pointed to a corridor to Shannon's right.

On the way to somewhere—to that mysterious "john"
that Clancy had been sent to search—they came through a
darkened room. Sweaters and towels covered the lamps.
Several young women sat around a table holding hands, eyes
closed. One of them hissed angrily when Benny entered. The
fat man began to tip-toe. He turned to Shannon, an index
finger across his pudgy lips.

"They're trying to raise Alkhazar," he said outside. "Do
you remember Alkhazar?" Shannon looked dumbfounded.
"Mary's Spirit Control," Benny added; then he shook his
head. "Either you're putting up a damn good show or else
you're really bonkers," he said. "Alkhazar really liked
you—and you don't remember him!"

"I told you. I don't remember anything. Who is Alkhazar?"

"Mary's Spirit Control."

"What is a 'Spirit Control'?"

Benny's shattered eyes expressed pain and agitation. He sighed. "A spirit. One of the dead. A voice from the Beyond. Come along, Raver. Either we can bring you back or . . . ''

Shannon would have liked to know the conclusion of Benny's thought, but Benny went on, down some steps again, and into a large room where rows of empty chairs faced a curtain across a stage. On the left of the stage stood a gigantic sculptured cross on which a sculptured man hung by nails driven through his sculptured wrists. Shannon recognized this figure from one of Benny's tattoos.

Clancy came in just as they were about to leave the theater. He looked triumphant and stopped with a balled fist extended toward Benny. He opened the hand; two oblong capsules lay on his palm; they were colored red and gold.

Benny pointed to the capsules with a thick, pale finger. Shannon noticed dirt beneath the fingernail. "There you are, Raver. Those are some of your PD's.'' His eyes flickered as he regarded Shannon.

"PD's are . . . medicine?"

"Medicine," Benny cried. His eyes narrowed. "Do you want them? Do you want some medicine?''

"Why should I? I don't feel sick.''

Benny chuckled. "Not yet. Not yet. But we shall see.''

Immediately outside the theater, Clancy opened a door.

"Okay," Benny said. "In you go. And do me a favor, Raver. When it hits you, try to keep the screaming down.''

Then Shannon was left alone in a narrow room. He discovered in a moment that it was a toilet from which human wastes were carried off somewhere using very large quantities of very pure water.

THE NEO-CATHOLIC CATHARSIS CHURCH

7

As Shannon awoke the following morning, he couldn't
place himself. He lay on the floor of a narrow cubicle, his feet
against the door, his head against a wall. The sink loomed
above him on one side, a waste-stool on the other. Drawings
on the wall next to the toilet depicted portions of the human
anatomy. Through the barred window he glimpsed an expanse of very thin, transparent membrane; beyond the membrane clouds moved against the sky.

His memories came with a rush. He was in the Purgatory
Zone. Held prisoner by thugs. In an institution called the
Neo-Catholic Catharsis Church. Reverend B. Franks, Pas-
tor. Benny Franks. The smuggler.

Shannon uncoiled himself and rose. He was stiff all over
and not in the best of humor. He had already tried the window
the night before, and he had found the bars strong, stiff,
unyielding, and sunk deep into stone. The door was locked.
He tried it. Still locked.

He looked at himself in the mirror. Beard bristles on his
chin; his hair was long and none too clean. Otherwise he was
clearly Ravi Shannon, no mistake about it.

''What kind of a mess did you get me into?'' he asked his mirror image.

It was a mess, all right. But he could hardly blame himself. He had stinkingly bad luck, was all. And he felt a little out of it. He hadn't read enough about the Purgatory Zone to know exactly what was what, but he guessed that he had hooked up with SD's—slum dwellers—and did not belong in such company. He had to get out of this neighborhood and up into those golden flowers at the city's center. But how?

It'll come to you. Just look for a chance to get the hell out of here.

He took off his shirt and washed himself as best as he could in the tiny, filthy sink.

Soon the house woke up around him, and the nature of the sounds he heard convinced him that something unusual was happening. Feet drummed up and down stairs; people shouted; buckets clanged. Above the growing din, Benny bellowed orders in a hasty, irritated, anxious way.

Some of the sounds came from the outside. Shannon climbed up on the toilet-stool and peered down into an alley. Three youngsters down below were dragging huge, green sacks filled with rubbish. They piled the sacks on top of overflowing barrels. One of them, a young woman, said that Parents' Day was, like shit—what a circle-jerk! An over-fat young man said that Pop never came anyway, the Smoosh, and where he was concerned all parents could suck his zork.

A fist then banged on the door behind Shannon, and a voice cried, ''Hey, Raver! How're you doing?''

''Fine,'' Shannon shouted back. He jumped off the toilet-stool. ''Are you going to let me out?''

The man outside gave no reply, but the door opened just a crack. Shannon saw a peering eye. The man outside was cautious. What did he expect? Attack? The door opened all the way. The man called Clancy entered. He carried a tray covered by silvery metal foil; wedged under his arm was a tubular container and some rags. He kicked the door shut. Eyes wrily on Shannon, he placed the tray on the box-like water container. Still wary, still observant, still holding the tube and rags, he stepped back.

Clancy was not an unattractive figure. His hair hung down on either side in stiff, long, dirty strands. The face recalled the cratered surface of the moon—extinguished pimples that had left him scarred. In the bright light of day he looked unnaturally pale and sallow—as if his skin had never seen the sun. The eyes had a hard quality, lacked depth. They resembled windows with pulled shades.

"Well, well," Clancy said, eyeing Shannon through those opaque eyes. "You look pretty good, kid, pretty good. Remember anything?"

"Is your name Roberts?" Shannon asked, remembering a Clancy Roberts back in Kibbutz.

"Well," Clancy said, "looks like your memory is coming back. Anything else you remember? Like PD's?"

"No. Are you going to let me out of here?"

"Don't get funny," Clancy said. "You've got Benny all upset—and besides, it's Parents' Day tomorrow. We can't afford to have you screwing up the works. Here," he said, holding out the tube and the rags. "Clean this place up—and I mean make it *shine!* And scrub these damn things off the wall," he said, pointing to clumsy sketches of sexual organs. Then Clancy Roberts turned to go.

"Wait just a minute," Shannon said. "I want to get out of here. You can't just keep me locked up here—without rhyme or reason."

"Without rhyme or reason!" Clancy raised his eyebrows. "You kidding? You're the number one raving maniac at N-triple-C, and you don't call that rhyme or reason? You got another think coming, Raver."

"I don't know anything about that," Shannon said. "I don't remember being a maniac, raving or otherwise. I'm not raving now. I'm as calm as anybody. I'm a reasonable man."

"Until it hits you."

"Until what hits me?"

"The crazies," Clancy said. "The heavie-jeavies." He

narrowed his eyes. "You're not exactly like you were before, but one can never tell with you. Who knows what pill
you popped this time. Get on with the scrubbing. I've got to
go." He turned toward the door.

"Come on, Clancy," Shannon said. "The least you can
do is tell me a little something."

Clancy looked back over his shoulder. "Like what?"

"Like—who am I? What is this place? Why do you people
keep me locked up—precisely why? What are PD's? Who is
Benny?"

Clancy looked at Shannon with a mixture of pity and
contempt. "Haven't got the time, Raver. It'll all come back
to you."

"Just a little," Shannon pleaded. "Tell me just a little
something. I've got to know. You owe me that."

Clancy glanced toward the door, seemingly unsure
whether to comply or not. Benny's voice bellowed somewhere near.

"All right," he said. He leaned against the door, arms
folded across his chest. "You're a loser, Raver, that's *what*
you are. A stinking PD addict and a trouble-maker Number
One. You were sent here by the Feds, and we've been busting
our guts trying to clean you up ever since. But you're just full
of happy little surprises. You kick PD's—or you claim
to—but now you lose your memory. You're a loser, Raver,
like I said, and I wish to God you'd never set foot in here."
He turned to go again.

"Who are the Feds?"

"Jesus *Christ,* Raver. Don't you remember anything? The
federales, the government, man."

"The government?"

"Yeah. What else."

"You? You people are the government?"

"Did I say that?" Clancy asked. "Raver, forget it. We're
a government contractor, not the government. There is a
difference, you know."

"You work for the government?"

"Oh, Jesus Christ. Look, Raver, I've got to go. I can't stand here all day long teaching you your ABC's."

"How can you be the government—or even work for it," Shannon said. "The government means law and order, stuff like that, and what you guys were doing last night was something else. I may be stupid, but I could see that, even so."

Clancy's face darkened. He settled against the door again. He tossed his head to move a stiff, greasy strand of hair out of his eyes.

"You know something Raver? You're dangerous. Downright dangerous. Memory or not. What you saw out there—listen, man. You were out there too. Just remember that. You're as guilty as all the rest of us. And if you so much as breathe a word of that . . ." His eyes tried to convey a threat. "We're a church, Raver. Not everything we do is Uncle's business. And you'd better get that through that crazy head of yours, right quick. It might be best for you if you forgot that too. I mean last night. Forget it—like every thing else."

Shannon failed to grasp the full meaning of Clancy's words, but he decided not to press the issue. "What are PD's," he asked.

Clancy snorted in dry mirth. "Fancy you asking that, you of all people. You really don't know?" Shannon shook his head. "Paradise dice," Clancy said. "You roll them, as they say; and if you're lucky you zoom off to paradise."

"What if you're unlucky?"

"Then down you plunge, down to the pits of hell."

"You mean—PD's are a hallucinogenic drug?"

"Hallucinogenic! Wow! You didn't forget everything, Raver, not everything."

Benny shouted angrily nearby, and the sound of the voice electrified Clancy. "Gotta go," he said and immediately left. A key turned outside, locking Shannon into the cubicle again.

Shannon stood in the room. He held the tube and rags

Clancy had handed him. Odd, he thought. Smugglers working for the government? Best if he forgot about it? The
Neo-Catholic Catharsis Church had things to hide . . .

He set down the tube and rags and turned to the tray Clancy
had brought. He removed the silvery foil and found beneath it
some sort of yellow mush in the tray's center flanked by two
shrivelled strips of burned protein. The food smelled syn-
thetic. Using the plastic fork that he found embedded in the
mush, he tasted and then devoured the food, suddenly ravenous.

Finished, he took up the tube and rags. The container held
some kind of scouring powder named Ajax. Unlike the food
this stuff was potent. On hands and knees, he began to cut
into a thick accumulation of filth encrusted on the base of the
toilet bowl. Working like this reminded him of housekeeping
detail back on Zen Richelem. Some things remained the
same, zone to zone . . .

He was not engaged long in this labor when loud yelling
and the stomp of feet interrupted him. After an angry rattle
of keys, the door flew open. Benny burst in. His face was
red, beaded with perspiration. He was furious.

"You don't say a goddamned thing to nobody," he
shouted at Shannon without introduction. A pudgy finger
shook in Shannon's face. "Not a goddamned syllable about
last night, Raver, or so help me God, I'll choke you with
these hands." By way of demonstration, he held his hands
forward and clawed his fingers around an imaginery neck.
Without explaining himself further, he left the room, slam-
ming the door so hard that the wall appeared to shake.
Someone else turned the key. Shannon was alone again.

He worked on the fixtures and walls of the toilet all that
day. In a way he didn't mind the isolation. It gave him time
to sort his impressions; and the simple task of scrubbing kept
his hands occupied.

He guessed that the Neo-Catholic Catharsis Church—and
Project DARE which it administered—had something to do
with housing and treating young people. That Parents' Day

meant a visit by the youngsters' parents and that such visits were not very frequent, else why the great clean-up? That the Church was inefficient . . . else why would the place get filthy enought to require an all-day scrubbing? That Benny ran a smuggling ring. That Raver was an inmate in this establishment—and thus denied freedom of movement. Why else the bars over the window? He guessed he was in trouble and had to get away. That he'd been careless in his conversation with Clancy Roberts and had infuriated Benny Franks, the Pastor. That he had stinkingly bad luck . . .

Late that afternoon Clancy came by once again. He inspected Shannon's clean-up efforts with unconcealed astonishment.

"I don't get it, Raver," he said. "I just don't comprehend you. What's come over you? You find some other kind of pill?" He shook his head. "If it weren't for the way you look . . ." He ran a finger over the bright gleam of the sink. "I said 'shine' and, boy, does it *shine*. You're making the rest of us look bad, Raver. Are you doing that on purpose?"

Shannon had no answer to that. Clancy shook his head again.

"All right, Raver," he said. "You're moving. Come along."

Clancy led the way out of the toilet and then through the mansion by a somewhat circuitous route. Shannon saw quite a transformation in the place. The house had been cleaned from top to bottom during the day. Holes in the plaster had been patched. He smelled paint, soap, disinfectant. The trash and litter he had seen the day before had disappeared. The windows gleamed. At one point he heard loud laughter, the rush of water, and saw billows of steam issuing from a room at one end of the hall. When he asked Clancy about that, Clancy said that the "animals" were bathing—had to smell good for Mom and Dad tomorrow.

"Do I have a mom and dad?" Shannon asked. "Are they coming tomorrow?"

They were walking up a circular stairway at this point, a

stairway Shannon guessed led to one of the small towers he had seen at the corners of the mansion yesterday. Clancy stopped above him on the stairs.

"*You*?" he said. "I guess that you must've had a mom—but I'll bet that she got rid of you in a hurry. No, sir. You don't get no visitors tomorrow—thank God! You're dangerous. You're a slum kid, Raver, a welfare case."

Clancy continued climbing.

Shannon didn't like the sound of that. A slum kid? Did that mean that he was an SD?

"What's a welfare case?" he asked.

Clancy did not answer. At the top of the stairs he took a key from his pocket and unlocked a door. He pushed it open, switched on a light, and pointed inside.

"There you are," he said. "Benny gave you a present."

Shannon looked in. The room was bare. A stained mattress lay on the wooden floor. Next to it stood a small cathode-ray device, a miniature version of the one that he had seen the day before in the room where the small child had been crying. He guessed that Clancy meant that.

"Benny wants you to watch TV," Clancy said. "Maybe that'll help you to remember. Watch it long enough, and I'll guarantee that you'll soon find out what you are. And all about the welfare system."

"Are you locking me up again?" Shannon asked.

"What else?"

"But why? I haven't done any harm—and you liked the work I did."

"No complaints," Clancy said. "But you've got to remember that I don't run this place. Benny does. And Benny says that I'm to lock you up. I don't blame him, either. You're dangerous, Raver. I've told you that."

"*How*?" Shannon insisted. "How can I possibly be dangerous? I won't harm a fly. Listen. I won't say a word—about last night. Not a word, not to a soul. Nothing. Mum. Okay?"

"Fine with me," Clancy said. "I'll tell Benny what you

said, but I'll bet you a Caddie for a nickel that he will keep you in here for a couple of days at least. At least until your memory comes back. Or something. Think, Raver. You've got to remember, see? If you don't remember—or something—Benny will get antsy. *Very* antsy."

"What do you mean when you say 'or something'?"

"Something," Clancy said, shrugging. "Get back to normal. You're Raver and yet you ain't. It's driving Benny up a tree. Hey, I've got to go. Go on in so that I can lock you up. I'll bring you some chow later; but now I've got to run along and tend my animals."

He nudged Shannon into the room, closed the door. The lock rattled.

Shannon inspected his new quarters. The room was spacious, empty, dusty. It hadn't been used for a long time. The windows were barred. Through them he could see the clay-covered front of the house. The volleyball net had been stretched taut and the poles on which it hung had been righted. He saw the street beyond the double fence. People moved about. A vehicle rolled slowly down the center of the street; it had an odd, red bubble on its top.

The tower in which he stood formed one corner of the mansion. He had been isolated. The Moms and Dads who would arrive tomorrow wouldn't hear Shannon's screams if—as Benny probably suspected—Raver began to crave those mysterious paradise pills. And the TV would help him get his memory back . . . lest Benny grow "antsy." He squatted down to inspect the various knobs of the instrument, guessing that it was a teaching machine.

A rush of sound—he turned it down quickly—and then ions crackled behind the glass screen, an image appeared. A smiling woman held an oblong box on a level with her ear; she glanced at the box repeatedly as she spoke. POTENTATE, said the box in letters of flaming red against an orange background.

" . . . great against fatigue, too," the woman was saying. "Don't settle for substitutes. POTENTATE is the sure-fire erector, and *He* will never suspect that those warm, amorous feelings that drew him to your bedside had a tiny little bit of help from POTENTATE, the *safe* hormonal stimulator.''

At every mention of the word POTENTATE, the letters on the box glowed and sparkled. The woman in the screen now made as if she had been interrupted. She hid the package behind her back, and, turning, she held up and puckered her lips as if expecting a kiss. A smiling man approached and took her in his arms.

''Available at your local drugstore,'' said a voice as the kissing couple faded.

Puzzled by the meaning of this message, Shannon settled on the mattress in a cross-legged position; he felt an intense desire to learn as much as he could.

8

Shannon watched TV that night until the last station went off the air. He slept at last; wild dreams about the Kibbutz Zone disturbed his rest, and he awakened early. He began to watch the TV tube again, stopping only to eat the breakfast Clancy brought him.

He was still watching when Parents' Day began around midmorning. Dazed and a little bleary-eyed, he shoved aside the food tray, rose from his mattress, and went to the window to see what the commotion he had just heard was all about.

He arrived just in time to see two buses pulling to a stop in front of the Neo-Catholic Catharsis Church. Men dressed in identical suits poured out of the first bus. Carrying small communicators—or perhaps weapons of some kind—they formed a tight circle around the second bus and a gate in the wrought-iron fence. These had to be bodyguards—real bodyguards rather than merely members of that caste.

The door of the second bus opened now. Men and women ducked out and made for the gate. In striking contrast to the drab-looking BG's, they were richly dressed. The women shimmered in tight fabrics or billowed in colorful folds. The men wore stately robes set with bright ornaments and jewels. The Beautiful People, Shannon thought, Purgatory's ruling caste.

Chatting leisurely, they streamed toward the gate in two's and three's. Benny bowed before them. He wore a long black robe, a round, white collar.

The youngsters of the Neo-Catholic Catharsis Church had lined up near the house to receive their moms and dads. They wore identical blue overalls and they were on their best behavior. Clancy stood near also dressed in a long, black robe. Presently the parents, youngsters, and Benny moved into the mansion. Only the bodyguards remained outside. Leaning against the fence and talking among themselves, they guarded the Beautiful People within.

Shannon watched the guards for a while, but when nothing happened, he sat down before the TV once again. The tube had begun to tire him, but with every passing hour he knew more about the Purgatory Zone—and less.

He did not like everything he saw. This was a complex culture, difficult to grasp. People here were very rich and very poor. It was nice to be on top but wretched to be on the bottom—and he seemed to be one of those on the bottom. Drug addict, slum dweller, inside an institution. And he did not see a clear way of escape.

Tension and division marked the culture. Hundreds of factions argued and fought. Educated people talked a great deal about problems, ''crises.'' The world had many nations, powers, blocs. Commentators talked about hot-spots, ''cold'' wars.

Shannon had learned most from programs of a dramatic sort the night before. He settled down to look for one of those. The heroes all came from the BG caste; their actions always won them the love of beautiful BP girls. In the pursuit of such love, they killed dozens of Mao-Mao's, SD's, squatters, and occasionally a bad BG. Was life really so violent in the Purgatory Zone? Shannon guessed that it had to be. He had seen a killing within an hour of his arrival.

He found a drama and settled down to watch it. This show was unlike the one's he'd watched the night before. Men and women engaged in endless conversation, talking very slowly about love, abortion, marriages, divorces. Scenes faded out slowly to oddly melancholy music while the picture focused on the face of one of the characters.

Noon came and went. Squatting on the sidewalk or leaning against the fence, the guards ate lunch from paper boxes. Judging by the sounds inside the mansion, the BP's and their youngsters also ate. Only Shannon was forgotten. His stomach growled.

Irritated by Clancy's neglect, Shannon went on watching the TV. Toward midafternoon, his eyes burning and his head beginning to ache, he turned off the television and laid down on the dusty mattress. In a while he fell asleep.

He awoke again as night set in. Hearing the sounds of a commotion, he went to the window of his tower room.

The buses were gone. The youngsters of the NCCC were piling from the mansion. Now they wore shirts and slacks self-tailored to adolescent taste and carried cans of beer. Already drunk, they behaved with wild abandon. They tossed empty cans, they argued, they made obscene gestures, they yelled insults at SD's out on the street.

"Hey, hey you," Shannon shouted through the window. He drummed on the window-frame. The window had been nailed shut or had become stuck years ago. He couldn't open it. Nevertheless, he knew that they could hear him down below even as he could hear them. But the youngsters did not want to hear.

He was getting mad. He had kept his peace throughout the day, but now he wanted food.

"Hey," he called again. Again he hit the window. But the youngsters disregarded him.

Some time passed. Shannon watched the youngsters, and they caroused below like drunken youngsters anywhere. Benny appeared at last. He had shed the long black robe and once more wore blue slacks and that tinted undershirt Shannon had seen before. Oozing letters on his back spelled the message of his church—TURN ON TO CHRIST, TUNE IN TO SALVATION.

Benny seemed to be aglow with happiness. His red face beamed. He held a can of beer in each of his fists. The neck of a bottle peered from one of his back pockets. Two young women ran toward him and hung themselves in his arms. With the women hanging on, he circled the yard. Then he disappeared into the mansion again, taking the girls along. He held a fat hand over the buttock of each girl; they carried his cans of beer.

Benny reacted to Shannon's shouts no more than the youngsters had. Disgusted and angry, Shannon went back to his mattress and sat down before the television set again.

The night before and during the day, Shannon had heard little in the way of noise from the rest of the mansion. Tonight, as the evening deepened and the youngsters went indoors, the Neo-Catholic Catharsis Church began to throb with the sound of a chaotic party. Benny's animals behaved now in a manner much worse than any drunken Youth Camp group. Could those youngsters really be diseased? They yelped and screeched through rooms and halls. Tremendous crashes resounded with such force that even the floors of Shannon's isolated tower shook. In the midst of all this, and for several hours, he heard the unrelenting screaming of that little baby he had glimpsed in a crib on his first entry into the mansion. Alone and neglected, perhaps as hungry as Shannon was, the child voiced its primitive needs unheard.

Quite late that night—Shannon had given up hope of being

heard when he shouted for food at the door of his room—
steps drummed up the stairs to his room. A key turned in the
lock, the door came open. Benny stood there. He was purple
in the face and so badly winded from his climb that he stood
gasping for some moments before he staggered in. Clancy
came in behind him.

Shannon rose from his mattress and faced the fat man.
Benny reeked of alcohol. Bits of food and droplets of liquid
clung to the tinted undershirt. The shattered eyes searched
Shannon's face with a vague kind of interest. Benny was
inebriated; he tried to concentrate but could not quite control
himself. He staggered where he stood.

"Well?" he said, and a moist burp escaped with the
question.

"Hello," Shannon said; he did not know how else to
respond. The look in Benny's eyes intimidated him.

"You ain't done it, have you?" Benny asked, staggering
in place again. "Have you?"

"Done what, Benny?"

Benny waved a hand in the air around his own closely
cropped head. "Your m'mry," he slurred.

"Nothing yet," Shannon said. Then he glanced at the TV.
"But I'm learning."

Benny exchanged a glance with Clancy; the turn of his
head unbalanced him; he staggered backwards, caught himself. Clancy looked more sober. Invisible shades down over
his eyes, he stared at Shannon. Clancy looked as if he had
participated in a meal where food had been tossed rather than
eaten.

"Shit," Benny said, giving the word a long, slurred intonation. A glance at Shannon—then a diversion of his eyes.
"We gonna have to deal with you," he said. "I mean to tell
you—*deal* with you." He stopped and looked at Shannon
again. Then at Clancy, nodding, nodding more than he had
intended, staggering. He set himself in motion toward the
door. He aimed his body at the door. He let inertia push him.

Clancy reached into a pocket. He tossed something at
Shannon. Shannon caught the object by reflex.

"Have yourself a ball," Clancy said, and then he turned to go.

"Hey," Shannon cried. "Hey, Clancy. Aren't you going to feed me?"

But Clancy had already gone. The door slammed and the lock turned. Shannon ran toward the door and began to shout and to pound on it, but the action seemed wasted. Cursing angrily, he turned toward his mattress again. Only then did he notice that he still held the tiny object Clancy had tossed to him. He opened his fist and looked at it. It was an oblong capsule colored red and gold. It was a paradise die.

9

Amidst howls, yells, crashes, shrieks, and the stamp of stampeding feet, the revelries continued into the small hours of the morning. The TV had gone dead a long time ago. The streets had emptied. Even the distant center of the city— Shannon could see some of the flower-like buildings from his tower window—lost its luminous blaze. Yet the party continued. Early light had begun to shimmer on the membrane dome again before the mansion settled into silence.

Nervous shivers passed over Shannon's skin as he paced across the room. Emotions jerked and zigged and zagged across his innards. His hunger had disappeared. In its place he had a searing headache, pinpoints of pain behind his eyes.

An argument went on inside of him; accusation, counter-accusation. He accused himself of carelessness and foolishness and impetuousity. He had rushed into this trip without a plan, goaded by circumstances, prematurely. The council might have ruled in his favor—not likely, but possible! Lillian loved him, she really did. She had called his hands intelligent and had kissed them front and back. Only a real idiot could have done what he had done.

"Not so," said another part of Shannon. "You're just complaining because it's a little rough. Be a man! You wanted battle and adventure. You've got it, sonny. Buckle in and fight. This is the *real* world, not the goody-goody Kibbutz that you never could stand."

Shannon did not like these arguments. Back home he had never had a doubt about himself, only about the world around him.

He settled down on his mattress, by-and-by. It was ancient, lumpy, and had a musty smell. Puffs of dust rose from its tears and holes when he moved his body. The dust also had an odor, an unpleasantly acid odor not unlike the soap that James P. Schuster had slapped with that bent brush over his skull. He dozed off thinking about that odor, the Time Van, and his Maturity Trip, feeling vaguely and drowsily that there was some connection . . .

He woke up with a start. Clancy stood above him, nudged him with a foot.

"Go on, get up," Clancy said. "Move, Raver. Benny wants to see you."

Shannon rolled off the mattress, came to his feet. He staggered a little. Sleep still weakened his limbs. He yawned and rubbed his eyes. He looked at Clancy and noted the man's dark expression. Clancy looked threatening.

"You didn't take it, did you?" Clancy asked, tossing his head, tossing a stiff strand of greasy hair.

"Take what?"

"The pill."

For a moment Shannon did not know what Clancy meant. Then he recalled the red-gold capsule. It lay in the pocket of his leather jacket.

"No," he said.

"Didn't think so," Clancy said. "You should've." He gave Shannon a flat look, tossed his head, and turned toward the open door. "Let's go," he said.

There was a bathroom at the bottom of the circular stairway. Shannon stopped there while Clancy waited. When Shannon was finished, they went on.

The mansion had been turned into a shambles during the night. Wrecked furniture and spent containers littered the halls and rooms. The youngsters lay about on the floor. Most still slept. A few had awakened and munched food. One youngster still lay between the widespread legs of a girl, his buttocks naked, his pants bunched at the crook of his knees. The couple had been overcome by sleep during or after copulation. Shannon stared at the pair, unable to look away; he hadn't seen a thing like that since his Youth Camp days, and then only once.

Clancy opened a door next to the theater that Benny had called the sanctuary and led Shannon into an office. Benny hulked behind a desk. He looked like a huge, sad frog; his skin had a greenish tint; his eyes stared fixedly down at hands laid flat on the desk. He did not look up when Shannon entered.

"Sit down," Clancy said, pointing to one of two chairs before the desk; he took the other chair.

The room smelled of alcohol and recent vomit. Behind Benny hung another sculptured cross with that same sculptured man suspended from it by nail-pierced hands. Shannon knew the figure now. It was a man—or god—called Jesus Christ. He had heard the television preachers rant and fulminate about this Christ. Christ had died for the sins of humanity. Shannon guessed that only SD's worshipped this savage god, and he had inferred that the Neo-Catholic Catharsis Church was but one haven of this cult.

Benny lifted his face slowly. The shattered eyes avoided Shannon. He groaned and reached up to hold his head. Recovered at last, he spoke to the wall opposite the desk.

"Time has come to deal with you," he said. Then he groaned. Even speaking seemed to hurt him. "You tell him," Benny said, addressing Clancy.

"What Benny means is that you're cured," Clancy said. "You've kicked your PD habit. Ain't no reason for us to hold you. We want to let you go. The only question Benny has is how to do it.''

"Is there more than one way?"

"Tell him about the Raddies," Benny said.

Clancy tossed his head to move that long, stiff strand of hair away from his eyes. He appeared to be thinking.

"There are two ways to go," he said. "By the book . . . or the other way. Benny thinks it might be best if you went the other way—on account of your memory. By the book—well, the way we would do that is to call the feds at Welfare. We would tell them that you're cured and so on, and then they'd come to fetch you and give you tests and so on, and before you could say one-two-three they'd stick you into the Raddies just like that—'' Clancy snapped a finger and Benny winced ''—and then within a year or so you're dead and gone, Raver. So that's not such a good thing is it? That's why Benny thinks that you should go the other way.''

"Wait a minute," Shannon said. "Why would they send me to the Raddies?"

Benny stirred, groaned. "Because of your memory. Tell him!''

"Couple of reasons," Clancy said. "You're a slum kid. And you're a dope-fiend, cured or not. You haven't got a chance. And you've got a record. You're a loser, see? I'll bet you a Caddie for a nickel that they sent you here in the first place because they had you pegged for Raddy-duty. But the Raddies don't take pill-boys. So they wanted to clean you up a little before they fed your ass to the Mao boys.''

"Tell him about his memory," Benny said.

"Then there is your ames—your ames—your loss of memory," Clancy said. "They'll pick that up, just like that, even if you try to hide it. And they'll figure that you're a natural for Raddy-duty.''

Shannon was puzzled. Raddy duty seemed to be the equivalent of death, the way Clancy sounded, yet based on what he had seen on TV, Raddies operated armored vehicles against irritating but poorly armed bandits. He had seen a program where cheerfully smiling Raddies in green uniforms had been given awards of some kind to the sound of music before applauding audiences. After that they had been discharged to take up promising civilian careers.

"If the feds put me in the Raddies," he said, "what's wrong with that?" He went on to tell about his observation on TV, thinking as he spoke, that his talent as a pilot might stand him in good stead; and a successful tour of Raddy-duty might wipe out Raver's ill-starred history that he, Shannon, seemed saddled with for now no matter what he did.

Clancy began to sneer as Shannon spoke. He gave a snort. Benny seemed occupied with his internal processes.

"Raver," Clancy said at last, "what am I going to tell you? Listen—that stuff you saw about the Raddies on TV is advertisement, propaganda. That's not how it is out in the boonies. They chew up more bodies out there . . . Hell, the casualty rate is eighty percent. You go to the Raddies and you're dead."

There was a pause.

"And what's the 'other way?" Shannon asked.

Clancy looked at Benny. The fat man pushed his chair back—carefully, gingerly. He extracted five narrow slips of greenish paper from a drawer and laid them on the desk, fanned out like cards.

"You tell him," he said.

"We figured out a way for you to get away," Clancy said. "Benny is willing to give you a hundred bucks to get you started. What we do is this. We make it look like you escaped. We cut a hole in the fence, something like that. We call the feds and tell them that you took off—but only after you're safely out of Phoenix, going the way we came in yesterday."

"You mean *out*? To the squattings?"

"That's right. You'll have a hundred bucks. A hundred bucks out there, Raver, hell, man, that'll keep you in bread and booze and broads for better than a year."

"I don't know," Shannon said. "I don't know about the

squattings." As a slum kid he was already very low on the totempole of Purgatory life—almost a retrograde. To be a squatter . . . and he had talent piloting the jumbo jets . . .

Clancy looked at Benny and Benny stared at the fanned-out money on the desk. In the silence, Shannon heard the wailing of the child again.

"Tell him," Benny said wearily. "Tell him."

"You're a little dense since you lost your memory." Clancy tossed his head again. "Benny doesn't want you going to the feds."

"Why not?"

Clancy made a face as if the question caused him intense intestinal cramps. He stroked the stiff strands of his hair; then he inserted a finger in his ear and moved it about rapidly. Done with this, he glanced at Shannon.

"Why not?" he asked. "Well, sir . . . Look, Raver. In the old days, when you were still a Trouble Maker Number One and popped the pills and swam in booze—back then we could handle you. But now you're different somehow. Benny says that you're a bomb. Just ticking, ticking, ticking. One fine day—boom." Clancy put his fingertips together before his face; then he flung his arms out wide, in a circle, to mimic an explosion. "If we let the federales have you, they are sure to smell a mink. They'll dump a ton of pressure on you. You're going to crack wide open. You'll go on a singing jag. And in the end they'll close the Center and send us into the Raddies too."

Shannon's face must have mirrored his bewilderment at the sound of all this slang. Clancy clicked his tongue in irritation.

"They will make you talk," he said. "They will get the goods on us—and they're already watching."

"But I don't know anything," Shannon said.

"Enough," Clancy said. "Plenty enough."

"So I don't really have a choice?"

"You might say," Clancy admitted.

"And what if I refuse to go along?"

Clancy pointed at Benny by way of saying that his question belonged to the Pastor. Benny sucked in his breath, looked up, looked down.

"Let me tell you a story, Raver. A while back a guy we had here died of an overdose of horse. Don't ask me how he got the drug or why he shot himself an overdose, but the fact is that he croaked. We found him in the basement. And you know what? He died the day before we were going to let him go."

Shannon waited, but Benny seemed to have completed his story. The silence lengthened. The baby wailed. The room stank of alcohol, vomit, heavy sweat.

"So I guess I'm going to the squattings," Shannon said at last. "When do I start?"

His statement rent the tension. Both Benny and Clancy moved. Clancy smiled, a little sarcastically.

"You're not as dumb as I thought you were," he said. "We figured that you'd leave tomorrow, after mass."

"After . . . mass?"

"Tell him about that," Benny said.

"We want you to do some witnessing," Clancy said. His skin seemed to be itchy. Now he rubbed a finger along his nose. "Tomorrow is Sunday. We want to put you on the stage to help with the mass."

"But . . . I wouldn't know what to do," Shannon protested. "I don't even know what a mass *is,* much less help . . ."

Benny now made a contribution. "Look, Raver. Relax. You won't have to do a thing but stand there. I'll do all the talking. The people will want to take a peek at you before you disappear. That's all. If any of them speak to you, you just say 'Amen, brother'—or 'Amen, sister,' as the case may be. You say 'Hallelujah, brother. Praise the Lord, sister,' That's all you have to do. I'll handle the rest. You don't remember this, but we have had you up there when you were high on your PD's—to show them what Satan does to sinners. But now you're healed, you understand. The Holy Ghost has come and perched on you. And the Lord's healing power has powerfully touched your brow.''

Then Clancy cried with a false flash in his hard eyes. "Praise the Lord, brother. Oh, hallelujah. Amen and hallelujah.''

10

Rain fell on Phoenix Sunday morning, and all the lights were dim. Electrostatic generators holding up the membrane dome worked overtime. The dome itself, despite its thinness, throbbed under the drum beat of a trillion drops. Shifting pressures on the dome engendered a peculiarly erratic breeze; it lifted and moved rubbish and debris in the slum neighborhood. In the center of Phoenix it caused structures and skyways to sway, but these marvels of architecture seemed designed for accommodating movement.

Shannon shivered at his tower window. A razor hummed across his chin as he shaved. He shivered from lack of sleep and involuntary frights. Dreadful rending sounds came and went in waves as the dome vibrated. He hadn't showered since his arrival in the Purgatory Zone and wouldn't get to shower this morning either. Clancy had just said that he didn't need to smell good, not for *this* congregation.

Clancy had brought the razor and a two-piece suit telling him to shave and dress and stand by for the mass—and never mind if he didn't know what a mass really was.

Shannon finished shaving. He had no trouble with the suit Clancy had left behind, but he had no idea how to knot the tie that came with it. He tried once or twice but gave up the effort and simply hung the cloth around his neck.

Presently he heard an organ booming. The music issued from the direction of that theater they called the sanctuary. Where the mass would soon be held . . .

He had gathered from Clancy's comments that "mass" was some kind of public event attended by a "congregation." He would be displayed to the people like some object . . . like some freak.

Thus far his stay in Purgatory Zone had been a sequence of humiliations.

He didn't even mind being a prize steer at an exhibition, but he wished he hadn't yielded quite so easily to Benny's threats. Had he lost his combat spirit? He had been a man of courage in his Youth Camp days. He should have tried resisting . . .

The trouble was—he knew so little about the Purgatory Zone. Time enough for courage later, after he had settled down and learned the ropes.

In the end, he told himself, only one thing mattered. He would get away from here. With money in his pockets. And he'd be better off than he had been upon arrival. He would start again and carry out his plan. He'd go to the authorities, claim amnesia, and tell about his memories of an aerial crash . . .

They're doing me a favor, he thought. *Damned if they're not. That's worth a little humiliation. Who knows. Maybe my luck is changing.*

Moments later the congregation began arriving down below. Benny met them at the gate wearing his long robe again. He shook hands with the men, nodded to the women. These were SD's and not BP's, Shannon observed—perhaps the reason why the odors of his body were acceptable. They seemed festively and colorfully dressed, but their garments merely imitated the raiment of Beautiful People.

The stream of people died down in time, and Benny left the gate. Mack came out and took up Benny's post. Shannon was about to leave the window when a sleek sedan pulled up before the entrance and three large men jumped out. Two made for the gate; the third one went to open the back door of the shimmering vehicle. Shannon did not see the passenger or passengers hidden from view by the glare of the glass. Clancy entered the room and called him urgently.

"Come along, hurry, now," Clancy called. "Oh, look at you. You haven't tied your tie. Can't you even do that? Come here, let me do that . . ."

Clancy wore a brilliant red robe; beautiful circles and crosses had been stitched into the fabric in golden thread. Beneath this outer garment, Clancy wore a ruffled shirt of questionable cleanliness and a black pair of pants.

With hasty motions, muttering curses, he knotted the cloth around Shannon's neck.

"All right," he said, patting the tie. "All set." He led the way. "Remember," he said, rushing down the circular stairway, "you just stand there. Don't do anything. If they speak to you—'Amen, brother; Amen, sister; Praise the Lord'—and so forth."

The speedy passage brought them to a narrow door outside the sanctuary. The organ boomed. Clancy opened the door and motioned Shannon up some steps into the dark confines of one wing of the stage. Shannon glimpsed the stage beyond a curtain; it was well lit; and he heard the loud roar of song.

Benny stood by a little table in the dark wing, his eyes on two flasks and a silver tray heaped with flat, white wafers. He listened to the urgent, breathless whispers of Mack who must have just arrived. Now he turned from Mack, passed Shannon, and fit his eye to a tiny hole in the wall. He inspected the congregation that sang with such gusto on the outer side. Then he turned to Clancy.

"We have a vistor," he whispered, sounding displeased. "A BP and three bodyguards."

Clancy frowned. "Really?" Then he went to the peephole himself.

The song ended at this point. Benny stood irresolutely for a moment in fancy robes exactly like Clancy's. Then he could wait no longer. He assumed a dignified posture, like an actor shouldering a role. Slowly and sedately, his arms folded across his chest and his fists hidden in the loose sleeves of his ruffled shirt, he marched out on the stage. His red robes flamed like blood under floodlights as he turned toward the congregation. Shannon saw his face for just a second and felt shock at its transformation. Benny now looked benign, and aglow with empathy—like that other Benny on another world. Even his shattered eyes had fused into awareness. Yet it was all a sham.

Shannon moved a little. On a table draped with a white cloth he saw a golden cup covered by a flat tray. Next to it stood an enormous open book. Benny loomed behind the book. Hands raised, thumbs and index fingers touching to form eggs, he read in a sing-song voice so rapidly that Shannon did not understand a word. The congregation responded at intervals with a mumbled reply.

Clancy left his peephole. He looked unhappy.

"What's the matter?" Shannon whispered.

Clancy just tossed his head and grimaced.

"BP's" he said. "Or at least one. Somebody's sister or sweetheart. I wish they'd stay the hell out of the slums. It always means trouble."

"Why?" Shannon asked. Clancy did not answer. Moving to the little table, he picked up a cloth and a pair of flasks. Standing at the curtain he waited. At the sound of a bell, he marched out on the stage. His demeanor did not change; his eyes remained hard and shuttered.

Clancy poured liquids from the flasks over Benny's fingers. Benny's fingers hung over the golden cup. He whispered words as Clancy poured. Setting the cup aside, he wiped his fingers on the cloth Clancy had unfolded.

Shannon glanced at Mack; the man sat by the little table oblivious of Shannon. Shannon found the peephole and looked out at a sea of faces in a darkened hall. Soon he found the slender figure in the back—a girl in shiny, clinging garments; her silver suit reflected light, but her face was shadowed. She sat in the last row, alone. The bodyguards stood behind her, their backs against the wall.

Now a voice announced a song, the organ boomed, people

stood up, and the girl dropped out of Shannon's view. He turned toward the stage again.

Nothing happened right away. The people sang their hearts out. Only after they had settled again did Shannon hear Benny's voice.

"A glorious good morning, folks."

"Good morning, Benny," roared the crowd.

"Who loves Jesus?" Benny called.

"We love Jesus," cried the crowd.

"Who died on this cross here, died for your sins and mine?"

"Jesus did," yelled the crowd.

"Amen to that, brothers and sisters, amen and hallelujah. He died for us, he died for your sins, he died for mine, he walked on up to Calvary, that hard old Mount Calvary, carrying that cross and sweating blood. He did that for you and me, yes, sir!"

"Amen, amen," cried the crowd.

"He died because you're sinners. He died because you're heavy with shame, with envy, with greed, with lust. And drunkenness and fornication. And because there's murder in your hearts, murder and adultery and foul fornication. Because you look upon your neighbor's wife or husband and you want to *get down* with them. Don't deny it, the Lord knows the blackness of your hearts, the secret shame that hides behind the whited sepulchers you are, the lusts that stir your limbs because you love old Satan more than you love Jesus, the itch that you can't wait to satisfy, grunting and sweating with your neighbor's wife, your neighbor's man, for-ni-ca-ting, wallering, sweating, grunting, groaning like animals while this man hangs there on that cross his hands pierced with *nails,* nails, folks, thick and heavy, right through his hands, right through the feet, but you don't care, Satan has you in his clutches, Satan points, Satan smirks, Satan tells you the fun you'll have down on your back, a slave to vile *lusts,* and *greeds* and *fornication.*"

Shannon listened to all this, amazed. Benny sounded like a television preacher, but he seemed obsessed with sexual themes, and the more he spoke the more explicit became his descriptions of the scenes of sin he so deplored.

He stalked before the audience, moving in and out of Shannon's view. Soon his voice grew hoarse; sweat brightened his features; his eyes had shattered again. He was entranced, entrancing—a frightening, fat apparition in a brilliant red robe, a snarling noise from a wide-open, raging, almost foaming mouth.

Shannon stepped to the peephole again and looked out over spellbound faces. Rigidly seated, the SD's were mesmerized. The girl glimmered in the back—a silver shining in the darkness. She seemed quite uninvolved.

This went on for quite some time. Then Benny paused. He pulled a handkerchief from his sleeve and mopped himself matter-of-factly. Then he faced his audience again.

"Sinners, filty, groveling sinners are we all," he said. "But shame, guilt, and the crud of iniquity that chokes us all—it can be washed away, cleansed, purified. Think of the Rock of Ages, folks, the Rock of Ages cleft for you, for me. The rock of grace and purity—not the rocks that Satan wants you to get off. The cleft of grace and purity—not that itching cleft you women like to pamper with all those creams and deodorants the TV people tell you to buy—and when it comes time to pay the Lord, when Jesus asks that you should give and generously for the great work of redemption—then you people have no tithes and offerings because you've spent it all on booze and creams and sweet-smelling powders for all those clefts and nooks and crannies of your lusting flesh, but there is that other cleft, the cleft of grace, and from that cleft flows Jesus Christ's sweet blood to heal, to cleanse, to purify, to make you whole, to let you walk with your head high, saying 'Yes, Lord, Amen, Lord, I'm all yours, Lord, I'm your servant,' saying 'Get thee behind me, Satan, Tempter, Foul Fiend, Scorcerer,' saying 'Bless me, Father Benny, let the Lord's grace flow out and cover me for ever more.' " Benny paused. "You want to see the way the Lord can heal?" he asked.

A few people in the crowd called "Amen" timidly.

"You want to see the *power* of the Lord? Let me hear you now!"

"Yes," cried the crowd.

"You want to see a devil turned into an angel by the grace of God."

"Yes," yelled the crowd.

"All right," Benny cried, slapping his pudgy hands together. "I'll show you Brother Raver now, the fiend you've seen before, rolling up here, shouting vile things, in the grip of Satan. But I prayed over the fiend, didn't I? Didn't I?"

"Amen," cried the people.

"I prayed to Jesus. Yes, I did. And the Lord heard me. He came down and shined his light on Raver's head."

Benny paused and looked toward the curtain hiding Shannon.

"Brother Raver," he called, "come on out and show these folks what the Lord can do."

A nudge from Mack, who had risen and drawn near, broke Shannon's paralysis. Hot in the throat, he lurched forward and out onto the stage. Glaring lights from overhead blinded him temporarily and he couldn't see the people, but he felt their presence like a choking fog of psychic life. Benny placed an arm around his shoulder and began addressing the people, explaining something. Blood sang in Shannon's ears. Caught up in a single thought—I'll faint, I'll faint—he could not concentrate on Benny.

A moment later he began to see the crowd, and now he noticed movement. The girl had risen and her bodyguards were moving toward the stage. Now they began to run. Benny stopped in midsentence. The congregation stirred uneasily.

Then things happened with eerie swiftness. Benny let go of Shannon. He stepped forward. "Hey, what is this—" he cried. Just then a guard leaped on the stage. He rushed at Shannon, Shannon retreated reflexively—but not quickly enough. The man—Shannon glimpsed a rocky face set in a determined expression—caught him by an arm, jerked, pushed. Shannon flew forward, toward the congregation. He lost his balance, stumbled, and fell down over the edge of the stage. Arms flailing, he fell toward the other bodyguards. They caught him neatly. Then they dragged him up the aisle, between astonished SD's, toward the exit.

EXCELSIOR, THE PHOENIX MIDTOWN HOTEL

11

Before he could recover from surprise, the men dragged Shannon from the Church, across the courtyard, through the gate, and out to the waiting automobile. They threw him against the vehicle, grabbed his arms, and forced cold clasps of steel over his wrists behind his back.

"All right," one of the men said. "In you go."

The man shoved Shannon roughly into the back of the sedan through an already opened door. The door slammed shut. Shannon struggled to right himself from a half-lying position when the car surged forward, its tires squealing, and Shannon fell against the cushions.

He wriggled himself into a sitting position, and as he straightened, he noticed the young BP-girl. She sat at the far end of the long and luxuriously upholstered seat and stared at Shannon with an expression of malice and amusement combined.

He stared back at her in some amazement.

The girl resembled nothing so much as a queen of cats— the queen of some breed of vicious, silvery feline. She sat

with her legs crossed. Leaning slightly forward, her arms
rested on her widespread knees. Her fingers were slightly
curled; tipped with dangerously long and blood-red nails,
they resembled claws.

She had black and shiny eyes marked by some kind of
hardness. Short black hair surrounded her oval face; it was
cut straight in bangs across her forehead and glistened silkily
despite the uncertain light. Her lips were soft but painted a
brilliant red. A pasty substance with an irridescent, greenish
sheen covered her cheeks, her forehead, and her neck. And
her eyebrows had been shaved or plucked, replaced by sharp,
penciled lines; some sort of black substance crusted her
lashes and outlined her eyes.

This fierce-looking creature was nonetheless a perfect
replica of Lillian. Shannon recognized her face and also the
unique undulations of Lillian's body—covered now by a
skin-tight suit made of some kind of silvery mesh—the
darkness of her nipples and of her pubic hair. A strong,
enticing odor enveloped pseudo-Lillian; it was a redolence of
mysterious musk tinged with traceries of rose.

"What is this?" Shannon asked hoarsely. "What is this all
about?"

The girl did not respond. She continued to stare at him.

The car, meanwhile, had reached some sort of ramp and
moved at a perilous pace up, up, and up toward a complex of
looping skyways leading toward the center of the city. Rain
had begun to drum against the dome again with renewed
intensity. The air shrieked as if cut. Unpredictable gusts of
air buffeted the car and frightened Shannon into a sweat. The
guard behind the wheel in front—separated from the back by
a thick pane of glass—seemed unconcerned and drove like
someone in a race. The other two guards, next to him, were
evidently also accustomed to such breathtaking speeds.

Shannon looked at pseudo-Lillian and tried again.

"Would you mind telling me what this is all about?" he
said. "Who are you? Where are you taking me? Why am I
shackled like this?"

The girl laughed to herself. Her laughter sounded like a kind of low grunting from the back of her throat. She did not say anything.

A shiver passed over Shannon's back. He found it damnably odd—suspicious—that a double of Benny and a double of Lillian should take him prisoner is succession so soon after his arrival in the Purgatory Zone. He found it suspicious that both of these people, his closest friends at Richelem, should appear before him now in aspects so alien and threatening. He wondered about the nature of the parallelism that controlled these parallel dimensions in that limitless ocean of time—and he meant to think about that soon, in a moment, but now he was much too excited and frightened by the speed, the sway of the unstable car, by the shrieking sound of the sky.

"Why don't you answer me?" he said again, sweating now and growing edgy with irritation. "What sort of funny business is this? . . . Hey," he cried when she still did not respond, "I want an answer!"

His words aroused the girl. She looked at him with a changed expression. Her mirthless smile faded, replaced by a mask of contempt. Then her features twisted themselves into a grimmace.

"Oh . . . you . . . scum!" she said. She spoke with feeling, from the gut. Then, so suddenly that she startled Shannon, she scrambled across the seat toward him. She stopped in a kneeling position immediately next to him and took his face in her hands. Shannon felt the heat of her skin and the sharp, dry touch of her artificially elongated nails. Her eyes hovered above his eyes; the dark, shiny orbs were so close to him that they blocked his view of everything else.

"This time I'm the boss," she whispered. Her breath touched Shannon's face; her fingernails sank into his skin as if testing its depth. "Do you know what will happen to you, Raver?" She asked. "I'll tell you what. They'll burn you, sweetheart. They'll fry you to a crisp." She shoved his head back roughly. "Pew," she said. "Where did those Holy

Rollers keep you? In a pen? You reek goatish, honey.''

With that she scrambled back to her earlier position.

Mixed emotions struggled for dominance inside Shannon—feelings of impotence, anger, and rage. The rage won out. He felt a sudden fury at her presumption—and at the whole mesh and weave of hatred, violence, and inhumanity that he had experienced in the Purgatory Zone thus far.

"How dare you!" he cried. "What gives you the right— who are you anyway? What gives you the right to abuse me?''

The girl's eyes flashed. "Auw," she snarled. Then she scrambled toward him again on hands and knees with wanton, animal abandon. She stopped with her knees against his legs, righted herself, hauled back a red-clawed hand and struck him across the face with all the power she could muster. The blow burned Shannon's cheek, but instead of dissipating the girl's fury, the action seemed merely to arouse her. Growling a low, "auw, auw, auw," she hit him again and again. Then she sagged back on her buttocks, breasts heaving.

"Beast," she hissed, a little winded. "How dare *you*. *You* have nothing to say. *You* have no right to question *me*. You have the right to *fry*!''

Tumultuous emotions now seemed to shake her frame. She raised her hands again. Her fingers curled like claws as if to scratch him. Her face moved under the momentum of some mad emotion; her mouth formed a rectangle of rage. And she came to him, growling—he cringed away but could not escape her—and then her lips pressed against his mouth, her tongue stabbed, her teeth worked. She kissed him with a bruising violence, but her kiss had other than amorous motives. Shannon could not understand what she was trying to do until she managed to get his lower lip between her teeth. Then she bit down.

Shannon yelled out in pain. The yell came out like a gurgling roar, a sound from his throat; it was muffled by her still pressing head and body. Tears filled his eyes instantly,

and he struggled reflexively to get away but couldn't. She
held on, mauling his lips. He was on the point of fainting
when at last she released him. He gasped for breath and
choked on blood. Tears blurred his vision. His head swam
with the onset of dizziness.

Moments later he recovered a semblance of self-control.
He tensed his muscles against the searing pain at his mouth.
He sobbed. He tore at the clasps that held his hands behind
his back in a futile effort to free himself, but all that he
achieved was to cause pain at his wrists; that pain, at least,
mitigated the agonizing flashes in his mouth.

Pain rolled over him in waves. His lip bled profusely,
discoloring the suit and the shirt he wore. The pain diminished after a while, and Shannon brought his shivering
body under control. Slowly and carefully, he tested his
wound with his tongue. The lip had already begun to swell.
He blinked his eyes repeatedly to clear them of films of
moisture.

Still moving at a furious pace, the car had advanced to a
high positon among coiling skyways. The architectural flowers Shannon had admired from a distance loomed near now,
slender towers swaying in the uncanny breeze of the dome's
cavitations. Sharply angled exit ramps led from this portion
of the skyway toward these towers. The buildings were
bright with lights; clouds darkened the sky beyond the dome.
Far beneath the highway, resembling some dark fungus
spread between bright clumps of birch trees, lay a vast
acreage of dreary slums.

Shannon looked over at the girl. She sat in her corner
again, arms crossed over her chest. She stared forward in the
direction of travel, and it seemed to Shannon that the girl
looked sad, tiny, and a little . . . empty now.

"You've hurt an innocent man," he said to her. His voice
sounded slurred and his lip hurt badly when he spoke. "I'm
not who you think I am. I've never even seen you, Miss. I've
never done you any harm."

"Hah!" she said.

He waited for the pain to subside before he spoke again.
"What have I ever done to you?" he asked.

"Don't pretend," she said, "oh, don't you dare! Either
you are Raver or you're Ra-Ra. You can't be both. I told you
I would find out who you really are. If you are Ra-ra—admit
it now! Go on, admit it."

"Who is Ra-ra?" Shannon asked.

"All right," she said, decisively, "have it you way. If
you're not Ra-ra—then you're Raver. And the Ravers of this
world—hell, sonny, the Ravers of this world are not supposed to cross the Lilly Waterfords. Understand? If you are
Raver, I'll see that they burn you to a crisp. So help me God.
And if you're Ra-ra, I'll sit there and see you admit it before
the whole wide world."

Raver, Ra-ra . . . Shannon was confused. The pain in his
lip, the swaying car, the sense of dizziness he felt—none of
this helped him think.

Who was Raver, to begin with, and what had he done to
Lilly Waterford? And who was that other person she wished
him to confess he really was. *Give it up,* Shannon told
himself. *Give it up.* He could not think straight in this
damned Purgatory Zone.

"I wish I knew who I really am," he said, "but I don't—
unfortunately." He paused. Speaking caused a burning searing, stabbing pain in his lip; it caused the bleeding to start
every time he opened his mouth. "I lost my memory," he
said. "But I know this much. I'm not Raver. And I've never
heard of, of this Ra-ra."

"Hah," she said. "You'll never get away with that.
Amnesia! Likely story. Do you think that that'll help you?
With me against you? Don't forget who I am, sweetheart.
Judge Noland owes his job to Uncle Fred. The Commissioner
of Corrections used to work for Daddy before he got his
job—before *Daddy* got him his job. Nothing will save you,
sweety, least of all amnesia. You tell it like it is. Raver or
Ra-ra. No third way for you. You try to wiggle out of this and
I swear I'll have them fry you."

"If you won't tell me any more than that . . ." Shannon began. Then he broke off. His lip had begun to bleed profusely again. He licked over it with his tongue. Dizziness gripped him again.

The car slowed down in a moment and turned off onto one of the steep ramps. The ramp led toward the upper portion of a very tall, slender structure. It was formed of eccentrically stacked white disks, each disk three stories high. In a moment, slowing even more, the car entered the building and dove into a dark garage. Cars were parked everywhere. In the relative darkness, Shannon noted that Lillian's face-paint had a phosphorescent sheen. Pseudo-Lillian glowed. She glowed like Lillian back home. But that other Lillian's strange radiance, glimpsed at times, rarely, had come from her insides and not from some tube of paint.

"I'm not any of the men you think I am," Shannon said.

"Good-bye, Raver," Lillian said with finality. "I'll be seeing you in court."

The car stopped before a luminous shaft. Its walls were made of Plexiglas. It seemed to be at the center of the building. Pod-like elevators moved slowly up and down inside it. Two of the bodyguards jumped from the car. The driver remained behind the wheel. One of the men went to the shaft and punched a button on a translucent panel. The other one came around and opened the door at Shannon's side.

"All right," he said. "Out with you. Come on. Move it."

Shannon got out reluctantly. He saw no other choice. The man glowered down upon him, ready to drag him forth. Shannon followed the guard to the elevator shaft.

"Where are we going," he asked, wincing, sorry he had spoken. That lip sent flashes of pain down to the pit of his stomach.

"You're off to jail, Raver," the bodyguard said. "And then into the frying pan."

12

Moments later, Shannon stood in one of the pod-like elevators moving upward smoothly. He had always been uneasy about heights and kept his eyes riveted to the opaque floor of the elevator, unwilling to gaze out through the pod's translucent walls at the yawning shaft through which they were moving.

The elevator stopped several floors higher up. Through Plexiglas walls, Shannon looked into some kind of lobby. A high counter faced the elevator shaft; above the counter hung a sign suspended from the ceiling by chains. OFFICE OF INVESTIGATIONS, said the sign. Beneath the sign sat a big man with a red face; he wore a blue uniform with golden buttons and seemed occupied with reading in a huge ledger of some kind. He did not look up when Shannon, flanked by his guards, entered the lobby.

Then Shannon noticed another person. He was a short, pudgy man in a brown suit. He had been leaning against the counter to Shannon's left. The man was balding and had a round face. His suit was flecked with the ashes of a thick tobacco tube he carried in his mouth; it was one of the objects the TV had called "cigars." The man advanced now and stopped before Shannon. He nodded to the taller of the two guards.

"Hello, Simpson," he said. Then he gave Shannon a flat look. "So you got him," he said, addressing the guard called Simpson again.

"Of course we did," Simpson said. "We always get our man. We don't slouch around like you characters in the public sector. The Old Man said to find him, so we found him for you, Murphy."

Murphy took the cigar out of his mouth and stared at its burned-out tip. Then he gestured with the object. "Big deal," he said. "We would have got him too. Sooner or

later. You should see my caseload. It's the length of my arm.
I've got a lot of *serious* crimes to deal with. Serious. I can't
pull out all stops just to help the Waterburgs with their little
personal vendettas. But don't tell the Old Man that. I've got
troubles enough without getting on his shit-list too.'' He
gestured with the cigar again. ''Undo this character. He isn't
going anywhere.''

The guard whose name Shannon still did not know stepped
behind him and released him from his shackles. Shannon
rubbed his wrists.

Simpson said: ''Don't you want to know where we picked
him up?''

''Not especially,'' Murphy said, ''but tell me anyway.''

''The Neo-Catholic Catharsis Church,'' Simpson said.
''Down on the east side.''

''That figures,'' Murphy said. ''Half the cons we're looking for are hiding in some cosy welfare nest. Mind you . . .''
He gestured with the unlit cigar again. ''If the Old Man
should happen to ask, tell him that we asked the feds about
this character. They said they'd never heard of him. We've
never come across a guy with fewer records in the computer.
Tell the Old Man that. I don't want my boss' boss catching
hell for something that isn't our fault.''

''I'll tell him,'' Simpson said. ''If he happens to ask. Take
good care of our buddy here.''

''Don't worry,'' Murphy said. ''Come along,'' he said to
Shannon. He waved casually to the bodyguards and moved
toward a narrow hall.

The corridor was long. Small offices lined it on either side;
most were empty; a few were occupied by men talking on the
telephone. Murphy stepped into one of the empty offices and
pointed to a chair before a grey metal desk. He moved behind
the desk, dropped into a chair, and lit his cigar. Clouds of
smoke soon hung about his head. He leaned forward through
the smoke.

''What happened to you?'' he asked. He pointed at Shannon's lip with his cigar.

"I got bitten," Shannon said. He expected a surprised reaction, but Murphy just nodded.

"She is a goldplated bitch," Murphy said. His round face was without expression. "You're out of luck, Shanty," he went on. "All I can say is that you're most unfortunate. We knew where you were hiding all along, but we played stupid. I don't know how they found you, but now that they did, there isn't much that I can do for you. I feel sorry for you, pal, but you should have stayed away from her. Any stupid SD punk that tangles with the Waterburgs deserves what he has coming, but I'm still sorry for you. I'll do the best I can—and not because I like you, either. But I've had it up to here," he said. He gestured with a flat hand beneath his chin. "Up to here. The Waterburgs have all the power, but enough is enough. You are the fifth punk they have dragged in here on some trumped up charge or other, and I've had it up to here. I'll try to spring you, Shanty. Somehow. But I might not be able to swing it."

Shannon understood the man—vaguely.

"What's supposed to be my crime?" he asked.

"She says that you raped her. My guess is that it was the other way around, but she says that you raped her, and that's a capital offense. And she is a Waterburg. If we can't spring you somehow, it's curtains for you, Shanty. Curtains, pal. Did you do it?"

"Do what?"

"Rape her."

"Not to the best of my knowledge."

"What is that supposed to mean?" Murphy asked. "You either did or didn't. Not that it matters, in your case. It's your word against hers, and she has a much bigger word—if you take my meaning."

"My problem is," Shannon said, his speech slurred and sounding odd, "I don't think that I am Raver Shanty. But I can't seem to prove it."

"Come again?" Murphy said.

"Everybody calls me that," Shannon said, "but I don't think that I am Raver."

"You're confusing me, pal. What are you trying to say? You don't know who you are?"

"No," Shannon said. "But I know I'm not Raver."

"Well," Murphy said, "this is getting better and better. You know who you are *not*, but you don't know who you *are*? Explain that to me. Nice and slow."

"Yes, sir," Shannon said. "You see, I lost my memory."

"You did, did you?" Murphy said. His expression began to change. He eyed Shannon. Then he examined his cigar for a moment; he laid the dark, frazzled stump into a dish filled with mounds of grey rings of ashes and other burned-down stumps. "Tell us about that," he said.

"I—I woke up a couple of days ago," Shannon said. "I was lying in a field, outside the city. I had no idea where I was or who I was. I still don't know who I am supposed to be. I remember flying an airplane, kind of vaguely—"

"Flying an airplane!" Murphy said, raising his eyebrows.

"Yes," Shannon said. "I seem to remember. I was flying an airplane and one of the engines was on fire."

"On fire," Murphy said. "Hmmmm."

"That's right," Shannon said, "but that's all I can remember. Then I came to, lying in a field. I started walking along this road, toward Phoenix, and then some people from the church came by. They picked me up and brought me back to the city. They've kept me locked up, ever since. This morning they took me to a thing called 'mass.' In the middle of that the guys that brought me here grabbed me and carried me out of there. She was with them. She bit me while we were driving here."

"Well, well," Murphy said. "Let's just take that from the top again, okay? You're not Raver Shanty?"

"I don't think so."

"You don't remember?"

"That's right," Shannon said. "And it doesn't sound like my name."

"Hmm. And you say that you woke up—where? In the Squattings?"

"No. Further out. Out along some road."

"In a field?"

Shannon nodded.

"And you don't remember anything that happened to you before that time?"

"Only that I was piloting a plane. And the engine was on fire."

"Ah, yes," Murphy said. "The engine. And you say that you came into the city? How?"

"We came by a tunnel."

"A tunnel? What sort of tunnel?"

"It was dark. Wet, too. There were all sorts of puddles."

"Old rails on the ground?" Murphy asked.

"That too."

"And the people who brought you belonged to the NCCC?"

"The . . . yes. The church."

"Was Benny Franks out there?"

"Yes. He was there."

"How did you get into the tunnel?"

"First we went into some hangars. Huge hangars."

"In the Squattings?"

"Yes," Shannon said.

"And where did you end up. Where'd you end up in the city?"

"In a warehouse."

"What kind of warehouse?"

"It was filled with old furniture."

"Did they carry something? Did they bring something with them?"

"Yes," Shannon said. "Some sacks of stuff. They smelled like hay."

"You sit right there," Murphy said, rising. "Don't move. I'll be right back." He hurried to the door. His feet shuffled off, down the corridor.

Shannon sat there. His lip had stopped bleeding, but it hurt worse than ever; it throbbed and throbbed and throbbed. He felt a little dizzy and very ill at ease in the narrow cubicle. It smelled of stale smoke in here, evoking memories of Youth Camp. The torn green cushions of Murphy's chair revealed aged foam rubber. The blotter on the desk was covered by dark doodles. Portions of the black telephone were covered by dust. Four posters on the wall, each one different but each depicting men on motorcycles, advertised the Police Circus of four successive years. A lone black metal helmet hung on a clothes-stand in a corner.

Shannon felt dizzy—and in more ways than one. He was confused. Things were happening too quickly. He knew too little. He had to navigate in darkness and in fog, without instruments.

Rape . . . rape . . . He had barely understood the word. Forcible sexual intercourse. Said to be one of the social evils of the past. Of the past of Kibbutz. Here it seemed more common. He? A rapist? No, not he. Raver might have raped, not Shannon, but he lived Raver's life now, like it or not, and he couldn't get himself disentangled . . .

God! That lip. It needed medical attention. Infection . . . Shannon touched his forehead. He thought that he might have a fever but his forehead was moist, cool. Cold sweat . . .

Something has to give, he thought. I've got to find someone to help me. Anyone. A person who tries to help me rather than always . . .

What a . . . violent zone this is.

He pondered Lilly Waterburg, the power of the Waterburgs. Was there such a thing as justice in the Purgatory Zone? Did they run psychoscans on people here to determine guilt or innocence? Did they have retraining camps for the mentally defective? Would he ever clear himself—clear Raver? Shed Raver? Shuck Raver off like some skin that wasn't his . . . ?

Time passed.

What was keeping Murphy? Why had he left? Would he order some kind of an action against the Neo-Catholic Ca-

tharsis Church? Probably. The smuggling would end. The
youngsters would be placed under proper supervision. That
tiny child Shannon had heard bawling hour after hour would
receive competent care at last . . . Maybe there was justice
after all. But what if Raver was guilty? And what if Shannon
couldn't shed that damned identity?

The office had no windows. A neon bulb overhead
hummed irritatingly. It reminded Shannon of the Time Van,
sitting in its lobby, waiting for James P. Schuster. The stale
cigars exuded a foul smell.

Hold on, Shannon told himself. *It can't go on, not forever,
not like this.*

He reached into the pocket of his suit. The PD pill Clancy
had tossed him two days ago lay there, an oblong plastic
capsule, oily to the touch. Maybe people took those things
around here to get away from things. He was glad that he had
brought the pill alone. He might need it if things went on like
this. No one to help him, no one *nice*, all these harsh men and
catty females . . .

More time passed. Shannon's lip throbbed and throbbed.

At last he heard steps coming down the hall, the steps of
several men. Murphy entered the room. He was carrying
a folder. He went behind his desk and sat down on the chair
with the torn, green cushions. Two men in uniform entered
the room behind him and stood by the door. They looked at
Shannon placidly.

"Funny thing about your memory, Shanty," Murphy
said. "You have a very convenient memory, pal. You remembered that field. You remembered the road. And the
air plane. And the engine. The burning engine. Let's not
forget the engine. By no means, Mr. Shanty. But somehow
or the other . . . " Murphy clicked his tongue. "Somehow
or another, Shanty, you didn't remember knifing George
Emerson to death. How convenient."

Shannon felt the blood draining from his face.

"I didn't do that," he said, almost whispering. "They
did. Benny's people. I had nothing to do with that."

"Ohh," Murphy said. "So you *do* remember. Just in the nick of time. Just in the nick of time. She remembers everything. Not like you." Murphy opened the folder. "Take a look at this, Shanty. Recognize him?"

Murphy held out a sheet. It was the drawing of a face, a long, dark, narrow face surrounded by long hair. A band across the forehead. It was not a perfect portrait, but it resembled Shannon.

"Mrs. Emerson made this," Murphy said. "She had a computer to help her. Not bad, is it. Not a bad portrait from *memory*. Mrs. Emerson has a damned *good* memory. You should have a memory like hers."

"I didn't do it," Shannon insisted. "She wasn't even there. She couldn't have seen me do it! They did it. I just lay there. They had knocked me to the ground."

"Amazing, isn't he?" Murphy said, addressing the two policemen who stood inside the door. "For a guy who has lost his memories, Shanty remembers lots. Lots. And to think that I felt sorry for you," he said, addressing Shannon again. "It'll be a pleasure to help the Old Man this time. I am going to get myself some brownie points—without a guilty conscience. All right, boys. Take him away."

"But I didn't do it," Shannon protested.

"Take him away," Murphy said. "Tell it to your lawyer," he said to Shannon. "Tell your lawyer all about it. Everything that you remember. Tell him about the airplane. And the engine. Don't forget the engine . . . ."

13

From the darkness of a van—one of the cops had called it a 'paddy wagon'—Shannon jumped down into uncertain light.

His trip in darkness had been brief, but it had brought him down to the ground again. He stood beneath the center of the city. Monstrous concrete columns and ramps rose above him forming platforms for those giddily high structures rising toward the apex of the membrane dome. Beneath that superstructure squatted ordinary buildings of a bygone era made of brick and stone. They were uniformly grimy, run-down, and neglected.

The cop who had let Shannon out again, inclined his head toward a large, grey building nearby. It had three wings and narrow, barred windows.

"There it is," the policeman said. "We call it 'Excelsior,' the Phoenix Midtown Hotel. For SD-types," he added. "Are you ready to be checked in? Ready or not, your time has come." He gestured with a yellow folder, inviting Shannon to approach the structure. The folder contained Shannon's record, presumably. Shanty's record. Shannon was still en-meshed, still captured in a spiderweb of Shanty's cursed identity. "Come on, Ralph," the policeman called. "Let's get a move on."

A second policeman emerged from the paddy wagon and joined Shannon. Then the three of them went up some steps toward the massive building's massive entrance. Shannon looked at the barred windows on the way and saw grey faces peering at him through the bars. The building was dark inside and the observing prisoners silent.

Before the door, the officer who carried Shanty's record pushed a bell. A voice then issued from a circular apperture above the bell. "State your name and business," said the voice.

"George Fletcher, here, MPD," the policeman said. "We're bringing you another guest, Charlie. One Raver Shanty. He comes recommended by Old Man Waterburg himself. Special guest. Special handling," So saying, Fletcher smiled to himself, then he winked at Shannon.

"All right," the voice said. "Stand by, George. We've been expecting you. I'll come and get you as soon as I find my goddamned flashlight."

Moments later the massive door came open. A thin man wearing a white shirt with a golden badge above his heart looked out and signalled with a hand inviting them to enter. Then, lighting the way with a flashlight, he led them down a pitch dark corridor. Only the ball of his light was visible, moving erratically over a stone floor, but Shannon saw that the hall was wide. Their footsteps echoed as they walked.

The man with the flashlight, the man called Charlie, knew George Fletcher well. The two talked as they walked, and Shannon gathered from the conversation that this building had been cut off from the electrical grid again. Someone by the name of Dalton was said to be enraged by that. Dalton was climbing the walls, Charlie said, but nothing could be done about it. Phoenix Electric had its priority schedule, and the penitentiary was on the bottom of the totempole. "Hell," Charlie said. "We don't count for much. The VIP's must have their hairdryers and electric massagers and God only knows what else, but we're 'interruptible.' Interruptible! Imagine that. We're supposed to do *our* job the same as always, but when it comes to money or electricity, we always get the short end of the stick."

He stopped before a door at last and pointed his beam of light at a narrow bench. "You can wait here," he said to Shannon. "George, you come along. Dalton wants a run-down on this guy."

Charlie and George Fletcher entered a room, leaving Shannon outside with the policeman called Ralph. As soon as the door closed, they were in total darkness. The only light came through the crack beneath doors on either side of the corridor.

"How long am I going to be here?" Shannon asked, settling on the bench. Many people had waited there. The wooden surface of the bench was smooth with the touch of many a body.

The officer called Ralph settled down as well. "All depends," he said. "If you ask for jury trial, you might be here for months. But it you accept a summary—a week or so, maybe less."

It was quiet in the corridor. Shannon heard the murmur of voices through the door but could not hear what was being said.

"What's a summary?" he asked.

"Well, sir," Ralph said, "in a summary trial, you get tried by a judge. If you accept a summary, you more or less accept whatever the judge is going to say. There is no appeal."

"And trial by jury?" Shannon asked.

"That's the whole show," Ralph said.

"Meaning?"

"Well, you know. They select a jury. The prosecutor prepares his case, your defense attorney prepares his. Both sides present evidence, and at the end the jury gives a verdict. It's the whole hog. And it takes a lot of time."

Shannon thought about that. He liked the sound of jury trial. He had read about that in his books—the adversary process. He knew something about trials of that sort from his Youth Camp days. When Ralph spoke about evidence, Shannon guessed that Ralph meant the testimony of a psychoscan or some equivalent device. If they used the psychoscan here in the Purgatory Zone, Shannon had a good chance of clearing himself. A psychoscan would tell the jury that he was innocent of both crimes—rape and murder. It would also reveal that he was from another time zone—but better that than being "fried," whatever Lillian had meant by that. Shannon guessed that he would opt for jury trial. He wanted to be rid of Raver once and for all.

"Do you have any money of your own," Ralph asked after a while.

Money? Shannon thought about the hundred "bucks" that Benny had promised but had never delivered.

"No," he said. "Money is one thing that I don't have."

"Oh, boy," Ralph said. "In that case you're better off asking for a summary. They'll assign you a lawyer, but without money you're not likely to get a good one. And you need a very good lawyer to get out of the mess *you're* in. It's an open and shut case—and double-barrelled charges. Rape and murder. Hell, you need a miracle-man, not a lawyer.''

Shannon brooded over that. He could not undersand why the quality of a ''lawyer'' would make any difference. If they used a psychoscan, his innocence would be established in the most scientific manner possible . . .

''Who is this man Dalton Charlie was talking about,'' he asked after a moment.

''Dalton? He runs this hotel.'' Ralph chuckled as he said it.

''What is his first name?'' Shannon asked.

''Malcolm,'' Ralph said. ''Malcolm Dalton.''

''Malcolm Dalton,'' Shannon repeated. He had guessed as much at the first mention of the name. Here was another figure from Zen Richelem station, another double. The Malcolm Dalton Shannon knew was a gentle biologist who had charge over the station's livestock back in the Kibbutz Zone. He wondered what Dalton's double would be like here in the Purgatory Zone.

They sat in silence. Voices murmured on the other side of the door.

Shannon reached up and touched his forehead. Yes. A fever had set in. His mouth felt like a hot, painful cave. His eyes sat in dry sockets staring into darkness. That bite needed medical attention soon lest . . . He thought about the phosphorescent paint on psuedo-Lillian's skin. He thought about blood poisoning.

Then steps approached, the door came open. The man called Charlie looked out. ''All right, Shanty,'' he said. ''The big boss wants to see you.''

Shannon rose and entered a large room.

Pale light fell into the crowded office from two narrow windows barred with rods of iron. A cluttered desk stood at one end. A kerosene lantern blazed on one corner of it, spreading a circle of yellow light. Malcolm Dalton leaned over the desk. He was writing something on a slip of paper.

Straightening, he handed the slip to Officer Fletcher.

"Here you are," Dalton said. "Now that I have signed for him he is officially mine." He noticed Shannon. "Sit down," he said. "Over there." He indicated one of three wooden chairs before the desk. Then he came around his desk. A hand on Fletcher's elbow, he led the policeman out. "Back at city hall," he said to Fletcher, "try to raise some hell, George. We've got to get some lights in this place. And tell that boss of yours that I don't want any more turkeys like this Shanty here. Do something creative for a change. Shoot them while they're escaping, or something. Get some brownie points with the Old Man. Don't always dump your problems on me."

"I'll do what I can," Fletcher said, "but you know how the system works."

"Do I ever," Dalton said, opening the door. "Charlie, you show these gentlemen out again. Don't let them get lost in the dark."

Dalton returned to his desk and stood behind it, his huge frame partially illuminated by the kerosene lamp. He looked very much like his double at Zen Richelem—a big man with a sagging gut. His uniform was open to accommodate the pot-belly. He hooked his thumbs into a wide leather belt and peered at Shannon with an expression of distaste. Unlike his double back in Kibbutz, this Malcolm Dalton had small black eyes, heavily oiled and pasted-down hair, and a pair of waxed moustaches.

"I'm Malcolm Dalton," Dalton said. "I run this place. And when I say I run this place, I mean just what I say. I'm the law around here, and I am the *only* law. Is that understood."

"I guess," Shannon said.

"Good," Dalton said. "Let me get right to the point. I don't buy your silly story about amnesia—no more than Murphy did." He unhooked one of his hands and tapped the yellow envelope on the desk before him. His fingernails gleamed with unnatural brightness suggesting that they had been lacquered. "And let me tell you something else. I want you out of my establishment right quick-like. Waterburg cases are nothing but trouble, and I have trouble enough without the likes of you. So don't give me any shit. Is that understood?"

Shannon felt very hot. He gathered saliva and swallowed to wet his throat. He wondered fleetingly why every person he met in the Purgatory Zone was invariably hateful.

"I'm innocent," he began. "I'm not sure—"

"Ah, ah, ah," Dalton said, gesturing with an index finger. "You're starting already. I don't want to hear any of that crap. It's none of my business. All I want to do is to get you the hell out of my little establishment. Okay? I've got six hundred people inside this luxury hotel, and you know what, Raver? Every last son of a bitch is innocent. Every last one. So what you are telling me is nothing new. I'm not interested. All I want to hear from you is that you're ready to cooperate. Well, are you?"

"I . . . How am I supposed to cooperate?" Shannon asked.

"Well," Dalton said, "about your trial. The Waterburgs want to see you in court—fast. No long delays, nothing like that. So I have to call the Prosecutor's Office today to tell them what you said. All right, what am I going to tell them? Are you going to be cooperative and ask for a summary trial? Or do we have a trouble-maker on our hands. What is it going to be?"

Shannon swallowed again. Dizziness assailed him. The room smelled unpleasantly of oil, of burning kerosene. The odor made him nauseous. Dalton exuded an air of violence, and Shannon feared opposing him; but he had to do it.

"I—I've got to ask for a jury trial," he said. "You see, I'm innocent and—"

"Stand up!" Dalton shouted with sudden vehemence and at the top of his voice. "That's right," he shouted when Shannon rose. "straight up. Put your shoulders back. Chin out. Don't you know where you are? You're in jail now,

Raver. Put your feet together. Arms down by your side. And when you address me, I want to hear 'sir' loud and clear.''

He came around the desk and marched up to Shannon. He stood so close that the heat of his body seemed to touch Shannon. His small eyes gleamed.

"All right," he said, "let me hear it again. Is it going to be a summary or jury trial?''

Shannon hesitated for a moment. Then he gathered his courage. "Jury trial, sir," he said. His voice came out sounding like a whisper.

Dalton stood foi a moment and stared at him. Then the big man began to pace up and down between the desk and the door, the desk and the door . . . Shannon stood stiffly. He felt himself swaying slightly.

"You're not very smart," Dalton said after the second or third turn. "I advise you to start thinking. Be sensible, Raver.''

"I'm not Raver," Shannon said. The words came out sounding like a croak, and no sooner had he uttered the words than he knew that he should have kept his mouth shut. But he couldn't acquiesce. He had to resist all these attempts to pin him with a name that was not his.

Dalton came to a stop before him. Dalton's exquisitely polished boots reflected pale light from the window. Mingled with the odor of kerosene, Shannon now perceived the smell of Malcolm Dalton's hair oil, and a momentary panic seized him. His mouth filled with saliva. He was going to be sick. Then the spell passed. Only his mangled lip continued to throb; it throbbed in rhythm with the beat of his heart.

Dalton's dark eyes peered at him with a glint of malevolence.

"Fine, Mr. X," Dalton said at last. "Mr. X, you've got a lot to learn. You've got a hell of a lot to learn. We know how to skin a cat around here. We've got nine ways to skin a cat, and you won't be the first one that we've skinned. We specialize in skinning cats like you. If you don't want to be cooperative—fine with us. We have our ways. You want a jury trial. Fine, Mr. X. You'll be sorry. You'll be very sorry. But it's your decision.''

Behind Dalton's desk, affixed to the wall with pieces of dirty adhesive tape, hung a large, faded chart. Dalton went up to the chart. He picked up the kerosene lantern on his way and held it high to illuminate the paper. The chart seemed to be a diagram of the penitentiary. Shannon saw the outline of the three-winged structure repeated three times—once for every floor of the building. Rectangular spaces subdivided each of the wings. Within each rectangle, variously sized cubicles had been marked off; names scratched in pencil filled the cubicles. Dalton studied the chart for a moment. Then he turned to Shannon.

''I'll tell you what I'll do, Mr. X,'' he said. ''I am going to be nice to you. I don't have to—understand that. But just for the hell of it, I'll be nice to you. I'll give you a day to think it over—and I'll put you in with a smart man, a man who knows the ropes around here. You listen to him. You've got a lot to learn, and he can teach you all you need to know. Tomorrow I want to hear what you've decided.''

''Sir,'' Shannon said, ''I think I need medical attention. My lip . . . ''

Dalton set the lamp down to the corner of the desk again. He shook his head slowly from side to side.

''You're a trouble-maker, Raver,'' he said. ''Now you're starting to tell me how to run my own business. I can see that you need help—and I don't need you to tell me.''

On Dalton's desk stood a silvery bell with a wooden handle. Dalton picked it up and shook it. Summoned by the clear tinkling of instrument, Charlie entered the room.

''Okay, Charlie,'' Dalton said. ''I'm all set with this unfortunate bird. Take him to the dispensary. And when you've got his puss fixed up, take him to the third floor, Wing A. Put him in with John St. John. Tell John that this man has not been too cooperative.''

''Yes, sir,'' Charlie said. Then he nodded to Shannon.

14

Some hours later, Shannon lay on the lower bunk of a double-decker bed. The bed stood in the smallest of the cage-like cells that occupied either side of a long, echoing, noise-filled hall. Narrow, barred windows threw weak light into this hall revealing a hundred or more shadowy prisoners. Some of these men rested, some played cards, some moved restlessly about. At one end of the hall, seated before a little table under a wall-mounted rack with guns, a lone guard, whose name was Higgins, leafed through a magazine in the light of a propped-up flashlight. Immediately next to him was a heavy metal door, the door through which Shannon had entered his new home some hours earlier.

Shannon's cell was on the dark side of the hall— illuminated only by the tips of glowing cigarettes some of the prisoners were smoking. One old, emaciated creature shared his cell—the man whom Dalton had called John St. John. St. John sat on a wooden stool by Shannon's head. Persistently inquisitive—and evidently schooled in what he had to do—St. John had drawn out Shannon right away. For some time now, he had been arguing with Shannon, arguing and pleading. Shannon had stopped responding quite some while ago. He was growing weary of this John St. John. Very weary.

"Accept the fact that you are Raver Shanty," St. John whispered now. "What other choice have you got. Look. You don't remember who you are, but everyone else remembers you. All right? So how can you be innocent? I don't mean the murder now. I mean your raping Lilly Waterburg. I'll accept what you say about the murder—after all that happened after you came out of it. But that rape . . . Listen, even if you didn't do it, how can you know that? And if you don't know it, not for sure, how can you deny it? It's her word against your word—and she is not only a BP, my friend,

she is a Waterburg. Okay? Know what that means? Every
person on that jury will stand to benefit from your conviction.
The Waterburgs have power, boy. It's like a spider's web.
The strands are all over the place. You get that? Those jury
men—they can't afford to vote for your acquittal. No way.
The word would get out. The'd lose their jobs or pensions or
whatever. They'd get evicted from their apartments. Their
credit ratings . . . You get the picture. And if you don't,
Raver, you've forgotten more than is good for you. And that
fantasy of yours? About that, that psychoscan? You got that
out of a comic book before you lost your memory. That ain't
going to save you. There ain't no such thing. And that jury
of your so-called 'peers' . . . don't make me laugh. They'll
send you to the chair like one-two-three. And if my guess is
right, you'll never even see a jury. Dalton will make sure of
that. Dalton always gets his way. Believe me. You might
think that you're a high-class kid; you might think that you're
a pilot and all that rot, but in reality you're just an SD-kid.
Really. No amount of fancy imagination is going to change
that fact. And Dalton isn't scared of you. He knows where
you're coming from. He can force you to do what he
wants—and nobody is going to blow any whistles. I assure
you. Not with the Waterburgs involved.''

This hissing, insistent sound went on. It was lulling Shannon into slumber. He wasn't cheered by St. John's words,
but at least this man seemed to mean him no harm.

He was groggy, dizzy, and nauseous.

He lay with his eyes half-closed, his head on a stiff, narrow
pillow, one hand in his trouser pocket. His fingers touched
the smooth and oily surface of the PD pill which he still had.
They hadn't searched him—not in the dispensary and not
here in this block of cells.

A bandage now covered his swollen lip. He had also been
given two injections—but the drug or drugs seemed to wors-
en rather than improve his condition.

Groggy, dizzy, nauseous.

Noise and stink swirled around him. The bare walls of the
cavernous hall threw back every sound—the shuffling tread

of prisoners, the harsh voices that rose and fell, the bangings and scrapings. The stink came from holes along the two main walls. They served in lieu of toilets. The stink of piss was especially powerful—a breathtaking tang of ammonia. The smell seemed to be growing stronger as the weak light from the windows opposite failed with growing darkness over Phoenix.

"There is a way out of this," John St. John was whispering. "There is a solution to every problem. There is a way to skin all cats. There are routes from every maze. There is a light at the end of every tunnel. What you must do is flow with it. You have to let yourself go. Stop resisting this experience. Let it happen to you, nice and easy. Stop fighting—but persist in *your* decisions. Let go of that cramped ego complex. Remember that you're not a person so much as a cosmic process."

Shannon sat up abruptly. A terror had seized him. Barely masked by the fumes of ammonia, he clearly smelled the odor of James P. Schuster's shaving soap. And the whispered words he had just heard did not belong in the Purgatory Zone.

"What did you say?" he asked.

St. John seemed to shake his head. "I didn't say anything," he said. "I saw your body jerking. I figured that you had dozed off."

Dozed off? Shannon had no memory of dozing off. And that damned smell of James P. Schuster's soap! The smell was fading now. He laid himself down again, puzzled but reassured. The fever and the drugs they had pumped into his buttocks created illusions.

"Pussy," yelled a shrill, high-pitched voice in a large and crowded cellblock across the way. A number of the inmates responded to the shrill shout by banging with tin bowls in which the soup had been served for the evening meal. "Pusseeeey!" screamed the high soprano again, and once more tin bowls clattered.

"Hold it down, back there," shouted Higgins, the guard, looking up from his magazine. "Keep it down," he yelled.

John St. John leaned closer to Shannon.

"Hear that?" he said. "That's why Dalton sent you here." A thin, white hand gestured in shadowy darkness. "Larry and his boys are over there. Dalton uses them to teach the likes of you a lesson."

"What kind of lesson?" Shannon asked, suddenly alert.

"You'll see for yourself," St. John said. "The fun will start after it gets dark and Higgins takes off for the night. Dalton leaves this hall unguarded. He claims he doesn't have the staff, but that's not really true. He leaves the hall unguarded so that Larry and his boys can do their thing."

"What thing?" Shannon asked. Every movement of his mouth caused pain. A thick-set woman in a white dress and wearing a peculiar white hat had washed the wound with alcohol until it had bled again. She had smeared a yellow ointment on the wound after the bleeding had stopped.

"A guy like you came in here about a week ago," St. John said. "Dalton put him in with me. A trouble-maker, just like you. By the name of Henry. Henry didn't want to see the light, so Dalton put him over there—" The pale hand gestured again. "With Larry and his boys. Larry calls him Henrietta now. They've just about fucked him to death over there, but Henry is stubborn, or crazy. I don't know."

Shannon sat up again. The fever and the drugs caused him to have illusions.

"They—they what?"

"You heard me," John St. John said. "You'll see it for yourself in a minute, after Higgins leaves. Dalton made sure that you'd have a ringside seat. He gave you a day to reconsider, and if you're smart, you'll do just that. Summary trial is the way to go. With a little luck, a federal recruiter will claim you for the Raddies, and that way you may have a chance at least. You'll end up in summary one way or another. Or dead. Over there." The white hand flashed in darkness.

"Chicken!" shrilled the high soprano from across the way. "Pusseeey!"

"Once Dalton makes up his mind," St. John whispered,

"there is no way out of it. Use your head, Raver. You landed yourself in this mess. No one else did it. You went into the Time Van on your own, nobody forced you—"

Shannon sat up so abruptly that his head swan with dizziness. He saw a thousand crackling stars and felt a searing pain in his head. He clutched his skull until the sensation passed.

"I heard you this time," he said to John St. John. "I heard you distinctly. You said 'Time Van' didn't you? How do you know about that?"

"*Pussy!*"

"*Quiet* over there."

"Are you all right?" St. John asked. He leaned closer in the almost total darkness. His musty breath smelled of James P. Schuster's soap. His thin, grey hair and small, sharp, penetrating eyes seemed phosphorescent.

"You said 'Time Van,' " Shannon croaked. Shivers passed over him. He turned his head with sharp, abrupt, crazy jerks, this way and that. He could not believe this. He had to reassure himself; he had to make sure that he was still here in the echoing, stinking hall.

"What are you talking about?" St. John whispered. " 'Time Van!' I've never heard of such a thing."

"You're lying," Shannon said. "I heard you distinctly. Something is going on. Don't you dare to lie to me or I'll—"

The wooden stool scraped as John St. John drew back.

"You're hallucinating," he said. "Take my word for it. And don't try anything. I'm not as old as I look, and you're not in the best of shape. I'm your friend. I want to help you. Go on, lie down. Rest until the fun starts."

Shannon sagged back on his bunk. He closed his eyes. The room began to go around and around and around and around. He opened his eyes again.

Going crazy. He counted. It was his fourth night in the Purgatory Zone. In that time he hadn't met a single normal, friendly person—except perhaps this St. John. Threats, violence, incarceration, abduction, violation. And now some kind of medication. He couldn't sort the real from the unreal.

His mind was like a burst barrel, seeping sanity between its staves.

Waves of ammonia wafted over him.

It seemed to him that the noise in the cavernous concrete hall had intensified. The muffled talk of the inmates had become a roar—like the crash of waves.

Henry, Henrietta. Larry and his boys. Summary judgment. Federal recruiter. Raddies.

The Raddies made him think of Clancy Robers. *You go to the Raddies and you're dead,* Clancy had said in Benny's office. The casualty rate.

He sensed movement. John St. John had drawn near again.

"There he goes now," the old man whispered. "It'll start pretty soon."

The harsh sound of a big key turning in a lock echoed across the cavernous hall, and then a dry hinge shrieked as the heavy portal opened. The door slammed shut with a dull report. Then the key rattled on the outside.

Suddenly an eerie hush fell over the hall. The talk stopped abruptly. Feet ceased to shuffle. Implements no longer banged. Shannon heard St. John's nearby breathing.

He sat up slowly and carefully, unwilling to disturb the menacing silence. The narrow windows across the way had become completely dark. Here and there in the giant hall, inmates smoked cigarettes; the red glow of these slender tubes revealed that most of them stood by the bars of their cages facing the central hallway between two rows of cells. They waited. For what?

Beneath the feverish heat of his skin, Shannon felt the electric movement of a shiver. Time passed. The silence deepened. Expectancy stretched across the gloomy space of the reeking hall, threatening to break. And then, at last, it broke asunder. Shannon heard that voice again, that shrill high voice. It shattered the brittle, expectant silence.

"*Pussy!*" cried the shrill soprano. Then again, "*Pussy!*"

And the hall exploded in noise.

Nudged by John St. John, Shannon got off his cot and

moved toward the front of his own cell. His hands around cold bars, he listened to the sound of some kind of chase in the large enclosure across the way. Men ran, clambered, and yipped excitedly. The high soprano acted as the leader of the hunt. "Pussy" was his hunting cry. It was too dark in the cavernous hall to see much more than shadowy movements.

Amidst the lusty yells of the prisoners, Shannon now heard the voice of the prey—the desperate sobs and mewls of a breathless man. "For God's sake," cried the man. "No. For God's sake!" Scrambling sounds, the thud of blows, angry shouts, and loud breathing obliterated the pleading voice.

"They've got him," St. John whispered. "They've put a gag in his mouth. Listen. Hear that? That's Henry."

Shannon heard a muffled moan.

After a moment of near silence, a lull in the general tumult, he heard the high soprano once again. The man emitted sharp, excited, rhythmic outcries; they coincided with violent, lunging movements of his body, barely visible in the darkness.

"He could be doing that to you," St. John whispered next to Shannon. "You'll suffer the same fate unless you cooperate with Dalton."

The outcries came faster and faster until at last Larry achieved his obscene objective. His outcries ended in a long, animalistic groan.

"That's not all," St. John whispered. "That was Larry. Now the others get their turn. They'll keep this up as long as they can keep him conscious."

Shannon let go of the bars. His palms were sweaty. He felt the onset of another dizzy spell. He stumbled back to his cot and fell down on his stomach; he covered his ears with his hands, but even that did not help; he continued to hear the brutal rape. Two, perhaps three other prisoners worked their way on Henry before the commotion, groaning, moaning, and cries diminished and subsided.

After a while John St. John shuffled near.

"Hey, Raver," he whispered. Shannon did not respond.

"Raver? Are you asleep?" Shannon did not stir. He was not in the mood for conversation.

St. John shuffled off. Shannon heard him urinating against the wall. Then the old man came back again. His boot depressed Shannon's mattress as he climbed up to his own bunk. The springs above Shannon sang metallically as St. John settled down for the night.

Around the hall, others were doing much the same. Little by little, the echoing sounds died down and out. Talk rumbled for a while, a receding tide. Sirens howled somewhere far away. Silence spread. Then a few men began to snore. The sounds of night were everywhere.

Shannon couldn't sleep. He turned this way and that. Wafts of stink nauseated him. He felt cold and hot in succession, dizzy and groggy in turns. His brain refused to settle down. Like a dull and terrible throb in his own head, he heard Henry groaning, sobbing, and moaning across the way. The sounds were muffled—as if Henry tried to hide his pain. But the more the man across the hallway tried to hide his desperation, the more Shannon heard it, and the prisoner's agonies became his own.

Hours passed in this way—Henry moaning and sobbing, Shannon turning and twisting, his fingers deep in his ears—but to no avail. He was weary, weary to his bones. His lip was hurting. The fever racked him. And yet he could not sleep.

In the early hours of the morning he could take no more. He could not leave his cell; he could not escape into sleep; and he could not avoid hearing the man across the way. But he did have one means of escaping all this, all this stink and violence and pain. He had the pill. Paradise dice. You rolled them, Clancy had said. If you were lucky—paradise. And if unlucky—hell. Shannon reached into his pocket and extracted the oblong, oily capsule. Could any place be worse than this cavernous hall? Even hell seemed a better, friendlier place.

He hesitated for a long time before, at last, he popped the

pill into his mouth and swallowed the little object. It went down hard. It left a track of sensation in his throat. Shannon lay there, feeling that track down to his stomach. Well, he had done it. He had acted as Raver might have acted. He wondered what would happen next.

Nothing happened for a while. Then he felt heat. The heat rose from his stomach and up, across his chest, toward his neck. Suddenly, and with a rush, he felt himself whirling. And then he was gone.

A TRIP TO PARADISE

15

Without warning, without preliminaries suddenly, unexpectedly, Shannon found himself suspended in mid-air. He floated at the level of the tree-tops above a bone-dry countryside in the early light of dawn. The land was yellow, red, and brown. Dusty bushes and lonely trees marked the rolling, rocky scene.

"I'm dreaming," he told himself. "This can't be real."

And yet it was very real and not like a dream at all. Shannon could see everything clearly, sharply, and in focus—and knew that in a dream the scene was more perceived than seen, a shifting texture of visible emotion rather than sense perceptions. The scene held still. The massed leaves of a tree were at his elbow; he saw a red bird on a branch; the brilliant creature rummaged beneath a wing, ruffled its feathers, flew away. The branch on which it had been sitting trembled; a dewdrop rolled from one of the leaves and fell toward the dusty ground.

For a moment nothing happened. Then Shannon heard a voice.

"You-who," cried the voice.

Shannon could not localize the sound. He felt a sudden rush of excruciating embarrassment hanging up there, in mid-air, without visible support, defying the law of gravity, seemingly encased in air. It wasn't real!

"You-who," called the voice again. "Ra-ver. Over here, Raver. Look up."

Raver? Was he still Raver? Even in a dream?

You can't think in a dream, not coherently. You can't concentrate—not in a dream. He held out his hands and looked at them and saw the pores of his skin, the flat-lying hairs of his hands, the pouching of his skin at his finger joints, the fine parallel lines in the horny substance of his fingernails.

"You-who!"

Shannon turned his head, and as he turned his entire body moved slowly and lazily as if it had no weight. Then he saw a whispy but huge apparition—a creature made of fog or some other vapory substance. He could see the substance quite clearly, sharply, unlike in a dream. He could concentrate on the moving, twinkling, smoky substance of the ghostly giant. The creature was a column of smoke, thick at the top and growing slender as it reached the ground in a curving swirl like a tornado's tail; but this mass of unsubstantial elements was relatively static. Sparkles played and danced within it.

A jinn, he thought. *Yes, a jinn.* He had seen a creature like this in a holographic film as a child—the ghost in the bottle found by the sailor on the beach. This jinn had no face, however, only a roughly head-shaped mass of foggy, smoky substance.

"Hi," the jinn said. "Long time no see, Raver."

The voice came from no specific aperture. It issued from the center of the cloud.

God, what a scene. Early morning sunshine lay over the desert landscape reflected in tiny bits of silicate in clay and dust and rock. And there he was, floating in baby-posture next to the crown of a Joshua tree. His suit was scuffed and filthy, its front encrusted with dried blood from his mangled lip. Near him swirled a blue-grey jinn with sparkles and tiny flashes in its interior mass. The creature threw no shadow, but in its vicinity, quite distinctly, time seemed to flow at a slow rate.

Time flowing? Slowly? It was unreal.

"Well, Raver, haven't you got anything to say?"

"Who are you?" Shannon asked. "What is this? Where am I?"

He spoke without difficulty. His lip no longer hurt. His voice was clear and rang out over the landscape. It startled another grooming bird, perhaps the same bird. The bird flew off with sudden rattle of agitated wings toward another tree—a bright, red missile—and disappeared in dark-green foliage.

"Welcome back to Paradise," the jinn said. Then it laughed. The miniature stars inside its vapory mass danced at the laughter. "I understand that you have lost your memory. I bet you don't even remember me."

"No, I don't," Shannon said.

"Look around you," the jinn said. "Surely you remember *where* you are."

As Shannon moved his head again, his body moved with him, describing a slow turn. The landscape looked vaguely familiar, but he couldn't place it until he saw a massive complex of buildings on top of a distant hill.

"Kibbutz," he murmured.

"Poor Raver," the jinn said. "Of course you're in the Kibbutz Zone. You've been here before. That much you remember. But you don't remember Alkhazar!" The jinn made the chiding sound of a clicking tongue. "Remember me? Alkahazar? Mary's spirit guide? And yours too, Raver. I am always with you on your OBE's."

OBE's? Alkhazar?

Then, in a flash, Shannon remembered Alkhazar. The name. He saw himself tiptoeing after a tiptoeing Benny Franks through a darkened room of the Neo-Catholic Catharsis Church moments after his arrival there. Twelve people sat around a table like numerals on the face of a clock, holding hands. One of the women had hissed in anger when Benny entered the room . . .

He glimpsed movement to his left. People approached from that direction walking in a long and scraggly line.

Embarrassment gripped him again. He had to get out of sight. Ludicrous to be suspended in midair. He moved his arms and legs awkwardly, half scrambling, half swimming. He tried to reach the sheltering shadow of the tree's crown, but he made no forward progress.

The jinn laughed—a booming sound. "They can't see you, Raver. You're perfectly safe. You're like me, now. Just a spirit. Heavens, Raver. It looks like we have to start all over again with you. You act as if you've never had an OBE. You don't even know how to move."

"What is an OBE?" Shannon asked.

"You see?" the jinn cried. Sparkles sparkled in the smoke. "Oh, my. Looks like we have to go back to basics. An OBE is an out-of-body experience. We've loosened the shackles that bind you to that body of yours just a little with three cc's of psilodenodrome. And consequently I can whisk you across a hundred skins of time—and right back to Paradise again."

Shannon considered this. His body was still moving from his earlier scrambling—toward the jinn and not toward the tree.

Was this a dream or wasn't it? A dream should not contain elements he had not experienced before. He had seen a jinn before—in a film, to be sure, but exactly like this creature. He had heard the name Alkhazar before, very recently. The place where he hung suspended like some weird balloon was in California, in the Kibbutz Zone, in the Youth Camp reservation of his teens. And that line of people moving toward him seemed oddly familiar as well. But he had never heard of psilodenodrome—or of OBE's.

"You got me over here . . . using a drug?"

"Yes, that what PD's are."

"But if I am a spirit," Shannon said, "what's all this?" He plucked at the fabric of his rumpled suit and grabbed one of his arms to demonstrate that he was real and made of flesh and blood—despite his gravity-defying suspension in midair.

"Patterns," Alkhazar said. "You're just a ghost now, just like me, but you can't imagine yourself that way. Your body is sleeping in Dalton's jail. You're still connected to that body—tenuously. But here you're just a pattern of your energies; you're just a projection. And it pleases you to see yourself dressed in those rags of fabric and of flesh."

Illusion? Hallucination? Dream? Paradise was *Kibbutz*? Was that really so? Or wishful thinking? A drug-induced reverie of a man in trouble in a jail?

"Are you ready?" Alkhazar asked.

"Ready?" Shannon asked. "For what?"

"Remedial instruction," the jinn said. "What else are OBE's good for?" Then it laughed again, this time in a high-pitched voice.

Shannon experienced anger at the laughter. The ghostly creature's ghostly whinny suggested amusement at Shannon's expense.

"I'm not sure I like this," Shannon said.

"If you don't like your OBE's, stay away from those PD's," Alkhazar said. Then came more laughter, but Alkhazar broke it off. "You can't get out of it, so do what I tell you. And try to get something out of all of this. In no time at all, you'll be back in Dalton's jail."

Dalton's jail . . . It seemed very far away just now.

"Are you ready?" the jinn asked again.

"I guess," Shannon said. "I don't seem to have much choice about it one way or another."

"Watch carefully," Alkhazar said. "And don't resist. Just flow with it and don't resist."

The jinn began to move. Almost immediately Shannon felt

himself in motion as well; he floated after Alkhazar feeling
drawn as by a magnet. They were making for the still distant
line of moving people.

As they came closer and closer to the column, Shannon
recognized both the scene and the occasion. He was looking
at a marching squad of teenage boys—ten or twelve young
men. Haggard and dirty, each boy carried a pack on his back
and a long, flexible stick in his hand. A war party out on
patrol. The boys had been in the field for three weeks now,
searching these hills for the "enemy," for a similar squad of
boys from neighboring Camp Winnetoo. This scene had
happened twelve years ago—and it was happening again.
And at the tail of the column, some distance behind the
rest—deliberately holding back—walked Shannon himself
in a younger version.

"Don't panic now," Alkhazar said. They floated above
the column now, but the youngsters seemed unaware of
them. "Go ahead and look at yourself," the jinn said. "It's
not going to harm you."

Suppressing a stir of anxiety, Shannon peered down at his
younger self. The boy marched slowly at the back. He eyed
the column ahead of him. And with quick, darting glances,
he searched the rough terrain around him.

Shannon looked strange to himself down there. His own
face—so familiar from a frontal view in the mirror—
appeared peculiarly foreign. *Am (was I) really so thin?* The
expression on the boy's face was unattractive: the eyes had a
sharp and calculating gleam; and the slightly parted mouth
and out-thrusting lower lip gave the youngster a greedy look.

He had been hungry that day—today. They had all been
ravenous.

"Watch now," Alkhazar said.

The column was passing a huge boulder on the right of the
barely marked path. Each boy passed the rock and moved on
beyond it, every boy except the younger Shannon. The
younger Shannon ducked behind the rock. Working with
feverish haste, he took off his backpack, rummaged inside

it, took out a flat, rectangular can. Using a metal key torn from the back of the can, he opened the tin with nervous haste. Then he poured the contents of the can down his throat—quickly and greedily. The can held sardines in a tomato sauce. The sauce ran down from the corners of the younger Shannon's mouth. The boy gulped sardines, barely chewing. He pushed the empty can into a shadowy hollow beneath the boulder. Then, wiping his mouth quickly, he picked up his pack and the long stick that he had dropped and hastened after the column.

"Well?" Alkhazar said, "what do you think of that?"

"What?" Shannon asked.

"What do you think of that?"

Shannon was puzzled. What *should* he think? Nothing. He had forgotten all about this Youth Camp war, one of the many he had been part of—a long, dull, stupid, and poorly planned affair. And the worst of it still lay ahead.

"What should I think?" he asked. "It's a Youth Camp war."

"What do you think about what you just did? Eating that can of sardines?"

"What do you mean—what do I think about it?"

"Why did you hide to eat it?"

"That's obvious. I didn't want to be seen"

"Why not?"

"I didn't want to raise a hue and cry. It was my can. I didn't want to have to share it."

"Why not? Some of those boys hadn't eaten in three days."

"So what?" Shannon asked. "It wasn't my fault if they hogged up all their rations in the first couple of days. Torrence was an idiot. I knew he'd lead us on a wild-goose chase; I knew that he would get us lost. I was smart enough to hold on to my rations. So why should I have shared?"

"You didn't want to fight this war?"

"Of course not. It was just a lot of childishness."

"And boredom. And hunger."

"That's right," Shannon said. "Boredom and hunger. And it wasn't a *real* war, just boys playing war."

"What would you have rather done?"

"I don't know," Shannon cried, suddenly cross. "I didn't ask to go to Youth Camp. I didn't want any part of it. Come *on*." he cried, impelled by a pulse of rage. "Let's get on with it—or get me out of this ridiculous position."

Maybe it was a vision, hallucination, dream. Maybe he was really just a spirit and a pattern of projected energies. But it didn't feel like that. His body seethed with angers. He had no wish to see this shit again, this stupid make-believe war. And be lectured by a pile of smoke. And float like a balloon.

"All right," Alkhazar said. "We shall get on with it."

Once more they were in motion, following the column. Shannon had no wish to see the battle that he knew would start within a minute or so, but he couldn't help himself. He had no way to control his own motion.

The boys moved down into a depression. The path led between a clump of woods and an irregular piling of huge boulders. And the boys from Winnetoo were hiding in the woods and behind that mass of rocks, in ambush. Torrence had been, still was, a fool. Incompetent. He led them right into the trap.

The battle started when the mass of the column had come abreast of the woods. Torrence, who carried the pennant at the front, and the younger Shannon, who straggled in the rear, were outside the main thrust of the attack.

With a bone-chilling shout, the boys from Winnetoo poured from the woods brandishing sticks; they rose up like a wall of bodies from behind the boulders, clambered over them, and leapt into the fray. They had assembled and infiltrated into Camp Calvin's territory an unusually large number of boys—eighteen or twenty at the least. And the younger Shannon saw the odds were poor at best.

The boys fought with sticks and stones and fists in a tumult of motion, shouts, and dust. A group from Winnetoo surrounded Torrence and the youngster fell. The pennant was ripped from his grasp and two boys from the opposition raced away with it.

The younger Shannon had left the path and had dropped to the ground. Now he crawled quickly toward a clump of low, dense bushes. He crouched behind them and observed.

The battle lasted for some minutes. The boys from Calvin fought valiantly despite their numerical inferiority. In the tumult and dust, both they and their attackers were unaware of the fact that Winnetoo had captured Calvin's pennant—and as a consequence Calvin had already lost. The boys from Winnetoo disengaged at last. They left behind a shattered column. Several Calvin boys lay on the ground, unconscious; most were badly battered; a number had broken bones.

Now the younger Shannon stirred in his hiding place. He took his stick and broke it in two over a knee. He scooped dirt from the ground and rubbed it over a portion of his forehead and one cheek. He balled his right fist and rubbed his knuckles roughly over the ground—once, twice, three times. He caused abrasions on his knuckles, inspected them. Proceeding on hands and knees, he then crawled in a wide circle toward the woods, and in a moment he disappeared into them.

The older Shannon watched all this from his embarrassingly helpless position in midair. Alkhazar hovered near him in silence.

Then suddenly the helicopters came out of the horizon buzzing toward the scene of battle. Shannon wondered again—as he had wondered in those days—how the camp authorities always knew when a battle had been fought. Somehow they knew. They always arrived within minutes to evacuate the badly wounded—and even worst cases emerged fully healed from the hospital within a week or two to fight again.

The helicopters landed amidst great upsurgings of dust.

During the noise and confused visibility caused by the landings, the younger Shannon joined the group. He stood with the rest, holding his broken stick, his face smeared with dirt, his knuckles bleeding. He boarded one of the helicopters with others who had only been lightly wounded. Then the whirlies rose up, one by one, and sped off toward Camp Calvin, the noise of their engines a receeding roar.

Suddenly it was very still in the desert. Shannon turned toward Alkhazar. The ghostly jinn hovered near him; sparks danced in his smoke.

"Well?" Shannon asked.

The jinn did not reply.

"All right," Shannon said. "So I didn't fight. So what's wrong with that? Only an idiot would've rushed out there to get himself clobbered." He paused to give Alkhazar a chance to react, but the jinn maintained its silence. "My running out there wouldn't have made the slightest bit of difference." No answer from the jinn. "As far as I'm concerned," Shannon said, "in a war—even in a phoney war like this—brains count for more than heroism. Look. I used my head. And not just in this battle. I told Torrence a hundred times what he had to do. But do you think he ever listened to me? No, sir. That kid would never stop to take advice from a mere fourteen-year-old second-year shrimp."

Shannon stopped talking. Suddenly it struck him as ludicrous that he should be explaining his actions of twelve years ago to a pile of *smoke*! Good God. None of this was real to begin with; it was just an unusually clear dream of past and present, a mixture of memories induced by paradise dice.

He closed his eyes to make the vision go away, but as he did he felt nausea and smelled James P. Schuster's revolting shaving soap. His lip began to throb. And he felt himself beginning to turn, turn, turn, and turn at an increasing rate of speed. Quickly, he opened his eyes again.

There was the desert. There was Alkhazar.

"Ready?" the jinn asked.

"Ready," Shannon said and sighed. He was ready for more 'remedial instruction' even if he didn't understand the meaning of it. Not in the slightest.

16

Shannon said "Ready," Shannon sighed, and Alkhazar began to move toward him. In the fraction of a minute, fog swallowed Shannon, and in reaction panic gripped him. He started to scramble again in midair, enclosed by sparkling vapor. He flailed his arms and scissored with his legs like a helpless baby, but despite these actions, he could not escape the jinn's embrace. Instead he felt a growing warmth and sensations of childish pleasure, and flashes of his earliest childhood memories flitted briefly across his brain.

Then he felt motion—a sensation of sliding. He seemed to be as slick as an ice cube; and the ice cube was sliding rapidly down a sloping plain that seemed to be made of mirrors. Time moved away very quickly now. The mirror plain curved up ahead of Shannon like the front of a toboggan. Then the motion slowed down. Alkhazar's embrace dissipated.

Shannon found himself floating in Outer Space, spread-eagled in velvety blackness. Sharp and piercing points of light sprinkled the darkness, trillions of points of light.

Shannon turned his head and glimpsed Alkhazar again. In a swirling curve that resembled a tornado's down-dipping tail, Alkhazar's body reached down, down, down, and down to the surface of a radiant planet, a ball of white, green, black, and blueish shade. It was home; it was the earth.

"You'll be on your own this time," the jinn said. His voice reached Shannon without the aid of airwaves; and Shannon also seemed intact; he was still capable of breath-

ing. But then, Shannon thought, this was just a vision and not
reality at all.

"I've brought you here," Alkhazar said, "but I am not
going in with you. When that thing rolls down on you, don't
resist the impact. Just flow with it. Nothing will happen to
you. Remember that you're just a spirit—no matter how you
look and feel."

"What thing?" Shannon asked.

"Behind you," Alkhazar said. Then he began to shrink at
an incredibly fast rate, moving down, down, down like
sucked smoke. "I'll be back," came the voice. And Alkhazar had disappeared, had merged with the earth below.

"Alkhazar!" Shannon cried. "Hey, Alkhazar!"

Shannon's heart was beating very rapidly now. The jinn
was just a figment, of course, a construct of Shannon's mind
and memories, but Shannon had found the ghost a reassuring
figment nevertheless.

No answer came. *God!* Here he was, spaced out, waiting
for . . . for what? Whatever it was, it was behind him.

He turned his head to see. He saw the thing immediately.
Brighter than the brightest of stars, the torus-shaped immen-
sity of a gigantic wheel rolled toward him. It was a satellite.
Shannon recognized this as yet another of his yesterdays. He
guessed that the satellite rolling toward him was *Saffire.* He
had spent his Maturity Trip on board of this celestial construct many years ago.

The satellite approached very rapidly, and Shannon braced
himself. *Don't resist,* he told himself, repeating Alkhazar's
advice. *Don't resist the impact.*

The wheel came on, blazing in reflected light—a bright,
metallic doughnut of such gigantic proportions that Shannon
was the merest speck of silvery dust in comparison. Then the
satellite rolled over him absorbed him. He passed through the
walls of the construct without the slightest effort. The satellite's walls were made of a honey-comb composite—metal,
membrane, metal, foam, metal; then came a space of vac-
uum; then once more metal, foam, metal, membrane, metal.

It seemed that he really was a spirit. Matter passed through him and he through matter. He moved through internal structures now—walls, piping, instrumentation, and finally several levels of floors. He broke out of this dense mass by rising up through the floor of a domed structure. Two people sat on chairs immediately above the spot where he emerged. He penetrated them as well; for a second his substance filtered through the flesh, bone, kidneys, lungs, and brains of a young woman and a young man.

His upward motion slowed down at last; he came to rest above an audience of youngsters, suspended in mid-air again. Above him curved a translucent bubble—the roof of the hall. Through that roof, he saw the hose-like interior of *Saffire*; it extended away into an up-sloping distance. Agricultural terraces jutted in tiers from either side of *Saffire's* skin; they were bathed in shafts of sunlight that originated from wide reflector slits in the vaulted "sky" of the satellite.

Immediately under Shannon sat forty or fifty youngsters of both sexes. They formed a semi-circle around an old man. The old man sat in a canvas chair. Behind and high above the old man was a curving screen.

The old man was very thin, emaciated—and now that he was thrown back into this setting, Shannon recognized him. The old man was John St. John, once upon a time Shannon's guide on *Saffire*. Shannon had forgotten the old man—both his appearance and his name. He had forgotten the old man to such an extent that even meeting his double in the Purgatory Zone had failed to stir recall. But now it was all back—suddenly, like a slap in the face. Shannon had spent many hours in this domed hall, listening to lectures and watching films on that curved screen behind the teacher. It was on that screen that he had seen vague and elusively rendered scenes of the Purgatory Zone. His resolve to visit Zone F-39—if ever he left the Kibbutz—had been born in this very hall! Looking down now, he was sure that an earlier self of his was sitting down there, toward the back, in the shadows. The youthful Shannon would be hiding back there, seated next to

Ronnie Rome, his friend. The two boys would be yawning at St. John's boring lecture, as usual.

And, as usual, St. John was lecturing. Shannon turned his attention to what the old man was saying.

"We showed you the earth again this morning," St. John was saying. "Have you ever wondered why we do that every morning—and from such a distance? There is a simple explanation. We want you to see the earth for what it is—a tiny speck in space, a beautiful little speck, a tiny cosmic egg, a dappled egg all green and white. It is the egg of the legendary bird, the Phoenix."

John St. John paused, seemingly collecting his thoughts. Then he continued.

"All of you have spent four years in Youth Camp. In those four years you have experienced what life was like in the old days. You have engaged in bitter wars and bloody feuds and politics. As the embryo passes through all the forms of human evolution—briefly a fish, briefly an ape—so now you've had a taste of the unregenerated times. You didn't experience them in their fullest bloom—but neither is the embryo really a fish. You've had the experience. You've seen through it. But now the time has come for you to make the leap onto the next ledge of evolution. The time has come for setting aside childish things. And that's why we show you the earth; that's why we call it a seed."

Shannon listened with interest. He did not remember this lecture—or not very clearly. Yet he was sure that he had been in this hall before. The thought caused him to look down and to his right. His gaze came to rest on a pair of young men seated side by side. Their heads inclined downward, they were absorbed in a game of warships played on their pocket calculators. One of them was the sixteen-year old Shannon; the other one was Shannon's friend, Ron Rome.

"A seed," John St. John was saying. "Well, what kind of a seed? How can I call the earth a seed—something so huge, something with oceans, mountains, cities? There is an explanation, but first let me remind you of something you already know."

"The universe is running down. The suns are burning up. It's as simple as that. The matter of the cosmos is expanding at a stupendous rate. Expansion. Diffusion. They are signs of decay, you know. The cosmos is still blazing with incredible energy, but time is a ruthless foe. All the suns will die some day. Thermodynamics teaches us that a time will come when nothing will move. The matter of the universe will lie in endless space like a hair-thin skin—like a shroud over the void. And then there shall be nothing out there but darkness. And silence."

The hall lay in silence for a moment. Then St. John resumed.

"So why is the earth a seed?

"Because we are gathering another form of energy down there. And more than that. We are spreading that energy through space. That same energy is gathering up here—in satellites and colonies. We are fashioning the substance of another and more subtle universe. It rises up from dying matter, from our bodies, from matter so complex in arrangement, in structure that each of you, every one of you, resembles the entire universe in sublety and power. And at the hour of your death, you will yield up that energy; you'll become that energy; you'll turn into a single, conscious atom of the *new* cosmos we are forming—the cosmos of personality."

Vaguely remembered concepts, vaguely recalled. So vaguely that Shannon wasn't sure that he had ever heard any of this before—not *he*, not his person. Clearly his ears had picked up the sound of St. John's mildly spoken words; his sixteen-year-old brain had processed the information; but it had not sunk in.

"Teilhard de Chardin was the first to see this clearly," John St. John continued. "He still lived in the unregenerated time. He was a biologist and a servant of the Lore. He talked about the evolution of the earth—first the lithosphere, then the atmosphere, then the hydrosphere, next the biosphere. And now, at last, we are working on the most important sphere of all—what Teilhard called the noosphere, the earth's psychic envelope. In his day it wasn't visible; but

since then man's power to smash the psychic atom has grown
by leaps and bounds. We do it as a matter of routine these
days with subtle programs of training, special environments,
and drugs. You too will see the noosphere—in another month
or so. And then you'll understand a lot more clearly why I
call the earth a seed.''

The younger Shannon still played warships down below
with Ronnie Rome.

"All right," John St. John said. He rose from his canvas
chair. "Enough for today. Gather outside and wait for your
assignments.''

The young people rose and made toward three exits of the
hall. The younger Shannon and his friend were among the
last to go; they had some trouble breaking away from their
game of warships. Shannon himself had no idea what would
happen next. He had no idea how to cause himself to move.
He hung up there in midair, watching the youngsters leave.

When the last of them had disappeared, John St. John set
out for a side-door himself. At the door he turned. He looked
straight up at Shannon, and the expression in his eyes revealed that Shannon was quite visible to him.

"Hi," he said, addressing Shannon. "I am glad that you
could make it, finally. The last time around," he said,
gesturing toward the spot where the younger Shannon had
been seated, "I didn't have your undivided attention.''

A shudder passed through Shannon.

"By the way," St. John said, "if you want to move, just
imagine your destination.''

"Imagine?" Shannon echoed in his thoughts.

"That's right," St. John said, responding to Shannon's
unspoken word. "Imagine the place where you want to be,
and you'll be drawn to the spot. That's the way to move in
OBE's.'' He turned to go but arrested himself again. Once
more he looked at Shannon. "You were never one to take
advice," he said, "but I advise you to tag along with your
predecessor. Today is his most important day on *Saffire*—
although you don't remember it that way. And good luck,
Raver. I really hope you make it.''

With that the old man passed through the door leaving Shannon suspended under a translucent dome and over an empty auditorium.

17

He hung alone inside the dome and wondered.

His most important day aboard the satellite? What could the old man mean?

The day fell into the early portion of his trip, his first or second week in space. Nothing much had happened in those days—although he did recall a string of mishaps and of accidents—so many that the kids had said that *Saffire* was accident-prone. More damned near disasters, more damned dangerous snafus . . . But the most important day? His most important day had been his last, the day he took that milky drug.

But now what? What should he do?

I'll follow him, he thought. Curiosity gnawed a corner of his mind. It would be nice to know exactly what this day had brought.

He closed his eyes and concentrated, picturing the area outside the domed assembly hall.

The method worked. His body floated across the auditorium, passed through the dome, and stopped above the younger version of himself. Dressed in grey overalls, the sixteen-year-old Shannon stood below in the company of a fair-sized group of youngsters with a bored expression on his face.

A young adult faced the group. "All right," he said. "All of you know what to do. See you again at noon." He had just made the morning's work assignments.

The younger Shannon and four other boys turned into one of the streets leaving the circular space outside the assembly

hall. Shannon found it easy to tag along. He floated right
above them like some kind of bloated kite.

Two-story buildings flanked the street. The boys entered
one of them—through a door. Shannon went in too—through
the wall. And when he saw the inside of the building he
remembered which day this was.

That day!

It hadn't been his nicest day in space. Not the nicest, not
the worst. But certainly not the most important.

Hovering just beneath the ceiling, he watched a man
issuing cans of paint, brushes, gloves, pans, scrapers, stirring sticks, and rags to the five boys. Then the youngsters
turned to go.

Shannon knew where they were going and decided to go
there ahead of them. He pictured the boiler room where
once—today—he had spend an hour painting pipes. He had
no trouble recalling a mental image of that boiler room. It had
left an imprint on his mind after all.

Under the impetus of his imagination, he began to move
ahead of the boys. Soon his floating body veered to the left,
passed over several more walkways and roofs, and floated
over some fields where agricultural workers tended what
looked like rows of lettuce. Then, passing through the up-
curving wall of *Saffire's* interior wall, he came to a stop
somewhere in utter darkness.

He wondered for a moment why it was so dark but remembered that the lights were off and would stay off until the boys
arrived.

The boys arrived a little later. Shannon heard them before
he saw them. They had to open the pressure lock as they
approached. The boiler room was close to the outer surface of
the satellite, and an airtight door—a heavy door—separated
it from the interior corridors. The heavy door was part of a
safety system—a sytem that, as Shannon knew, would be put
to a test in about an hour.

The lights came on at last. Shannon saw three boilers to his
left—squat circular tanks fed by a mass of piping. The boilers

had been shut down so that the work detail could paint the piping. Shannon glanced at the heavy metal door. It was still closed. Someone—probably Ronnie Rome—would now be opening it from the other side by working a crank.

The heavy door opened slowly, and the boys came in. They looked at the pipes running against the wall. Some of the pipes were painted red for steam, some white for make-up water, some blue for condensate return. The paint was old and peeling. Seeing all the work that lay ahead, the boys let out a mock-groan. They did not know, as Shannon knew, that a heavy, ugly, jagged, and huge meteorite was hurtling through space even now—on a collison course with this very spot of the satellite. The careless adults who ran the colony were failing to detect it even now, despite its size. The work would be rudely interrupted.

The boys set to work, and Shannon watched.

The younger version of himself, in company of Ronnie Rome, worked on the far side of the room. They began to scrape loose paint from steam pipes.

Shannon regarded the other three. They worked near Shannon. They would be heroes before the day would be over, Shannon reflected. Everyone would jabber about their bravery. But in truth they weren't brave so much as stupid— stupid and damn lucky. *Damn* lucky.

Time passed. The boys near Shannon scraped and painted and talked about girls. They hadn't had a lot of luck in "making a connection," as they said. The girls up here, they said, were hard to score.

"They say that girls turn prissy during their Maturity Trip," one of the three said.

"It's true," said another. "From now on it's love and marriage and that stuff."

"Give me Youth Camp," said the third. "Easy come, easy go."

"Easy come," said the first. "Above all, easy come."

The three boys laughed.

Just stupid kids, Shannon thought, *not heroes at all.*

He floated across the room to hover over his younger self and Ronnie Rome. Those two, he thought, had brains. He wondered what had become of Ronnie during the last ten, twelve years.

Ronnie and the younger Shannon were also talking.

"What were you during your last year?" Ronnie asked.

"Commander. Commander-in-chief," the younger Shannon said.

"You're kidding,"

"No, sir," the younger Shannon said. "It took some doing, but they elected me in the end."

"Commander-in-chief," Ronnie said; he was impressed. "Where'd you go to camp?"

"At Calvin. That's in California. We fought against Camp Winnetoo. We shared the reservation. And let me tell you! They were something else. They had nearly twice our strength, but we didn't let that stop us. We whipped them more times than we lost. There was this time—let me tell you about this time when they laid an ambush for us . . . ."

The older Shannon listened to the story thinking that in his Youth Camp days he'd been a lusty liar!

More time passed. Shannon wondered when the meteorite would strike. Why not look? He moved himself through *Saffire's* honeycomb skin and into naked space again.

He hung in velvety darkness. Silvery walls gleamed nearby. He saw the sun—a sharp, bright light. He glimpsed the meteorite at last. A big chunk of molten rock, its irregular surface scarred and pockmarked over eons of time, the giant boulder rolled toward the satellite. You could barely see it, but surely they had radar in this craft . . .

He went back in. The rock would hit within a minute. He looked at himself and at Ronnie. He looked at the three "heroes" over on the other side and wondered how they had survived.

Then the big rock hit the satellite, crashing partway through *Saffire's* outer skin. The temperature inside the room dropped in a flash. Moisture froze against the wall; the paint on the boys' brushes turned to rock. The atmosphere escaped into the void with a hissing sound through some crack.

Sirens took up a frightened wail immediately. Shrill bells began to ring.

Thrown to the floor by the impact of the rock, the boys scrambled up and rushed toward the heavy door and through it. Shannon followed. Then a man's voice came over the loudspeaker arresting the running boys.

"Boiler Room 38, Boiler Room 38. Can you hear me, can you hear me?"

"We hear you," Ronnie Rome answered.

"Shut the door, for God's sake. Hurry."

Ronnie ran toward the door and bent down to work a crank designed to open and close the heavy portal. He turned the crank, he tried to turn it, but the crank was jammed or damaged. Ronnie grimmaced with exertion, but he couldn't move the handle more than a quarter of a turn.

"The crank won't work," he called, exasperated.

"All right," the voice said. "Disengage it. Then you boys must close the door. You'll have to push it closed from the outside." None of the boys moved. "It's the only way," the voice said. "The safety of the colony depends on you."

The boys stood stiffly. Tense faces mirrored a rising comprehension. The outer skin was ruptured, the air was rushing out. The heavy door might seal off damage if closed from the outside. But those who closed it . . .

The younger Shannon was the first to move. He turned and looked down a stretch of corridor—toward safety!

Saffire was very big—with lots of air in many places, even if some of the air was escaping here. The colony had crews of men whose job it was to seal off ruptures. Why should he sacrifice himself? The crank didn't work. The door might not even seal. Then he would die for nothing.

He turned and ran. Ronnie hesitated for a second longer. Then he rushed after his friend.

The older Shannon stayed behind to see what the "heroes" would do. He had always wondered how they had escaped.

With Ronnie's steps receding down the hall, the three boys

looked at each other, faces grey. Then they moved through
the heavy door again and back into the boiler room.

Fools, damn fools. Shannon thought, following them. But
now he wished that he had joined them. After all they had
escaped. And had garnered lots of glory. But he hadn't
known that in advance.

Gasping in the extreme cold of the room, the boys pushed
against the door with all their might. The door moved slowly,
one of its hinges screaming. Air rushing through the opening
pressed against the door and prevented its closing.

One second, two seconds, three seconds, four seconds.
The boys pushed, shouted, cursed.

And Shannon knew that they could not succeed. They
weren't strong enough. Too much air was pushing through
that last, slender, obstinate crack. That air would prevent
their suffocating, but surely in another two, three minutes
they would freeze to death.

"You-who."

"What?"

"It's me. I've come to get you. Time's up, Raver. High
time I got you back."

Unaffected by outrushing air, Alkhazar's smoke filled the
boiler room.

"No," Shannon cried. "Not yet. There's something I've
got to see."

"Sorry," the jinn said. "No time for that. You're wanted
back in Dalton's jail."

"Just a minute," Shannon said. "Just a second. Damn
you," he cried, "I said just a second."

The smoky mass enveloped him. He waved his arms
frantically to clear away the sparkly fog, without success.
Damn. It seemed as if he had just heard a blast and seen a wall
cave in. And figures in space suits had come through the gap
thus created. But he could not be sure. He had drawn an
inference from sounds and motions barely glimpsed through
Alkhazar's enveloping substance.

"Damn," Shannon cried. He was in motion, carried by
the jinn.

"Looks like you've enjoyed your trip," Alkhazar said. "Looks like you didn't want to leave. Maybe next time. Maybe you can get your hands on more of those PD's. Then I'll see you again. For now, it's good-bye."

The smoke cleared suddenly, and Shannon found himself hurtling down toward a very distant earth. He couldn't judge the speed of his descent, but he was falling very fast. The green-white ball below grew larger with every fraction of a second. In a moment it filled the entirety of his vision. And then he plunged into the atmosphere.

Made of spirit rather than of flesh, contact with the atmosphere should not have caused him to ignite—yet he burst into flame. He hurtled down, burning, blazing. His spirit burned from contact with the noosphere rather than the atmosphere. He woke up, screaming, in Dalton's jail.

18

Shannon lay on his bunk and listened; his heart was beating rapidly. Slowly, he relaxed. He had only screamed in his vision, not in reality. The prisoners in the adjoining cells gave no sign that they had heard his outcry.

God, what a dream. It felt like a dream now, despite the clarity and seeming order of what he had experienced. Nevertheless . . . it had to be a dream, although quite evidently it had been a dream strongly influenced by drugs. There was no other way to explain the presence of Alkhazar or St. John's words . . . His most important day aboard the satellite? That made no sense at all. It was a random thought, an irrational notion.

The dream and its mood, especially the fright that he'd experienced in plunging down into the earth's atmosphere, lingered for a moment or two. Then the reality of Dalton's

jail asserted itself. The stink was overpowering. The grey,
gloomy light of morning streamed through the narrow window again. The prisoners were stirring. And Henry no longer
moaned. Shannon sat up. His body was drenched in sweat,
his head ached slightly, all sounds seemed magnified and
harsh . . . a consequence of the PD capsule that he had
swallowed? Otherwise he felt all right.

Looking about, he noticed that something was happening.
The heavy door stood open. Two men wearing white coats
were just entering the hall; they carried an empty stretcher
between them. Dalton came behind them. And Higgins, the
guard, accompanied the master of the jail.

The prisoners were rising from their bunks and moving
toward the front of their respective cages to see what would
happen next. As curious as all the rest, Shannon also rose. He
went to stand by St. John who already stood up front, his fists
around a pair of bars. John did not look at Shannon; he was
peering down the walkway between the cellblocks toward the
entrance from whence the stretcher-bearers came.

Shannon stood and watched. He felt rested despite his PD
visions. He had sweated heavily during the night, so much so
that his underwear was clammy; but his fever had broken and
he felt almost normal again.

The men in white stopped before the cell where Larry and
his boys were quartered. Higgins had stopped by the entrance
and had taken a short-barrelled gun from a rack. Now he
hurried forward to unlock the cell-door. He stood so that his
shotgun pointed at the inmates in the cell, but neither Larry
nor his boys seemed intent on breaking out. They stood about
and watched as the stretcher-bearers made for "Henrietta's"
bunk.

Malcolm Dalton had also arrived by now. His dark hair
pasted down flat and glistening with hair oil, his uniform
tunic open, revealing his huge, sagging gut; his legs apart,
his thumbs in his belt, Dalton stood and watched.

The victim of last night's multiple rape lay unmoving on
his cot. The medical technicians grabbed him by his legs and
arms and laid him on the stretcher—none too gently. They

lifted the stretcher and came out, and Higgins locked the cell door again.

Now Dalton stirred, "Set him down for just a minute," he said to the bearers, gesturing, "No, no. Over there. I want Mr. X to look at Henry."

The men complied. They crossed the walkway between the cells and placed the stretcher immediately in front of Shannon.

Henry looked awful. He was a pudgy fellow in his twenties. It was obvious that he had been very badly treated. Those portions of his skin exposed to view were disfigured by huge, black bruises caused by internal bleeding. The color of his skin was a sickening shade of blue. His eyes were open and stared up at the ceiling with a fixity so rigid that Shannon became convinced that the man was dead. He stared at Henry's chest to see if the man was breathing. Nothing heaved, nothing moved. The man had died during the night from his violent maltreatment over a number of days—or else Larry and his boys had murdered him to stop his moaning.

"Have you seen enough?" Dalton asked. He gestured to the bearers. Led by Higgins, they carried the stretcher toward the door.

Dalton hooked his thumb back into his belt again and stepped a little closer to Shannon. The odor of his hair oil reached Shannon's nostrils. His small eyes peered malevolently.

"Well, Mr. X," Dalton said, "what will it be? Summary trial or trial by jury? Just say the word. Tell me what I want to hear, and I might be persuaded to give you nicer quarters. You will be all by yourself. I might even get you a TV if they plug us back into the grid again. And they might. Miracles are known to happen every now and then." He paused. "On the other hand," he said, "and this is strictly up to you—I might put you over there." He inclined his head toward Larry and his boys. "It all depends on what you say . . . Well, Mr. X, what will it be?"

After the briefest of hesitations, Shannon said, "Summary trial."

Dalton nodded. "Good," he said. "I knew you'd see the
light. Higgins," he called, "we're moving Mr. Shanty.
Second floor. Wing B, Cell 35. Call Duggins and have him
fetch the prisoner." Then he nodded to Shannon by way of
approval and farewell.

As Dalton let himself out of the hall, St. John pulled
Shannon's sleeve. Shannon looked at the old man seeing him
properly for the first time. And in the grey light of morning,
he saw in those gaunt, emaciated features a clear re-
semblance to that almost forgotten old man aboard *Saffire*.

"Well," St. John said, "you've made your decision. Not
the gutsiest decision you've ever made, I'd guess, but probably the right one."

The statement irritated Shannon. "What do you mean by
that?"

"You had made up your mind, hadn't you?"

"About what?"

"Jury trial," St. John said.

"Well—yes, I had," Shannon said. "But under the circumstances . . ."

"Oh, I agree," St. John said. "I agree entirely. Still—you
did not vote your convictions, exactly, did you?" Then he
withdrew a step. "Hey," he said. "Don't get mad. I'm not
blaming you. It was a crummy test, if you ask me."

"Test?" Shannon asked. He glanced around. The prisoners were milling around in a dozen cells. Higgins was dialing
on a wall-mounted telephone. It was clearly day now and
Shannon wasn't feverish. Why then did it seem as if St. John
was voicing riddles. "Test?" Shannon repeated. "What do
you mean by that?"

"Well," St. John said, "it *was* a test—in a manner of
speaking. You know what I mean."

"No, I don't" Shannon said. "I certainly don't. Explain
what you mean."

St. John made a dismissing gesture. "There is no time for
philosophizing," he said. "They'll take you away in just a
minute. Before they do, I want to tell you something, some-

thing that may help you." He regarded Shannon for just a second. "Do you want to hear it or don't you?"

"Go ahead," Shannon said a little reluctantly, his mind still on the "test."

"Do you have any money?" the old man asked.

Shannon shook his head.

"Didn't think so," St. John said. "So listen. They'll assign you a lawyer from the Public Defender's Office. Now remember this. You have the right to pick your own lawyer from what they call the PDO 'pool.' Got that? Ask to see a list of the lawyers. You'll see Bill Fadden's name on the list. Ask for him. He isn't very clever, but at least he isn't scared of the Waterburgs. The Fadden's have a bit of clout around here. Bill's daddy is a senator. All right. Pick Fadden as your lawyer and tell him to call the Federal Recruiter. Remember that. The Federal Recruiter. It's your only chance. If the recruiter shows up at your trial, you might save your life—at least for a while. Otherwise you'll end up in the chair for certain. You were never one to take advice, but this time do as you are told."

"You did it again," Shannon cried, reacting to St. John's statement. *You were never one to take advice.* He had heard that very phrase in his PD vision. "You can't deny it this time," Shannon said. "You know something about the Kibbutz Zone. All right, what is it. What do you know."

Saying this, Shannon stepped forward and grabbed St. John by the filthy collar of a tattered shirt. He twisted the collar to choke the old man just a little.

"Talk," he said. "Talk or you'll be sorry."

For a moment only, St. John's ancient eyes stared up into Shannon's eyes, and Shannon detected in their depths an awareness that shouldn't have been there. Then, catching him by surprise, St. John punched him in the stomach, on the kidneys—swiftly and more powerfully than Shannon would have imagined possible from so frail and so old a person. He let go of St. John. Doubled over, he groaned with pain. St. John drew back.

"You're a fine one," St. John said. "Ungrateful son of a

bitch. I try to help him, I try to give him good advice . . .
You've got a lot of guts when it comes to beating up old men
. . . Let me tell you . . . You'll end up in the chair, my
friend, you'll end up in the chair . . . ''

Shannon straightened himself slowly. He felt nauseous
again and very confused. Vaguely, half-submerged, the
thought came to him that these temporary confusions were
unnatural, inexplicable, but he could not pursue the thought.
Pain made a hollow in the pit of his stomach. He stumbled
toward his bed, hands over his stomach. He was just about to
lie down when he heard the unoiled hinge screaming again.
Looking up, he saw that another guard had entered. And
Higgins, rising from his desk, was pointing in Shannon's
direction.

19

Still surrounded by a fog of confusion, Shannon followed
the guard out of the hall. The guard was a stocky and taciturn
fellow. He'd called himself Duggins. He led Shannon to
another floor in another wing. They walked in complete
darkness, Duggins' flashlight beam their only guide. Duggins stopped at last before a door, unlocked it, and pushed it
open with a foot.

A match flared up. Duggins had dug a candle from his
pocket. He lit and held the candle until the wick burned
brightly. Then he handed the object to Shannon and grunted
something Shannon did not understand. Shannon guessed
that he was to enter the darkness beyond the door. Shielding
his candle with a hand, he went in. The door fell shut behind
him with a heavy, metallic sound. He was alone.

The cell had no window to the outside world. With the
exception of a cot built into the wall and a malodorous hole in
one corner, the cell was empty.

He placed the candle on the floor—anchored into a little pool of wax—and sat down on the cot.

It was very still in the cell. The light from the candle made a small circle in the darkness. Movements flickered on the edge of the light, but Shannon knew that these were merely the work of his imagination.

Time to think, he told himself, lying back on the cot. *Time to sort things out.* He folded his hands behind his head and began the process of taking stock.

The first day passed uneventfully. Before the candle had burned out entirely, Duggins returned with a meal. He brought a list of names with him—the lawyers assigned to the Public Defender's Office. He handed Shannon a pencil and asked him to pick out the lawyer he wanted. Shannon quickly found William D. Fadden's name and placed a check-mark opposite. Duggins grunted something, took the list and pencil, and left Shannon alone again. The candle died soon after Shannon had finished the soup and the slice of bread Duggins had left behind. Then he laid himself on the cot again in total darkness to resume his cogitations.

He had many things to think about—too many to keep straight in his head. He wished that he had pencil and paper—and a light—so that he might make himself a list of his concerns, but having none of these, he turned to making mental lists, lists of questions, lists of worries.

The center of all his concerns turned around the Kibbutz Zone. It seemed to him that the Kibbutz Zone was interfering with his life in Purgatory in some odd and subtle way. He was sure of that—without being able to pin it down.

Take John St. John, for instance. The old man seemed to know something. His colorless, moist eyes had been full of some kind of awareness. He had spoken about tests. What tests? Was St. John really from the Kibbutz Zone—another traveller through those skins of time?

Take the fact that Benny Franks, then Lillian, and finally Malcolm Dalton had made their appearances in rapid succes-

sion in this realm—each one an ugly carricature of his or her
Kibbutz self, each one a ''jailer,'' in a manner of speaking.

Was it design or was it coincidence that Shannon had been
''captured'' and held prisoner in Purgatory from the moment
of his arrival?

Was it pure coincidence that Shannon had—as it were—
fallen into the identity of Raver Shanty, a good-for-nothing
trouble-maker and a drug addict?

And speaking of drugs, why had the PD pill transported
him back into the Kibbutz Zone and back into his own past
. . . to witness what amounted to humiliating episodes of
his own life?

Humiliating episodes? Shannon thought about that, unhappy with the thought. But, yes, upon consideration . . .

Face the facts. He had not really distinguished himself in
his Youth Camp days. And he hadn't exactly enjoyed the
instruction aboard the satellite. But—so what? Why dig up
all that old stuff? He never thought much about the past. Why
had he started doing so now? And here?

And what about Raver Shanty? Who in the hell *was* the
guy? Was he Shannon's double? Schuster had assured him
that he wouldn't meet himself in the Purgatory Zone. Schuster had been right—so far. But he hadn't warned Shannon
sufficiently about the other possibility—that Shannon might
be taken *for* his double!

And even if he was Raver Shanty—who in the hell was
Ra-ra. Lillian had mentioned the name—and more than
once. Ra-ra. Who were all these people? Why couldn't he
find clarity in all this murky murk . . . ?

Something funny is going on. Something is fishy.

Fishy? The word recalled his sensitivity to smell these
days. He was always nauseous around here. The reek of
James P. Schuster's soap still lingered in his nostrils. Why?

And come to think of it, the Purgatory Zone had not
''behaved'' the way a society really should, either. Think
about it for just a second: Wouldn't a proper police department do what the books about the old days always talked

about? Fingerprints? Body-searchers? Why had Murphy's people failed to search him? And if not Murphy's people, why not Dalton's? It almost seemed as if they had meant for him to take that PD pill? Why? So that he could have 'remedial instruction'?

That's it, that's it! Shannon felt excitement. He was on the track of some discovery. *Remedial instruction.* Alkhazar's words.

He began to probe the implications of that phrase, but suddenly his lip began to hurt; a dizziness swept over him; his stomach seemed to lurch; nausea began to spread up from his guts toward his brain. He began to moan. He was getting sick. He rolled off his bunk and stumbled in the darkness toward the smelly corner of his cell. Bent over, he vomited out the food that he had just consumed. His stomach heaved and heaved. He retched, spat. Thin strings of saliva hung from his still aching lips. Only slowly did he recover a sense of moderate comfort. He wiped his mouth. He took a deep breath. God . . . He stumbled back to his cot.

Lying down again in darkness, he tried to find the lost strands of his thought. Where was he? Something about Alkhazar. Yes, Alkhazar. A childhood memory of a dramatic piece about the Thousand and One Nights. A figment of his mind, a piece of his memories. Strange.

He felt a little weak. He didn't feel like racking his brains just now. It was very still in the cell. His mind kept seeing movements. He thought about sensory deprivation and the power of the mind in filling up such vacuums. He grew drowsy thinking about that, and eventually he dozed off.

Time passed. Perhaps it was hours, perhaps days. Certainly more than hours, but how many days? Shannon lost track of time. Every now and again, at irregular intervals—or perhaps they merely seemed to be irregular—Duggins came with trays or bowls of food. Sometimes he brought a candle, sometimes he did not. The candles lasted a shorter and shorter time—or perhaps that too was imagination.

Shannon slept a great deal. He could not help it—although he tried. His dreams were troubling and disjointed—and recurring. One dream bothered him more than the others. He seemed to be back at Zen Richelem station, in the station's auditorium. All the people were assembled there. They crowded the seats, the floor. They wore peculiar headsets; most of them had their eyes closed. Some moved about with trays of food and jugs of coffee. Shannon, meanwhile, naked as a newborn babe, stood on the stage of the auditorium, as if on display. The dream came time and time again in one guise or another. At the end of each dream, he ran naked from the stage and away into the night.

Sometimes he came out of such dreams in a state of great fear and agitation, convinced that the dreams refused to pass away merely because he was awake. He saw movements in the darkness—ghostly movements that always eluded him when he turned his head to catch them. And voices whispered in the stillness—ghostly voices without sound—but he could never catch the meaning of the words they hissed.

Sometimes, to fight off the panic that gripped him, he walked up and down inside his cell, rapidly, from wall to wall, talking loudly to himself, or whistling, or even singing songs vaguely recalled from his Youth Camp days.

Sometimes, bringing great relief, Duggins' key creaked in the lock, the guard came in—solidly real, carrying a candle, bringing food. And then, for a brief spell at least, Shannon was himself again.

Then came another night—or night it seemed—and once more Shannon dreamt. Alkhazar had come to fetch him and carried him in a helter-skelter trip through a maze of crazy, jumbled memories. Toward the end—cringing in anticipation, knowing what would be coming next—Shannon found himself before the people of Zen Richelem again, up on the stage of the auditorium. The people sat as if they hadn't moved since his last nightmare—headsets covering their hair, eyes closed in some kind of trance. Shannon felt tower-

ing rage. He shouted at the people. "I'm my own man," he
shouted. "I don't need any of you. To hell with you. God
damn you. I can take care of myself. I want freedom! I want
action! I want to do my own thing. I want to be me!" Then, as
always, he ran away, off the stage, through the station, and
into the night. Angry, skeletal figures clothed in rags chased
him brandishing broken bottles that glittered menacingly in
moonlight. Shannon escaped them just in time by running
into the Time Van that suddenly loomed up ahead of him.
James P. Schuster waited for him. Schuster grinned demoni-
cally and held a huge knife.

Shannon woke. His heart was beating at a tremendous
rate. He was sobbing uncontrollably. Little by little he
brought himself under control and sat up on his cot. The
words he had just shouted in his dream still echoed in his
mind. *I'm my own man . . . I can take care of myself . . . I
want to be me.* Against the backdrop of terror he had just felt,
the words sounded hollow and empty, plaintive and childish.

I'm my own man . . .

Thinking those words, Shannon had a sudden vision of
himself, struggling under the weight of a huge and heavy
object. It was the statue of a man. As soon as the image
surfaced, Shannon realized that it had been part of another
dream he had had during this night—if night it was. The
dream came back to him now.

He saw himself carrying the gigantic statue. He was
struggling up a grassy slope under a cloud-flecked, sunny
sky. Ahead of him stood Benny and Lillian. They had
stopped and they had turned to look back down on him. And
Lillian had beckoned to him, in the dream, but Shannon had
been unable to take another step. The statue he had carried
had been too heavy. He had tried to take another step, but just
then the statue had toppled forward. He had recognized it as it
fell—it had been a statue of himself.

Shannon reached out and touched the concrete wall. Yes,
he was awake. It was quiet in the cell, but for once he did not
hear the maddening whisper of ghostly voices. Moisture

around his neck told him that he had been sweating again.

"I'm my own man," he whispered, puzzled by the two dreams, convinced that he should try to understand them. He hoped that he'd be able to hold his thoughts together. He had not been too successful thus far. Something about this dark cell prevented him from thinking properly for more than an hour at a time.

He sat and brooded, seeking for some meaning. And this time his mind focused briefly, just long enough to yield an insight.

"Alone and frightened," Shannon told himself, voicing the essence of his discovery. The sound of the words echoed hollowly in the cell. "Alone and frightened," he said again. "And that's all."

It was very simple, really, now that he thought about it. He had always been alone and always frightened. Why lonely? Simple: he had lived in a world where everybody else was strange. But why had he been frightened?

Frightened? Sure. He had been frightened throughout his life because he had been protecting something. Protecting what? That statue, of course!

The statue of Ravi Shannon, hero. Ravi Shannon, champion of the old order. Ravi Shannon, commander of the troops at Youth Camp—but in reality he'd never even made it to captain. Ravi Shannon, pilot—sweating at every landing, every take-off. Ravi Shannon yielding to the threats of Pastor Benny. Ravi Shannon, hero, yielding to Malcolm Dalton's threats!

Maybe I am *Raver Shanty* . . .

He recalled Benny's words, back at Zen Richelem. *Ranting and raving, ranting and raving* . . .

He stood up and began to pace. He felt unusally clear in his mind this morning—if it was morning. He liked that dream about the statue. *Hell, yes,* he thought. It was hard to be a hero when your courage always failed you in the clinches . . .

"Raver Shanty," he muttered to himself. "Raver the SD. Drug fiend. Loser."

He made another turn or two.

"Jail bird," he murmured.

He paced back and forth, back and forth.

He sat down on his cot again. It felt strangely pleasant to think himself a coward and a loser. Light. No statue to carry about. He guessed that he might as well accept the fact that he was Raver. Everybody else did. He had agreed to summary trial. Sure enough they'd fry him sooner or later anyway. Why pretend?

Then, timed in such a way that it seemed to punctuate the rhythm of his thoughts, he heard the faint shuffling tread of Duggins' feet. And in a moment the key creaked in the cell-door lock.

20

Shannon stood before a mirror dressed in a cheap but clean suit. He adjusted the clumsily knotted tie again—he had wound it himself. Then he took a final look at himself, not pleased by what he saw.

After brief and cursory medical examination in the dispensary—where a woman in white had checked the progress of his lip—he had been allowed to shower and to shave. "Make yourself pretty, Shanty," a guard had told him. "You will see the judge this morning." Shannon had cleaned up, but neither the shower, nor the shave, nor yet the clean underwear and shirt he wore helped.

His face was gaunt and grey in the light of the kerosene lamp and looked a little strange. His eyes had a cringing, fearful look. But worst of all was the expression on his face. The mangled lip was healing now and bore a thick, encrusted scab, but somehow it distorted his face so that it had a permanently sneering expression.

He stood for a moment, recalling his reflections in the cell.

He didn't like the thought of being Raver Shanty and starting
all over again, as it were, by accepting that identity—and yet
now he looked a lot more like he guessed that Raver might
have looked . . . than Ravi Shannon ever had.

Sighing, he turned from the mirror to present himself to the
guards again.

Guards drove him to the Municipal Court. The court was
in yet another of those magnificent buildings that seemed to
compete for light, like flowers, beneath the Phoenix dome.
They reached the pink-and-blue structure by a series of
skyways. The court occupied a floor of this building, a floor
decorated in imitation of some venerable past with marble
floors and marble columns and dark oil portraits of dead
judges on the walls. Shannon's steps echoed over marble as
he approached a security gate. He passed through. The cops
who had brought him turned about. Court clerks directed him
to a waiting room and told him that he would be called by a
loudspeaker in there.

The room was relatively small, crowded, and filled with
smoke. People sat around on chairs in various poses of
boredom. Shannon spied an empty chair and sat down.

A garishly painted but not very young woman sat next to
him. She sucked smoke from a very long and very thin
cigarette. Her smeared lips left a red imprint on the tip of the
tobacco tube. She turned to Shannon blowing a stream of
smoke.

"What're you in here for?" she asked.

"Murder," Shannon said.

"Murder," she cried. "Hey! That's what I call class!
Whad'd you do? Axe your old lady?"

"I didn't kill anybody," Shannon said. The lady wore a
strong perfume. Its odor, mingled with that of tobacco
smoke, made a disgusting melange of smell, but Shannon
couldn't see another empty chair nearby and wanted to stay
by the door. "I didn't do it," he added.

"Of course you didn't, dearie," the woman said. She

gestured with her cigarette to indicate the roomful of people. She shed a length of ash in the process; it fell into Shannon's lap. "Nothing but innocents in this room," she said. "Purer than the driven snow. Murder," she said. "And you're taking a summary? You must be bonkers, baby. Suicidal. Are you suicidal?"

"Not that I know," Shannon said. He brushed ash from his crotch. "Are all these people prisoners?"

"You are," she said. "I can see that by your suit. Most of these turkeys are here on their own. Bail and things like that. How long have you been in the cooler?"

Shannon was about the answer when he heard his name called. He guessed that now it *was* his name, like it or not.

"Shanty? Raver Shanty?"

A young man stood by the door of the waiting room, a very young man, almost a boy. He had cherubic cheeks and sandy hair and wore an expensive suit made of metallized fabric. He held a slender folder underneath one arm. He had read the name from a slip of paper he held in his hand.

"Here," Shannon called.

The young man gestured. "Could you step here for a second?"

Shannon complied.

The young man glanced at his slip again. "Raver Shanty?" he asked. Shannon nodded. "I'm Fadden," the man said. "I don't have much time to talk, but I wanted to have a word with you before we're called. Now here is how I see your case. I think it's pretty hopeless, all in all. I'd be inclined to fight the rape charge. Lilly wouldn't have a leg to stand on—if we could get a change of venue. But you've agreed to Summary, so that's out of the question. The murder charge is quite another matter. Open and shut. Ferguson has a witness, and if we challenge the murder charge, he will just produce her. She's bad news, Mr. Shanty. I've seen her deposition. She intends to swear that she saw you stab her husband repeatedly. With Noland up there and the Waterburgs in the background, that just about seals it, so what I'd suggest is that we plead *nolo* to all charges and just hope to Christ the federal recruiter isn't having early lunch. I called him earlier this morning after studying your case, so that's all set—and your only hope. All right,'' he said, after the briefest of pauses ''so that's settled. We plead *nolo* and we hope for the best. I'll see you in the courtroom, but now I've got to run. See, they're fingering me now.''

He was gone before Shannon could even voice his questions. He looked after Fadden for a moment, shrugged, and returned to the waiting room.

''Was that your lawyer?'' the painted woman asked.

Shannon nodded.

''Indigent, aren't you?'' she said. ''I tell you,'' she said, ''I'll steal, borrow, beg, do anything to get a *good* lawyer. Those kids with the defender's office are barely dry behind the ears. Fadden isn't bad. He tries at least. And it helps to have a daddy in Washington. What did he tell you?''

''I'm not sure I understood him,'' Shannon said. ''He kept talking about pleading 'nolo' to the charges.''

''Oh, boy,'' the woman said. ''Oh, boy. Doesn't sound too good to me.''

''Why? What does it mean?''

''No contest,'' she said. ''It's just about the same as pleading guilty, but a little more polite, I guess. Just the same, but not quite—if you see what I mean.''

Shannon wasn't sure he did. ''What happens if I plead this 'nolo'?'' he asked.

''It isn't 'nolo,' '' she said. ''It's 'nolo contendere.' Oops, that's me.'' The loudspeaker system had called for a Sally Becker. The woman stubbed out her cigarette in a dusty, crusty, rattling, freestanding ashtray. ''Be seeing you. And good luck to you.''

She left. The cigarette she had left behind smoldered in the ashtray spreading a suffocating reek. Shannon reached over and put it out properly. He had a squeamish look on his face. Bad smells were everywhere—of stale tobacco, human sweat—and he felt nauseous again.

A disembodied voice called for Raver Shanty about an hour later. Fadden waited for him at the entrance of the courtroom, and judging by the expression on the lawyer's face, Shannon guessed that something was wrong. The cherubic lawyer's face was pale, he peered anxiously down the wide and echoing hall outside the courtroom as if looking for someone. People moved about, but Shannon guessed that none of them was the federal recruiter.

Fadden glanced at his watch. "I guess we'd better go on down," he said. "We're next."

"Is the recruiter here?" Shannon asked.

"He will be," Fadden said grimly. "He'd better be."

The courtroom resembled a theater with a high bench down below and spectator seats rising up from it in tiers. Flags made of richly colored silks flanked the bench. Affixed to the dark panelling behind the bench, above the judge, hung an elaborately carved seal, the seal of the City of Phoenix. The judge was an old man with sparse grey hair and a lined face; he wore a black robe. Leaning forward now between a stack of books and a pitcher of water, he spoke in low tones to a husky young man and another of those richly dressed men, a man in the luminous garb of the Beautiful People, another lawyer.

Fadden led the way down the sloping walk between the spectators toward an open area before the bench. He told Shannon in a whisper to sit behind a little table on the left. A similar table stood across the way as well; a man in BP garb sat behind it.

"Who is he?" Shannon asked, also in a whisper.

"The prosecutor," Fadden answered. He sat down next to Shannon.

A minute or so passed. The judge, the lawyer, and the husky man up front were still talking in murmurs. Fadden glanced at his watch. He craned his neck and looked back up toward the entrance. Shannon felt a peculiar sensation, something like a tingling at the back of his neck. He looked back as well. His gaze came to rest immediately on Lilly Waterburg.

She sat all by herself toward the back of the near-empty spectator area on the prosecutor's side. Amidst the dark wooden benches, she stood out brightly, a golden shining in her clinging suit. She stared at Shannon with a dark expression.

Shannon leaned over to Fadden. "The federal recruiter hasn't arrived, has he?"

"He will," Fadden answered, displaying more faith than conviction.

The judge now lifted a wooden hammer Shannon had not noticed before. He banged it on his bench. "Next case," he said. Shannon barely understood the words. The courtroom had terrible acoustics. The shuffle of feet and movement of bodies echoed from every wall, but voices sounded obscured and hollow.

"What happens if the recruiter doesn't come?" Shannon asked his lawyer in a whisper.

"Shhh," Fadden said. His eyes toward the bench, he laid a restraining hand on Shannon's arm.

As the lawyer and his husky client left the bench, evidently pleased with the outcome of their murmured discussion, the prosecutor rose from his little table across the way.

"May it please your honor," he said, "the next case is that of Raver Shanty, SD, charged with murder in the first degree and rape. Counsel informs me that the accused is present and has consented to summary judgment."

The prosecutor sat down again.

The judge lifted eyeglasses from the bench, bent his head, and looked down at papers. Then he turned toward Shannon and Fadden.

"Are you prepared to enter a plea, Mr. Fadden?"

Fadden rose. "With your permission, your honor, I request a conference."

"In chambers?"

"No, your honor. That won't be necessary."

"You may approach the bench," the judge said. "You too, Mr. Ferguson."

Fadden went to the bench arriving there just as the prosecutor did. Fadden spoke first, pleadingly. At one point he looked back up to the entrance; he gestured toward the entrance; he gestured toward a clock that hung on one of the courtroom's walls.

Then the prosecutor spoke.

The judge murmured something, got a reply. He leaned back in his chair and rubbed both of his eyes with long, thin, fingers. He leaned forward presently, and as he spoke, Shannon detected a very slight shake of the head.

Genuine fear suddenly panicked him, an instant, cold instinctive but very reasonable panic. His fingertips were icy. He felt a hollow in his gut.

Fadden's face, upon returning, confirmed Shannon's fears.

"I asked for a postponement," Fadden whispered, "but he turned me down."

"What do we do?"

"There is nothing we can do," Fadden said. "Damn that Watson! I told him to be here on time."

"Are you prepared to enter a plea, now, Mr. Fadden?" the judge asked from the bench.

"Your honor," Fadden said, half rising, "May I consult with my client?"

"Go ahead," the judge said, "provided it doesn't take too long."

"Thank you, your honor."

Fadden sank down again. "Under the circumstances," he whispered, "my advice to you is that you withdraw your consent to summary and ask for a jury trial. Noland doesn't mean you well. He is linked with the Waterburgs. We could plead 'not guilty,' but like I said before, they've got you cold on murder. But switching to a jury trial will gain us time."

"Will I be sent back to prison?"

"Yes," Fadden said. "it'll take some weeks to get you on the docket."

"Then I don't want to switch," Shannon said.

'We're waiting, Mr. Fadden,'' the judge called from the bench.

"One moment, your honor,'' Fadden said. He turned to Shannon; his eyes mirrored incredulity. "Why not?'' he asked. "Don't you realize what'll happen to you? They'll put you into the electric chair.''

"Is that what people call 'frying'?''

"Yes,'' Fadden said. "That's the colloquialism. But hurry. Make up your mind.''

Shannon shrugged. He seemed doomed in any event. Dalton on the one side, the electric chair (whose function he had read about back home) on the other. What the hell. He felt a cold, dull, resignation. His resistance had snapped. He was a loser. In this world as much as in the other. He was Raver Shanty, and like Raver Shanty he would come to a bad end.

"Go ahead with summary,'' he said. "I don't give a shit.''

"You are absolutely sure?'' Fadden asked.

"May we have the plea, now, Mr. Fadden?''

"Yes,'' Shannon told Fadden. "Go ahead.''

Fadden rose. "We are ready, your honor. My client pleads *nolo contendere* to all charges.''

Like an explosion, a sound came from the back of the courtroom. It was a laugh, partially suppressed. Shannon turned to look at Lillian and saw her doubled over. She pressed a handkerchief against her nose and mouth.

"Very well,'' Judge Noland said, disregarding the noise, "I will entertain arguments relating to sentencing.'' He nodded to the prosecutor. "And relating also to mitigating and extenuating circumstances.'' He nodded to Fadden.

The prosecutor rose to speak.

Shannon sat in something like a trance. The prosecutor spoke briefly but colorfully about Shannon's supposed crimes, Shannon's violent nature, criminal history, the widow's grief, and other things as well. Then Fadden rose and argued against capital punishment in favor of Shannon's employment in activities useful to the state, naming several categories, citing Shannon's relative youth, physical strength, and other attributes.

Shannon barely listened.

He was Raver Shanty—a retrograde in Kibbutz, an outcast in the Purgatory Zone. With the blind force of a natural phenomenon, each society had moved to destroy him. And he sat there impotently, unable to oppose the process . . .

I never had a chance. Not back home, not here.

He was innocent of crimes but lacked the courage to fight for his innocence. He feared Dalton and his jail more than he feared death itself. What was the point of living in a world like this—so filled with hatreds and with tensions? Or back home in the Kibbutz Zone where he was only half a man? Death seemed like relief from all of this—the blind sleep of sweet oblivion . . .

Fadden shook him and Shannon came out of his brooding.

"He wants you to come forward," Fadden said.

"What for?"

"Sentencing."

Shannon got up and walked to the bench. Ferguson was already there. Shannon stopped before the judge and looked up. The old man was very high up. Noland was quite old, his face heavily lined; the skin at his neck lay in flat folds; his old eyes were devoid of expression.

"Are you ready to receive sentence?" the judge asked.

"We are, your honor," Fadden said. He stood at Shannon's left hand now, Ferguson to Shannon's right.

"Very well," the judge said. "Raver Shanty, after due consideration and study of your case; and after hearing arguments on behalf of the government and from your counsel; I find that you are guilty as charged. You are a menace to society, a continuing threat to public order and safety, and hence I sentence you to death by electrocution. Have you got anything to say?"

"Your honor, if it please the court."

The voice came from the back, from the direction of the

spectators. The judge looked up. His eyes had suddenly taken on a frightened, almost hunted expression.

"What is it, Mr. Watson?" he said, looking over the heads of the three men before him.

"May I approach the bench?"

"In what connection, Mr. Watson?"

"An an intervenor in the case before you."

Shannon turned and saw a man dressed in the drab suit of the BG caste. The man carried a hat in his hand. He was moving with long strides down the central aisle.

"This case is closed, Mr. Watson," Noland said. "I'm afraid that you're too late."

"With due respect, your honor," the man called Watson said, arriving, "I am late because I was detained by the servants of this court. I was refused parking, and when I arrived on foot, I was subjected to a lengthy body search— despite the fact that I am very well known in these halls." He gestured with the hat he carried.

"Mr. Watson—" the judge began.

"Furthermore, your honor," Watson said, raising his voice and overriding the judge, "the federal code does not specify any particular point in time for intervention. I am entirely within my rights. Under the rights and privileges accorded by Congress to the United States of America under US Code XIV, Section D, Article 5, I claim this prisoner for service in the Regional Defense Forces."

"This is most irregular," the judge said.

"Not at all, your honor," Watson said. "I would remind your honor of a very similar case three years ago. The superior court, in that instance—"

"Never mind, Watson," the judge said, waving a lily-white hand. He turned to the prosecutor. "What is your opinion, Ferguson?"

The prosecutor cleared his throat. He looked unhappy. "Mr. Watson was about to cite *Landris vs. The State of Nebraska*," he said. "The court found in that instance that Article 5 affords the federal government almost total discretion in such cases . . . '' His voice trailed out as he saw the slow change in Judge Noland's expression.

The judge stared down at Watson, and his old eyes reflected fear and anger and pain. The look in Noland's eyes surprised Shannon: this old man with power over life and death—and himself advanced in years beyond recall with his own death very near—yet seemed now to writhe unmoving under the same fear Shannon often felt. The silence lengthened. Then color rose into the judge's sagging cheeks as if some ancient fire deep within him had reignited.

"Very well, Watson," Judge Noland said. He sounded venomous; his tone promised future retribution. "This court will yield the prisoner into federal jurisdiction." Then he lifted his wooden hammer and banged it with unusual force against his desk. "The court will recess until three p.m.," he said and immediately rose.

As Judge Noland left the bench in a swish of his black robes, Ferguson turned to Fadden. "Congratulations," he said dryly. Then he nodded and moved toward his own table to gather up his papers.

Fadden radiated with a pleasure he could not quite suppress. His cherubic cheeks glowed now with inner heat. "Wheew," he said, half-whistling. "That was close."

"You don't know *how* close," Watson said, stepping near. Watson had craggy features and wore a troubled expression. He looked at Shannon for a second, then turned his attention back to Fadden. "The next time you yelp for federal help," he told the lawyer, "check out your client first. This man is a drug addict and a trouble-maker. If those bastards hadn't given me such a hard time . . . They searched me down to my goddamned *underwear*. If they hadn't been so heavy-handed, I wouldn't have lifted a finger to help this creep." He turned to Shannon. "But now I guess I've got you—for better or worse." Then back to Fadden, "I hope you'll remember this some time when it counts," he said.

"Hey," Fadden said. "I really appreciate this. This case had political overtones."

"You're telling *me*!" Watson said. "Listen, Fadden. When they start coming after me, I hope you can produce your daddy. I'm going to need him. Okay," he said, addressing Shannon again, "say good-bye to Houdini here and come along. The sooner I ship you out of my territory, the better it'll be for all of us."

Shannon shook hands with Fadden, murmuring his thanks under his breath. The sudden change in his fortunes had caught him by surprise. He was still in a state of shock. And when it came to saying heartfelt thanks, he had almost no experience.

"Don't mention it," Fadden said, beaming. "It's my job. And good luck to you." He waved a hand.

As Shannon turned to leave the courtroom with Watson, he saw Judge Noland's black-robed figure in the spectator area. Noland sat next to Lilly Waterburg. The two figures struck Shannon like grotesque beasts—an ancient, dried-out black crow and a golden feline. In a breathless and anxious manner, the old crow was explaining something to the cat queen of Phoenix.

THE RADDIES

21

He flew high above the land and wondered idly why people back in Kibbutz called this the Purgatory Zone. What did "Purgatory" mean? He still didn't know. He'd posed the question to James P. Schuster without getting an answer.

The question rose into his mind when he saw how people farmed around here. For the last hour, give or take, he'd seen vast tracts of desolation and enormous areas of cultivation devoted to single crops. Monoculture, this was called—a practice much abhorred back home. You could fly for hours in the Kibbutz Zone and see only gracious swirls and curves of variegated vegetation—like dragons coiling and uncoiling some silent dance. That was called the Chinese Mode—and it required lots of people. In this Zone he saw no people, no agricultural stations—just desolate reaches of abandoned land and monstrously uniform cultivations.

He turned toward the pilot of the two-seat helicopter on the verge of asking him what "purgatory" meant. Then changed his mind. The little craft made too much noise for conversa-

tion. The pilot would think him nuts for asking such a
question. And he wanted to make a good impression in the
Raddies.

He felt better than he'd ever felt this side of that skin of
time.

Only a couple of hours had passed since he'd escaped
Judge Noland's grasp. He was headed for the Raddies now
by Watson's speedy arrangement. Camp Bridges was the
destination, a training camp of sizeable dimensions: three
hundred soldiers lived there, per Watson. In a matter of
minutes, Shannon would be one of them.

He was thrilled to see that Raddies operated aircraft. His
pilot wore a uniform and the helicopter had military mark-
ings. He'd seen the letters RDF painted on the side of the
bubble followed by a number. "Regional Defense Forces,"
the Raddies.

Shannon planned to drop a hint when he arrived. He'd
suggest that he had been a pilot. Surely they would test him.
And then he'd demonstrate his skill and end up in a whirly-
bird like this one.

Things are looking up. Things are looking up.

To think that he'd been ready to accept the worst earlier
that morning! His luck had turned at last, he thought. Even if
Clancy was right about the casualty rate, surely pilots had a
better chance. The Mao-Mao's had no aircraft.

Then the pilot tilted the helicopter forward for descent.
Pointing ahead, he nodded at Shannon by way of saying that
they had arrived.

Shannon peered forward. Still in the distance he saw a
large expanse of bald and rolling land crisscrossed by concrete roads. In the center of this scalped terrain he saw a huge
fenced complex.

Odd! A wire fence enclosed Camp Bridges—if this was a
camp. He saw a lot of little tanks in rows and rows and rows
and rows—little tanks painted in brownish-greenish swirls.
For camouflage? He also saw some helicopters, their bubbles
bright in the sunshine. But what about the buildings? There

was a warehouse down below and two little buildings. The buildings resembled huts—they were no more than that. Where did all the soldiers sleep?

The helicopter described part of a circle as it came in for a landing. Firing ranges lay beyond the camp littered with the wreckage of vehicles used as targets. Small groups of tanks were firing. Others maneuvered on the bald terrain.

The copter landed before the warehouse. The noise level dropped as the pilot throttled down the engine.

"Duck as you get out," he shouted. "Go over there." He pointed to the smaller of the tiny buildings.

Shielding nose and mouth from flying dust, Shannon ran clear of the aircraft. The helicopter rose at once, tilted forward, flew away. Shannon had arrived. He was in the Raddies now.

He looked around. The place was . . . desolate. Not exactly homey. Hundreds of little tanks stood side by side on an enormous concrete apron, their muzzled cannons pointing up. The warehouse had a gloomy aspect. Rust stains marked its concrete walls. The little buildings were in need of painting; their grey walls were peeling, their windows dark with grime. The only lively object in the camp was a fluttering flag on a pole, a blue-white cloth with stars and stripes.

Shannon walked to the small building and entered a room furnished by two desks facing the door, a row of green filing cabinets, a little table with a coffee pot. Yellowing sheets were tacked against one wall. He could see the other building through a filthy window to his left. Another door, now closed, led into the interior of this shabby place.

For some reason that he couldn't fathom, Shannon thought about the Time Van's grimy lobby.

Behind the desk to Shannon's right sat a man in his late forties dressed in the green RDF uniform. Stripes on his sleeves marked his rank. His hair was cut closely to his skull; he lacked an ear. And as he stared at Shannon, it was plain to see that one of his eyes was made of glass.

"Shanty?" the man said. When Shannon nodded, the man

pushed himself back. He rode a wheelchair, had no legs. The lower portions of his trousers were neatly folded under stumps. He wheeled himself to a file, wheeled back, and laid some sheets of paper before Shannon.

"Sit down," he said. He tossed a pencil from a cup. "This is an IQ test. First thing we do is find out just how smart you are."

IQ? "What do I do?" Shannon asked.

"Easy," the soldier said. "Read the questions, read the answers, then pick the one you think is right." He wound the spring of a timer on his desk. "You've got twenty minutes. You better get on with it."

Shannon read the first few questions. The test was elementary. Simple math, basic science, geometry, pattern recognization. He began to make his marks.

"You can have some scratch paper if you need to figure something," the man said after a while.

Shannon looked up, surprised. "I'm almost finished." He went to work again. Done at last, he handed the sheets across the desk.

The earless soldier peered suspiciously with his healthy eye. "This ain't no joke," he said. "You're supposed to think about these, not just mark down chicken scratches. Anywhichway."

"I did," Shannon said. "I mean, I thought about it. Check it."

Raising his eyebrows, the soldier took a pencil and began to check the test. He shook his head from side to side when he was finished, scratched the scar where once his ear had been, then began all over again. He looked up at Shannon at last.

"By God," he said. Then he wheeled around and passed through the door behind him with Shannon's test on his lap. "Hey, Lieutenant," he called. "This guy just maxed the IQ test. In five minutes flat."

"*Maxed* it," a voice said. "Let me see that!"

Someone turned pages. Slowly. "By God!" the lieutenant

said. A chair scraped. Steps approached. The half-open door swung out. A man appeared.

"Schuster!" Shannon cried involuntarily.

Dressed in Raddy-green, silvery bars at his shoulders, the man was nevertheless James P. Schuster, or his living image—the same ratty-looking creature in need of a shave. Holding the test in his hand, he looked at Shannon uncertainly.

"Do I know you?"

"I—I don't know," Shannon said.

"But you know my name."

"I—I guess I must," Shannon said. "Maybe I've met you before. I don't know for sure. You see, I'm an amnesiac."

"Amnesiac," Schuster said. "And you maxed the test? Harmsworth, let me see what we have on this man."

Harmsworth had followed Schuster out. He wheeled to his desk, held out a file. Schuster shuffled through the meager contents of the folder pausing to peer and read. Shaking his head, he tossed the file on Harmsworth's desk.

"Pretty kettle of fish," he said. He reached for a chair, sat down. "I've never seen anything like this." He looked at Harmsworth, looked at Shannon, shook his head. "You're a murderer, a rapist, dope addict, and an amnesiac." He hit Shannon's test which he still held. "And a genius, judging by this. Where'd you go to school, Shanty?"

"I don't remember."

"He doesn't remember," Schuster told Harmsworth. "Pretty kettle of fish." He turned to Shannon. "You're an SD, aren't you?"

"Everybody tells me that I am," Shannon said, "but I don't think I am. I remember flying an airplane; I remember a crash."

"Really?" Schuster said. He sat for a moment and stared into thin air. "Any other records?"

Harmsworth shook his head. "This is it," he said, tapping the folder. "Nothing else came through."

"Hmm," Schuster said. He stared some more. Then he

turned to Harmsworth. "Are you thinking what I'm thinking?"

Harmsworth nodded slowly. Then he reached under his desk.

Silence. Schuster sat and stared. Harmsworth sat and stared. Shannon looked from one man to the other. What now? What was this all about? Why the fuss over the test? Had he done or said something he shouldn't have?

Then he saw movement through the window to his left. Men ran from the building next door—ran, hobbled. Some hobbled on crudely fashioned wooden legs, some lacked an arm, some wore eye-patches. Six or seven soldiers in RDF uniforms. They burst into the office and made a line behind Shannon.

Now Schuster stirred.

"Sorry about this," he said. "You might be innocent for all I know, but I can't take any chances. Something tells me that you're a Mao infiltrator, so I'm going to oyster you right now. Don't resist. Just take it easy."

Shannon turned—too late. Someone placed a cool object against his neck. There was a hiss, a pain. He swooned away.

He came out of the swoon strapped to a chair and facing a blank wall. They had stripped him while he had been out. His legs and trunk were naked, but he wore a funny pair of rubber pants. The pants seemed to be open just beneath his rectum; and his genitals were laid into a hose that fell down between his legs.

People moved about behind him but he couldn't see them.

"Let's just play it safe," Schuster was saying. "He is smart as a whip and probably an infiltrator."

"Level Four?" someone asked.

"Level Four at least. By the way, Jenkins . . . "

"Sir?"

"Get a new set of massagers. I don't want to lose a lot of time testing these damn things. I want to get him put in before dark."

Shannon had a sinking sensation. Panic gripped his throat. Bound, confined again. Self-pity surged up from his stomach. His control was slipping, he was about to sob.

Then Schuster moved into his view, and Shannon stared at him in fright, astonishment. Schuster held a shaving cup, a shaving brush. He was whipping lather in the cup with rapid motions.

Irrational now, unable to believe this, fearing that his sanity had slipped, his nostrils wildly sucking up the smell of Schuster's shaving soap, Shannon struggled against the straps that held him.

"Get away from me," he shouted. And again. And again.

"Relax," Schuster said, still whipping. "Nobody is going to harm you."

"Get away, get away, get away!"

Schuster turned. "Jenkins," he called, "our buddy needs another shot. Make it a triple this time."

Shannon came out of his swoon again in darkness, still naked, still wearing rubber pants. Some kind of mesh covered his body. Objects had been stuck into his ears. Flat strips of tape held metal discs against his shaven skull. Wires ran from his skull to somewhere; they were loose enough so that he couldn't stretch them taut by movements of his head. His hands were on the far side of some panels pierced by holes just large enough to accommodate his wrists.

He had swooned away in a state of near-insanity, but now his mood was high and hopeful. He wondered why. Of course—he had been drugged. Beneath that false euphoria he detected his real state of mind—as desperate as ever. But now the singing of his blood held that mood in check. His desperation kept turning into mirth.

Well, what the hell. What's wrong with being happy?

It had been some time now since he'd been happy for any length of time. Not since his Kibbutz days.

He laughed.

Happiness. Kibbutz.

Oh, Raver, he told himself—calling himself Raver again, Raver the loser—*you really are a hopeless case, Benny knew what he was saying. No matter where you are, you can't seem to be happy.*

He had joined the Raddies in the morning . . .

He laughed again. His laughter sounded dull and flat in that narrow cubicle.

Damned funny! *Oystering,* Schuster had called it. He was in the oyster, the little tank the oyster's shell. He knew now where the soldiers were, all three hundred men. Oysters every one. Why build housing for a bunch of oysters? God, it was funny—so funny that it made him want to cry.

Little by little, he settled down.

He was seated in a tank, his movements restricted, cut off from the world . . . or not quite. He noticed that there was a screen immediately in front of him, and when he peered into the screen, he saw the tail ends of a row of little tanks. He peered some more and made out the scene. Tanks, sky, concrete. It was a starless night. Clouds had gathered since they had put him out . . .

He stared at the screen for a long time waiting for some movement, change in the light. Confined as he was, the screen was his only link to reality, a very slender link; he feared that if he failed to peer into that darkness, he might miss something.

Lulled by a steady but pleasant hum, he fell asleep a little later.

22

He came awake abruptly the following morning, feeling movement all over his body. Shocked at first, even a little frightened, he soon understood his predicament. The wire mesh that covered him had begun to move; it had begun to send out painful flashes; and the flashes had awakened him.

A moment passed before he understood exactly what was happening to him. He was being exercised.

It was a peculiar—and soon an unpleasant—experience. As the mesh squeezed and released him in sequence, and as electrical impulses from the wire reached his body, his muscles contracted and relaxed in various rhythmic patterns. He felt as if he were engaged in a dozen sports at once. In a minute he was huffing and puffing and sweat poured from his every pore.

It was day now. In the screen before him, he saw little tanks. Clouds striped the sky in a diagonal direction from his perspective; the rising sun colored them pink.

He began to curse after a while. The exercising went on too long; his lungs were hot; sweat lathered him. He itched ferociously, but he couldn't scratch.

He understood now the full extent of his predicament. He had been installed into the tank permanently, with everything provided for. The wire mesh would exercise him; his wastes would be removed by way of those peculiar rubber pants; no doubt he would be fed by some equally devilish method. He was more of a prisoner now than he had ever been in Dalton's jail. Whatever dignity he had enjoyed as a slum dweller or as a prisoner had been taken away. His brain and body had become a thing, a part of this tracked vehicle.

The exercise ended at last. It left him gasping. Then a fine spray of ice-cold water hit his body. He gasped again. Pinpricks of moisture blasted him. Water also ran into his rubber pants from some apperture and bathed the covered portions of his lower body. Suddently the water grew scalding. Shannon burned now, gasping, groaning. Then cold again. Then hot again. At last it stopped.

You bastards. You sons of bitches!

He was angry but his body felt loose and refreshed. Despite his confinement, he tingled with a feeling of well-being—which added to his anger. He did not want to feel good in this miserable oyster-shell. He resented the power of the Raddies to make him feel well.

The oysters in the other tanks had undergone much the same experiences, evidently, because in moments they came alive with many roars. Someone had ordered the engines turned on—but Shannon hadn't heard the order. Then the little tanks moved out. Engines racing, treads clicking on the concrete pad, they rolled ahead, turned, and rolled away.

As he watched the tanks' departure, Shannon had a peculiar realization. He knew how to operate his tank. He *knew*! Somehow, during the night, information had been fed into his brain without his own awareness. He reached out with his left hand tentatively, moving his fingers over buttons. He knew the function of each button, but something held him back from activating the tank's engine, computer, targeting system. He realized that his right hand had been trained to operate the tank's weapons systems, and his feet had a peculiar familiarity with two banks of pedals which he hadn't even noticed the night before.

Sleep-instruction. They trained me in my sleep . . .

He had also been given subliminal commands not to operate the tank—hence his aversion to push any of the buttons and pedals.

The tanks moved out, row after row, engines rumbling, treads clattering with chainey noise on the concrete apron. Shannon was left entirely alone. He also knew how to operate the video system using his left hand; he could have directed the camera and observed the tanks after they moved from his view. But he didn't dare to do so. He waited. He guessed that someone in authority would soon tell him what to do.

His guess turned out to be correct. After a while the tiny globe in his left ear crackled. Then he heard a man's voice.

"Raver Shanty?"

"Yes, sir," he said. He knew that he must address the man as 'sir.' He had learned a lot during the night without even trying.

Then a man walked into his view and faced the little tank. The man was short in stature, muscular. He wore the green uniform of the Raddies with stripes on his arm exactly like those that Shannon had seen on Harmsworth's sleeve. The little man wore a bright red helmet shaped like a bubble. A tiny microphone held on a stiff wire hung before his lips. The man's face was as red as his bubble helmet.

"Okay, Shanty," the man said. "I am Sergeant Donaldson. I run Baker Company, and you are one of mine."

"Yes, sir."

"Your number is 205," Donaldson said. "Remember it."

"Yes, sir. 205"

"Good. Did Schuster tell you about gigging?"

"Gigging, sir? No, sir."

"Well," Donaldson said flatly. "That little matter is still ahead. Okay, 205. We run a tight ship around here, and you're supposed to do as you are told—no more, no less. And with precision. *Pre*-cision. Got that?"

"Yes, sir."

"I'm going to give you a taste of gigging so that you know what's in store for you when you fuck off. Are you ready?"

Shannon had no idea what gigging was. "I—I guess so," he said uncertainly.

"No guessing," the sergeant said. " 'Yes' is the word."

"Yes," Shannon said.

"Dammit, 205," Donaldson cried. "The word is 'sir,' don't you forget it. I'm going to gig you for that." With that Donaldson reached up to touch his tunic, reached up to what seemed to be merely a button on his uniform-jacket.

And something exploded inside Shannon's brain. It was a blinding flash of nerves caused by an excruciating pain. Every fiber in his head seemed as if ignited, red hot, white-hot, incandescent. He felt the root of every tooth; the insides of his mouth felt as if he had just breathed in fire; his tongue felt as if a hundred razor blades had just sliced across it; his skull appeared to crack. He screamed involuntarily, but the pain continued. It rolled down from his head, and across his body—so intense, so shocking that he screamed again. His bowels opened. Helpless as a baby, he soiled himself, but water rushed into his rubber pants to flush the waste away. The pain seemed to pass out at the tip of his toes—with a feeling as if his toenails had been ripped away with a pair of pliers. The gig left him shaken, gasping.

When the film of tears over his eyes cleared away, he saw Donaldson again. The sergeant smiled faintly.

"Now you know what a gig feels like," he said. "And that was just a little gig. Just a single blast. How did you like it?"

"I didn't," Shannon gasped.

"*Sir*!" Donaldson shouted. "*Sir*, you blockhead."

And it happened again. Shannon's body arced inside the little tank. He screamed. The pain rolled over him as it passed out of his body at the toes, taking his toenails along. He was sobbing as the gig ended.

"Sir," he gurgled, "sir."

"All right," the sergeant said. "Any more mistakes, and you know exactly what'll happen to you. Now start your engine."

Shannon's fingers flew over the buttons in a desperate attempt to please. The excruciating pain that he had felt left no residue except in his mind, but his mind was filled with an unspeakable dread of yet another repetition. As the engine roared into life, Donaldson approached the tank and thus moved out of the range of Shannon's vision. Shannon heard the sergeant clambering up on the tank.

"Okay," the sergeant said, speaking from the turret of the tank. "Move out, 205. Head for the gate. We're going to join the company out on the firing range."

Shannon drove the tank through a wide-open gate in the fence, across a low bridge over the moat around Camp Bridges, and then along a concrete highway spanning the desolate terrain. The area had once been forest or agricultural land. The trees had been shorn away, bushes burned to blackened stalks; the earth on either side of the concrete was torn by treads and hardened to such an extent that only the toughest of grasses clung to the sides of thousands of ruts old and new.

"I understand that you're a smartie," Donaldson said after a while.

"I am not sure I am. Sir." Shannon said.

"Your test score says you are," the sergeant said. "And I hope you really are—for *your* sake, Raver. That ain't no picnic out there, and only the smart ones survive. Smart as a whip, that's what you've got to be."

"Yes, sir."

"You're the only smart guy in Baker Company," the sergeant confided. "All the others are stupid as stirred shit. You have to set a good example."

"I'll try, sir."

"Not *try*, 205, You'll do it. Or you'll wish you had."

"Yes, sir."

They rode along in silence for a while. In the distance Shannon saw clouds of dust marking the passage of a column of tanks over terrain. He heard the dull, faraway explosion of artillery shells. The streaky sky had lost its pink coloration as the sun advanced.

"If you're smart and if you're a killer," Donaldson said after a while, "you'll do all right in the Raddies. Now I know you're smart, 205, and your record says that you're a killer. Is that true?"

"No, sir," Shannon said—with some trepidation. His body cringed in the expectation of a gig. "I've never killed a soul."

"That right?" Donaldson said, still invisible, still riding Shannon on top of the turret. "Well, you'd better turn into a killer quick, 205. Killing is what this is all about. Kill five Mao's and you get a weekend off, out of the tank. How about that? Kill ten and you get a week off. After you kill twenty-five, you're eligible for promotion. Schuster says that you're a flyer. Kill twenty-five and you might make corporal and fly about in a chopper. Killing is what this is all about. Remember that."

"Yes, sir," Shannon said.

"It's kill or be killed," Donaldson said. "If you don't do

it, *they* sure will. And if you think it's bad to get a gig, wait till you're burning alive inside that tank of yours. All right, turn down there."

An intersection loomed ahead. Shannon approached it and turned to the right.

"To the left, the left!" Donaldson shouted—and once more spine-cracking pain swept over Shannon, once more he screamed.

"Teach you a lesson," Donaldson said after the gig had passed over Shannon. "Never accept an ambiguous order. Always ask. 'Which way, sir?' That's what you should've asked. Okay. Go down the hill now. See them down there, to the left? That's Baker Company."

Sobbing under his breath, tears streaming down his face, Shannon backed the tank a little and then turned down the road, to his left.

The firing range, to the right of the road, was a flat, dusty area bounded on the near side by a line of rectangular bales of straw. A flat area of perhaps two thousand meters extended outward from the bales. At various distances stood blackened hulks that might have been cars or trucks. Some of these smoked. The tanks of Baker Company had been firing under the command of a corporal.

The company consisted of four tanks marked by large numbers painted on their backs—201 through 204. They stood in a row facing the smoking targets. To the back of them stood a large truck. Soldiers lounged near its open end.

"See the truck?" Donaldson said as they arrived. "Back up to it and take on a load of ammunition." Then his feet scrambled off the tank and he came into view again.

"All right. Cease fire," Donaldson said. "Men, we've just taken on a new recruit. I'll give him a chance to show you cripples how to shoot. Go ahead, Raver. Take on the shells. Then I want you to roll over next to 204 and shoot five rounds. Aim at the nearest target and work your way out. Got that?"

"Yes, sir," Shannon said, backing his tank.

"Permission to speak, sergeant,"

"Go ahead, 201," Donaldson said.

"Sergeant, could you repeat the name of the new recruit?"

"His name is Raver," the sergeant said. "Raver or 205, as you wish,"

"Is his name Raver Shanty, sergeant?"

"That's right," Donaldson said. "Why? Do you know him?"

"You bet I do, sergeant," 201 said. "If it hadn't been for that son of a bitch, I wouldn't be in the Raddies now. None of the rest of us would either."

There was silence for the fraction of a second. Then Shannon heard a scream, a blood-curdling scream, followed by a series of moist sobs. Donaldson spoke.

"I advise you to keep a civil tongue in your head, 201," he said. "You'll refer to Raver as 205 or Raver. And if he got you into the Raddies, I bet that you deserved it. Got that?"

"Yes, sir," 201 said. This time Shannon recognized the voice, but he couldn't think about that now. Shells clanged as soldiers slammed them into his ammunition port. The port clanged shut, and he lurched forward to take up a position next to 204.

"Aim to hit, 205," Donaldson said. "Show them how sharp you are. I want to see a little talent around here. I want to show these pudding-brains that *somebody* can shoot. Hit 'em all, 205, and you won't be gigged for forty-eight hours. But if you miss, I'll gig you for each miss."

Fingers slippery with nervous sweat, Shannon aimed for the first hulk and squeezed a handle to release the shell. He knew exactly what to do. His tank rocked. His ears rang with the report. A smoky ball rose from the distant hulk. Pieces of its metal flew through the air. Shannon relased his breath, relieved. He aimed again, fired. A hit. Thank God. Again. A hit.

"So far, so good," Donaldson said.

The fourth target was far away. Shannon remembered something—without really remembering. He took a rapid distance reading this time and fed the data to his computer for a range-trajectory calculation. Then he aimed and shot, and another hulk flung its pieces into the air.

"Good," Donaldson said. "Tell these turkeys what you did, 205."

Shannon described the firing procedure he had just followed.

"Hear that?" Donaldson said. "Use the computer, you turnips. That's what it's for. You can't aim at something that's a thousand meters out with your bare eyes. Follow the training, don't override. Okay, 205. Shoot your last round."

Shannon did so, and once more he scored a hit. He sank back in his seat. Sweat covered his entire body. No gig for forty-eight hours, he thought. No gig. A time of peace, a time to take it easy.

"Very good," Donaldson said. "Looks like you're going to cut the mustard, Raver. As for the rest of you balls of shit, I want to see some shooting now. It's your ass if you don't learn. We're going on patrol tomorrow and that ain't no tea-party out there. Three gigs for every miss. You're on first, 204, and you'd better make it good this time."

Relaxed in his crowded cabin—as relaxed as you could be with arms and legs confined—Shannon watched the others shooting. They shot with desperate accuracy. Only two of the "oysters" earned a triple gig. Their screams of pain came over the radio.

Shannon wondered who was who. Tank 201 was Benny Franks. That much he had discovered already. Which tank was Clancy, which one was Mack, which one was Goulash. All were here, the entire leadership of the Neo-Catholic Catharsis Church. "Busted," as they said on the TV. Detective Murphy had cleared out that gang and James P. Schuster had "oystered" them for this reunion.

23

Late that afternoon, Shannon returned to camp riding at the tail of a column of small tanks arranged in numerical order, with 201 in the lead and 205—Shannon—bringing up the rear. Donaldson rode in the truck with the soldiers behind Shannon's tank.

As they came closer to the camp, Shannon saw streams of tanks converging on Camp Bridges from all directions. They merged into a mighty column of roaring engines and clattering tread. Directed by their sergeants, they filed into the camp over the bridge and through the gate Shannon had used that morning and found their appointed positions on the huge concrete apron. The engines died one after the other, and as this large detachment settled, metal crackled everywhere as engines cooled. Soldiers, most of them maimed or deformed in some way by past battles, moved among the tanks checking on mechanisms and lubricating tread-bearings with cannisters attached to pressurized injectors. Then James P. Schuster's voice came over the radio.

"Attention Battlion," he said. "We are going into action tomorrow, and as a special treat, you will be shown a movie tonight. Otherwise, I intend to enforce strict radio silence."

Soon after this a hose-like device came out of the ceiling of Shannon's tank and stopped immediately in front of his mouth. Even if he hadn't been ravenous, Shannon would have understood the function of this rubbery tube. He leaned forward and took the thing between his lips. Energetic sucking produced a flow of sweetish pap that tasted a little as if it had been laced with alcohol. The strange food did not entirely still his hunger, but it left him refreshed and elated. He knew that he was being drugged again, but he could not help that. He had to eat.

The movie came as night began to fall and the setting sun

painted cloud-shreds a virulent pink while the horizon
glowed like gold. The movie told the story of three courage-
ous Raddy tankers who, by dint of heroic efforts and mind-
less self-sacrifice, won a battle against tremendous swarms
of hateful Mao-Maos. For their courage and their devotion to
duty, they were decorated before cheering crowds and discharged to take up promising careers in civilian life. Shannon
had already seen that movie on TV in the Neo-Catholic
Catharsis Church.

Early the next morning, he awoke again while being exercised. An air of tension lay over Camp Bridges now. Soldiers
and sergeants, the latter in red bubble helmets, moved about
nervously in twilight. Orders crackled over the radio. The
Raddies were going out on patrol. After some confusion—
orders given and then rescinded—Baker Company started its
engines and, with Benny Franks in the lead again, it rolled
toward a railroad siding on the edge of the camp. There, by
way of ramps, the tanks clattered up to flatcars, two tanks to a
car. Fifty tanks were loaded in this manner, ten companies of
Raddies. Other trains, presumably, would come later to carry
off the rest of the battalion.

The train moved out around mid-morning. It lurched along
slowly at first but gradually took on speed. An hour passed,
two hours. The iron wheels beat rhythmically against poorly
jointed rails—ka-tuck, ka-tuck, ka-tuck, ka-tuck. The sun
rose higher and higher.

Going on patrol. Going on patrol.

Shannon watched the countryside in a half-dreamy state.
Images of the enemy seen in the movie the night before came
and went in his mind. He wondered what battle would be
like; he wondered if the film that he had seen was really true.
Would they really promote him if he killed twenty-five?
Magic number. Or was that a lie? He didn't trust the Raddies
anymore. He didn't trust a thing. He didn't trust the Purgatory Zone. Thus he brooded. Meanwhile the flat, dry plains
they had been crossing turned gradually into a lushly vege-

tated, hilly scene. Shannon guessed that this would be a long patrol. Camp Bridges lay very far behind.

Early in the afternoon, something happened toward the front of the train. They were moving now on a straight stretch of rail and Shannon could not see ahead. The locomotive pulled some forty cars, twenty-five loaded with tanks, the rest with ammunition, other vehicles, and ten small helicopters. His group was toward the tail of the train, and all he could see was a cloud of black smoke up ahead. The train had lurched badly in two or three spasms. Brakes had screamed. Then the train had stopped.

Maimed soldiers hobbled into view now led by Sergeant Donaldson. They pulled heavy ramps from beneath the railcars using small, earth-anchored hydraulic lifts. Shannon and his company were told to turn on engines and to get off.

Shannon had rolled down the ramp and came to a stop in high grass on moist, soft ground. He could see the front of the train now and noted that the locomotive lay in two gigantic, smoking pieces next to the track, on its roof. Several cars immediately behind the wreckage were in flames. Soldiers fought the blaze by squirting foam into the flames, and judging by their frantic efforts, Shannon guessed that fire threatened boxcars loaded with ammunition.

"All right, all right," came Donaldson's voice. "Fan out, you pumpkins. Fan out and move out. Head due south, and watch it. We've been detached to teach these punks a lesson. Move it. 201, you take the lead."

With the others, Shannon maneuvered himself into a spot in a wedge-shaped formation with Benny Franks leading at the tip. Shannon was on the left flank. Immediately to his right was 204. The oyster inside 204, he had deduced, was Clancy.

"You can kiss your ass good-bye now, Raver," Clancy said over the radio now. "We're about to see a little action."

Shannon said nothing. He still had a few more gig-free hours, but he didn't want to take unnecessary chances.

"You can talk," Clancy said. "I saw our leader taking off

his helmet. He is going to get into his whirly-bird.''

''Whirly-bird?'' Shannon asked.

''What else,'' Clancy said. ''You don't think that our sergeant is going to expose his precious skin to the Mao's, do you? *We're* the cannon fodder. He'll just direct us like an eye in the sky.''

A berm rose about a hundred meters from the railroad track. The five tanks labored up its steep sides and then down again. Shannon saw rough terrain—high, unruly grasses, dead trees aslant, and dusty bushes. A line of trees formed a distant wall, hiding the horizon. Thin clouds tried to cover the sky like a tattered blanket, failing, but they diffused the sunlight so that everying was bright and all the colors faded.

The tanks crashed over the terrain, moving in the direction of the woods ahead.

''I have one consolation,'' Clancy said. ''You know what it is? . . . Hey, Raver. You know what it is?''

''No, I don't,'' Shannon said.

''It gives me no end of pleasure that they've got you too. With a little bit of luck, I'll see the Mao's fry you to a crisp inside that tin can of yours.''

Benny now came on the air. ''Shut up, you two,'' He said. ''If Donaldson hears you, I'll be the one he gigs.''

''Shut up yourself, blubber-gut,'' Clancy said. ''You're the one who really landed us right up this creek of shit—you and your phoney religion. If you'd've wasted Raver like I told you to—but no. You had to show him to your stinking congregation. The day you tell me what to do is long gone, baby-fat. Long gone. If you and I ever get out of this alive, I'll make you pay for it.''

After that Clancy fell silent—and wisely so. In a moment or two Donaldson came on the air again. The sound of engines and of treads crashing through dry brush was such that the sergeant's helicopter could not be heard, but his airborne bubble appeared ahead of them in a moment.

''Turn east a little,'' Donaldson commanded. ''This way. I see the road ahead.''

He flew on and came to a hover above the woods. The tanks wheeled and moved ahead on a new course.

Ten minutes later, they reached the woods and entered it by a narrow track that Donaldson had spied from his helicopter. But the wood was deep and the track soon ran out. The tanks, moving in single file, ground to a halt.

Donaldson was high above them somewhere, hidden from view by thick foliage. He heard Benny's report and told the company to fan out again. "Make your own path," he ordered. "Move slowly. I'll scan the area for heat and I'll get back to you."

Shannon crunched ahead, picking a path for himself between the trees. Heavy underbrush, many fallen and rotting trees, disorderly curtains of vines, and vast, trembling cobweb patterns suspended between the trees revealed an untended, almost virginal forest such as he had never seen back home.

Back home . . . When he least thought of it, the Kibbutz Zone rose up in his memories to taunt him. Back home . . . where once he'd dreamed of freedom.

If I didn't have some kind of drug in my blood, he thought, *I'd be miserable.*

Somewhere deep down, beneath the surface of that drug-induced well-being he had felt continuously since his oystering, he *was* miserable. But he didn't feel it too keenly. It was a dull pain.

"Turn southwest," came Donaldson's voice. "Directly southwest. And get a move on. They spotted my copter and they're making a run for it. Full speed ahead."

The slowly crawling tanks came alive. Their noses lifted as the treads bit down. They roared through the forest now at a reckless pace, felling smaller trees, chewing off the bark of larger ones, raising dust, crashing, leaving trails of crushed brush and pulverized branches.

It was fun, in a way, this chase. Shannon's feet moved expertly on pedals directing his tank like a missile, threading the small vehicle through the woods. He moved so fast that

he took chances every other second. His blood sang with
excitement. For the moment it was all forgotten—his brutal
imprisonment, the savage pain his new masters administered, and the hopelessness of his future.

The chase went on for quite some while. Then, almost side
by side, the tanks roared out of the woods into a narrow but
long clearing. Directly before them rose a steep bank of
earth. Cave-like dwellings had been hollowed out of the
naked clay. Shannon saw rows of windows, some lined with
flower pots. Wooden ladders had been mounted between the
levels of this construct to allow access to the upper stories. To
his left, and already distant, Shannon saw men running.
Donaldson's bubble buzzed nervously above the clearing.

"All right," Donaldson said. "201, 202, 203, and 204—
chase those men. Raver, you stay here. Your job is to shoot
up the structure."

Shannon did not know what Donaldson meant, at first.
Then he grasped the situation. As the others raced away, he
aimed his cannon at the top-most storey of the clay structure
and released a shell. Metal and hard clay flew in all directions
as the blast sounded. Large quantities of dust boiled from the
structure and obscured the view. As the sound of the blast
faded, Shannon heard voices—shrill cries. He had been
ready to shoot again, but now he hesitated.

The dust raised by the shot settled slowly. Even before it
cleared away altogether, Shannon saw movement. Figures
were clambering out of the cave complex. Good God! Shannon saw women and children. With expressions of utter
terror on their faces, they hugged the lower wall of the
complex. Most of the women held their hands above their
heads. One woman was waving a white cloth in her hand.

Donaldson spoke. "What's the matter with you, Raver?
Blast those caves."

"Sergeant," Shannon said, "a bunch of women and children just came out."

There was just a second's pause. "So what?" Donaldson
then said. "Wipe them out."

"Wipe them out?" Shannon almost laughed.

"That's right. Use your machine gun. And be quick about it. They won't wait for you all day."

"But sergeant—"

"Do it, Raver. Don't *ever* question an order."

Shannon activated his machine gun. Drills he had learned in his sleep and practiced the day before had taught him what to do. He could have done it easily enough, even with his eyes closed. But he couldn't. These were ordinary people—women and little children. Thirty women and children—at least that many. They exceeded the magic number. They were poorly dressed, skinny, and terror distorted their faces. His finger was clasped around the trigger, but it refused to squeeze.

In the bright sky up above, Donaldson had begun to move in the direction where the rest of Baker Company had disappeared. He must have seen that Shannon's tank stood before the structure of caves inactively; he stopped his forward movement, turned the helicopter, came back, dropped a little, and surveyed the scene.

The women and the children still stood in a tight clump before the partially destroyed complex of caves. They were terrified. Only the woman waving a white flag seemed to be in control of herself.

"205," the sergeant said. "I meant what I said. Wipe out those Mao's or you'll wish you had."

Shannon said nothing. His mind seemed as if split apart. Deep down inside him a part of him screamed and clawed invisible walls. It urged him frantically to do what the sergeant had ordered, for the sake of *God!* He didn't give a damn about these skinny people. They were just Mao's, like the rest, what difference did it make. Squeeze, damn you, before it starts.

But while that voice raged deep inside him, fighting to gain control of Shannon's arm, of Shannon's hand, and struggling to take over Shannon's body, Shannon felt an odd, peculiar calm. It seemed to him almost as if Alkhazar were present and watching. And Alkhazar made time flow very, very slowly, giving Shannon time to think.

And in that moment—it was nothing more than that although it seemed like endless, silent ages—Shannon considered what he was about to do, what it was that Raver Shanty screamed and begged of him; to yield once more, to dissolve himself in fear. The loser was about to lose again . . . only to dream up some big lies to cover up his failure later. The memory of a statue came to him, the heavy burden he still carried, the mask of his own heroism.

You or they, he thought, staring at what seemed now a still picture of skinny women, naked children. The woman with the white cloth in her hand was frozen in mid-motion; Donaldson in the air above was fixed, unmoving; the smoke that but a moment ago had billowed richly from the upper caves had stopped flowing.

You or they. Even his thought seemed frozen.

And then it came to him that he could no longer live as he had always lived, in a world of you and they, in constant polarity—cringing from the pain and contact and subject to the whims and pride of Raver Shanty. He couldn't kill these people—no, not even to escape the tank! He wouldn't shoot. Raver wasn't worthy of such sacrifices. If now he squeezed the trigger resting cool against his finger, he would condemn himself forever. After this vile deeds would seem more easy, more justifiable—and act by act, failure by failure, he would lose ever more of the dwindling substance that he was, the Ravi Shannon he refused to be.

He took his hand from the trigger, and time began to rush again. The woman waved her white cloth. Smoke gushed richly from the broken wall of clay. Donaldson buzzed angrily above.

"You're a stinking infiltrator," the sergeant rasped over the radio. "Nevertheless, my boy, you'll do exactly what I tell you."

Pain racked Shannon—once, twice, three times. The sergeant repeated his order, but Shannon just sat in a slump; his throat hurt from screaming.

"Listen, Raver," the sergeant said. "The lieutenant wired you for level four—figuring you were a spy. If you think that ordinary gigging hurts, wait till I crank up the voltage. You want me to do that? Are you ready to obey?"

Shannon said nothing. He had arrived at the end of the road and there was nothing left to say.

"You asked for it," the sergeant said.

The pain that Shannon now experienced was beyond comprehension. His body arced inside the chamber. And arced! Vomit spurted from his mouth like water from a statue in a fountain. The wire mesh tore from portions of his body. His hands bled from an involuntary and mindlessly violent effort to pull them through the narrow ports that held them. He should have fainted but didn't, and a part of him admired the devilish cunning of the engineers who'd fashioned this incredible torture. He sagged back when the pain was over. He noticed, inexplicably, he had an erection inside those now torn rubber pants. The smell of his involuntary defecation filled the cubicle.

Donaldson was speaking again, but Shannon barely heard him. One thought filled Shannon. He could not endure too many more such gigs at level four. His left hand groped. He called up a schematic of his instrument board and studied it for a moment. The he reached out and activated a switch.

"Get away from here," he called. "Run. Run for your lives. If you don't run he'll make me kill —"

The pain's resumption cut him off. But his message, amplified by the tank's loudspeaker system, had had its desired effect. A long time later, barely conscious and whinnying insanely, Shannon came out of his peculiar hell. The women and the children had gone. So was Donaldson and his helicopter.

Shannon laughed hysterically—half laughter, half tears. His body rocked oddly. Tortured nerves jerked, tingled, and glimmered with remembered pain. The cubicle reeked of James P. Schuster's soap. He was nauseous. He tried to vomit, but nothing was left in his stomach, not even a gram of that sweet pap. Then, activated by smell—or perhaps by something else—the water jets came on. Very cold pin-pricks. Cold. Hot. Cold. Hot.

Shannon felt a little better. He wondered why that was but found no answer. Perhaps because he had survived; he had survived Level Four twice in a row.

It was very still in the clearing now. Birds noised in the trees behind him. He could hear a breeze rustling in the foliage. He felt very, very tired. He closed his eyes and fell asleep.

He awoke only once, briefly, a little later. It had seemed to him that he had heard Benny and Clancy and Mack and Goulash screaming in strange agonies, but those screams could have been a part of his dream. The radio transmitters had fallen from his ears and lay somewhere in the darkness at his feet. Shannon dozed off again.

24

The forest noised. Wind moved the crowns of trees. Birds chirped all around. Squirrels and rabbits fed and played with rustling sounds. A fire had raged inside the cave-complex but had died out at last, and now only one thin stream of smoke rose from one of the windows.

The time had to be late afternoon, but Shannon was not altogether sure which day it was. He had slept uncommonly soundly and had awakened unusually refreshed. The drug no longer polluted his blood; he felt as if he had shed a burden. It seemed as if his cells rejoiced, as if they were all singing. He was still confined, but now that didn't bother him. He felt oddly certain now and sensed that he would be released, but nothing around him so much as hinted at the manner of his release. He had been abandoned. The forest was empty. The Mao-Mao's had fled or had been killed by Raddies more

obedient than Shannon. Nevertheless, Shannon had a feeling
of certainty and consequently a sense of calm.

As the afternoon wore on and evening and then night set
in, he tried to understand the change that had overcome him.
Now that he had defied the ruling powers of the Purgatory
Zone, he should have felt despair. Dreadful things would
surely happen now—leading to his extinction. So why didn't
he tremble and rage in anticipation?

He puzzled over that for hours, searching for clues to his
present and his past. He shook his head from time to time. He
didn't comprehend it. The best explanation was that he had
gone insane and now lived in some kind of wild euphoria
caused by the disordered balance of chemicals in his brain.
He had been irrational in refusing Donaldson's orders. No
sane man in his circumstances would have acted so foolishly.
The Raddies existed, after all, to destroy and to kill. And no
healthy organism would deliberately choose unmentionable
pain. Nevertheless he was glad that he had acted as he had.

Come on, Raver, he thought at one point. *Where are you
hiding?* But Raver wouldn't answer, wasn't there.

He fell asleep that night thinking that he would awaken in
possession of his old self again. It was not a pleasant pros-
pect, but this odd state of calm and certainty felt a little
frightening.

The sound of engines and the chop of helicopter blades
roused him the following morning. Two helicopters had
arrived—a small one and a large machine with double sets of
rotors. The aircraft came purposefully and landed in the
narrow clearing. The air-blasts of their whirling blades flung
a storm of leaves and dirt across Shannon's video sensors.

Men jumped from the larger aircraft and marched up to
Shannon's tank. They carried tools and clambered up on the
tank. Then came the sounds of mechanical manipulation.
Heavy nuts were turned; armor plating scraped against

armor plating; a series of clamps were loosened and removed
with snapping sounds.

Meanwhile the helicopters had risen from the ground
again. The smaller of the two hung just over the complex of
caves—observing. The larger one positioned itself immediately above Shannon's tank. The men on top of the tank
directed the helicopter with shouts. Then Shannon felt his
cubicle jolt. With screeching noises, he was being lifted from
the tank—possibly by a cable. He had no idea what had
become of the men and guessed that they had clambered into
the helicopter using the cable from which he hung suspended.

Shannon's video equipment had not been disturbed by
this maneuver, and as the helicopter rose and changed direction, he saw his erstwhile home below. A rectangular opening gaped in the front of the little tank; the cubicle, meanwhile, swung like a pendulum beneath the craft that took him
. . . where? Shannon didn't know.

Out of the tank. He had escaped the tank, and soon now he
would leave this funny box as well. Vague but oddly
"hard," the premonition filled his mind. Sleep had failed to
bring back Raver.

The helicopter buzzed along above him for more than an
hour. The smaller craft kept them company; it flew to the
right and at a lower altitude. The sky was clear, a deep and
soothing blue. The land below lay in a faint haze. The sound
of engines and of whirring blades made a drowsy hum, but
Shannon was alert and very curious. He had the irrational
conviction that now he could control his future and that the
only question was what he would choose to see. The thought
was so unusual that he set it aside.

At last and with a change of sound, the aircraft slowed and
dropped. More of the immediate surrounds came into Shannon's view as the angle of his vision changed. Down there
was the scalped terrain around Camp Bridges, and then he
saw the camp itself—the warehouse, the two shacks beyond

the fence, a small formation of Raddy tanks. His aircraft made toward the warehouse.

Moments later he had been set down. Then a front-end loader approached and lifted his cubicle at a tilt. It carried him into the shadowy interior of the warehouse.

Voices now echoed and steps shuffled. Then he heard clangs and bangs. Men worked on his cubicle. Something hissed sharply moving from point to point on the outside of his prison. Then came a sharp call, and with a crash the entire frontal portion of Shannon's chamber fell away. Faces peered in on him, among them James P. Schuster's ratty, ill-shaved face.

Schuster raised his eyebrows. "Well," was all he said. Then he nodded to the other men, stepped forward, and began to work bolts that Shannon couldn't see. Moments later Shannon's hands were free. He drew them to himself and rubbed his bruised wrists. Schuster moved into the cabin.

"Hold still now," he said, leaning over Shannon. "Let me take these off." Schuster reached for Shannon's skull and began ripping tape. Shannon winced; the tightly adhering strips tugged at tiny shoots of hair that had come up since his oystering. "You can get up now," Schuster said, stepping back. "Everything else is pretty much ripped loose."

Shannon ducked out of his chamber. His legs almost buckled under him, and he staggered for a second before he found his balance. He stood in a work area with tables against a wall. Various electronic instruments crowded the tables. The cubicle he had just left was a low, rectangular construct, its sidewalls gouged and scraped from many insertions and retractions. Three soldiers lounged next to it staring at Shannon with a kind of curious interest that Shannon found difficult to understand. Did they take him for a freak?

"Well . . . " Schuster said again. He seemed on the point of saying something more but changed his mind. Instead he pointed to a door between two workbenches. "You can shower in there," he said. "We've also found you some appropriate clothing." He turned and gestured to one of the soldiers. "You keep an eye on him, Jenkins. We don't want anything to happen to our precious Mr. Shannon."

Shannon? There it was, suddenly, his Kibbutz name. Shannon stared at Schuster, a question on the tip of his tongue, but then he became aware of his own condition. He was half naked, still wearing those ridiculous rubber pants. Pieces of torn wire mesh adhered to his arms and legs. He wanted to be dressed again before he asked his questions.

Led by Jenkins, a sallow soldier who hobbled on a crude rubber-tipped wooden leg, Shannon went off to the showers wondering. He wondered why it seemed so proper and so fitting that he should be released—and to be called Shannon now instead of Shanty. His feelings were quite sure of everything, but his mind still lagged behind events.

Soon he stood under a stream of rushing water, sighing with pleasure. It seemed wrong that he should be enjoying himself, but he was. Logic told him that dreadful things now lay ahead, but his feelings continued to assure him. He soaped himself from head to toe and noticed, by-and-bye, that the soap had a sweetly, fragrant smell. He didn't even catch a hint of that nauseating odor that had haunted him off and on since his arrival in the Purgatory Zone. Finishing his shower, he decided to put some questions to the guard Schuster had assigned to him, Jenkins with the wooden leg.

Immediately outside the shower stood some narrow benches painted green. Jenkins sat on one of these, his wooden leg extended stiffly ahead. As Shannon stepped from the shower stall, Jenkins rose and handed him a thick, long, fluffy towel.

"Tell me something," Shannon said, drying his neck and chest and arms. "Why did Schuster call me 'Shannon' just now?"

Jenkins made an expression as if he were sucking on an aching tooth. He had a long face, sparse hair and wore a rumpled uniform that seemed to have been washed by hand, dried on a line, and donned without ironing.

"He found out who you really are," Jenkins said.

Shannon had a momentary shock. Had Schuster somehow learned about the Kibbutz Zone? But that seemed very improbable.

"How?" Shannon asked. "How'd he manage that?"

"Simple," Jenkins said. "He asked for a record check. After what happened out there . . . " Jenkins gestured. "Schuster figured that you were a commie all along, so now he was sure, see? So we sent your prints and picture to the NABA for a check."

"NABA?" Shannon asked. "What's that?"

"National Data Bank," Jenkins said. His eyes peered curiously at Shannon. "You really don't know? You really don't remember anything?"

"I don't," Shannon said. "I told Schuster when I got here—and that sergeant in the wheelchair."

"Harmsworth," Jenkins said.

"Harmsworth," Schuster said. "I don't remember having my picture taken."

"We do that just before we seal you in. You were out at the time."

"So you sent my picture," Shannon said. "So what happened?"

"So Schuster found out who you really are—and then the shit started to hit the fan."

Shannon had never heard that phrase before; he smiled when he understood the meaning. He had finished drying himself and threw the towel on the bench next to the rubber pants and bits of wire he had peeled off before his shower.

"What did you find out?" he asked.

Jenkins gestured. "This way," he said, leading Shannon from the shower room. "You don't know, do you?"

"I told you," Shannon said. "I've lost my memory." He wondered how many times more he would have to repeat that explanation. Then he stopped and stared.

They had entered another room lined on all sides by little lockers. More narrow benches stood before them. From the

latch of one of the lockers hung a suit, and on the bench lay
underwear, a folded shirt, rolled up socks, a pair of shoes, a
wig. Shannon was staring at the suit. Woven of rich, expensive, and almost luminous fibers, it was a suit of the sort worn
only by Beautiful People.

"There's your answer," Jenkins said, pointing to the
clothes. "Turns out that you're one of *them*. One of *the*
Shannons. But don't suppose that means anything to you."

"It doesn't," Shannon said. He reached for the underwear and began to dress.

"Well, sir," Jenkins said, "I didn't either. Not till Schuster clued me in. It turns out that the Shannon's are the money
behind Desirium Incorporated." Responding to Shannon's
blank stare, he went on, "That's the big drug company. And
I mean *big*! They make venisol, thalmarpa—and desirium."

"What about PD's?" Shannon asked.

"Yeah," Jenkins said. "PD's too. But those you can't
buy over the counter."

Shannon slipped into the exquisitely soft, fragrant shirt
and began to button it. "So what'll happen to me now?" he
asked.

"What do you think?" Jenkins answered. "You're going
home, of course."

"But I thought I was in the Raddies."

"Not you, sir," Jenkins said. "We thought that we had
somebody else. BP's don't serve in the Raddies." Suddenly
Jenkins laughed. His laughter made him curiously memorable, and Shannon saw him now as a person for the first time.
Jenkins had a hard laugh, and his eyes expressed some kind
of scorn. "No, sir," Jenkins said. "BP's don't serve in the
Raddies. That's why Schuster's all unglued."

"What about Raver?" Shannon asked. "Raver Shanty—
the guy everybody took me for?"

"We found out about him too," Jenkins said. His eyes
shifted; he smiled. "Turns out that you look a lot like Raver.
But Raver is dead. He died a couple of weeks ago. Or so they
say." Once more Jenkins laughed in his hard, metallic,
memorable way.

"Why do you laugh?" Shannon asked. He was sitting on the bench now, putting on his socks.

"Why do I laugh? Well, sir, it just strikes me funny, is all. It seems that you disappeared just about the time when Raver started making trouble in Phoenix. And you lost your memory just about when Raver is supposed to have died. And Raver is supposed to have died right after killing a man. Kind of a neat coincidence."

Shannon looked up at Jenkins. "Did they ever find Raver's body?"

" 'Course not."

"Of course not? Oh," Shannon said. "You think that I am Raver, don't you."

"I don't think anything," Jenkins said. "I'm not supposed to think. Just follow orders. But I know a thing or two. When a company like Desirium wants to fix a little problem for one of the owners' precious kids—why, things just sort of happen."

"Do you think they did something to get me out?" Shannon asked. It surprised him how calmly and quickly he had accepted the fact that he *was* getting out.

"I'm not thinking," Jenkins insisted. "I just find it funny, is all. You're just lucky Schuster ran a NABA check. If he hadn't, you'd still be out there in the boonies riding around inside a tank. And I reckon that you wouldn't be around come a week or two. Donaldson had a way with guys that refuse to shoot when they are told. And then you'd *really* be dead. Mr. Shannon." Jenkins laughed. "Like I said. You sure is lucky. Luck is what it's all about. Luck makes all the difference between a guy like you and a guy like me. All the difference. Some are born to lose, some are born to win . . .

"Come on, now," he said after a moment. "Put on that fancy suit of yours. A chopper is waiting to rush you into Mama's arms."

Shannon finished dressing. Ready at last, he looked at Jenkins again. "What about the others?" he said. "The other guys in Baker Company."

"Them?" Jenkins said. "Oh, those boys are gone. They

were a bunch of losers, right from the start. They ran into a Mao ambush and got burned up.''

''Burned up?'' Shannon asked, frowning.

''Sure enough,'' Jenkins said. ''The Mao's knocked them off their treads, poured gasoline through all the cracks, a little match. Poof. Burned to a crisp.''

''Benny and Clancy and . . . ''

''The whole shooting match,'' Jenkins said and turned to go.

Shannon followed him, thinking of Benny and the others, remembering some screams he thought he'd heard over his radio. Burned to a crisp? Jenkins had asserted it, but Shannon's feelings weren't sure at all. In fact he rather doubted the truth of Jenkins' assertion.

THE BEAUTIFUL PEOPLE

25

He walked from the helicopter to the smaller of two terminal buildings. The reddish bubble of Phoenix glittered nearby in sunlight. He had left this very airport two or three days ago bound for the Raddies. Now he was back—as a BP! His sudden change in fortunes was no more explicable than his long string of mishaps, but this was a great deal easier to take.

As he approached the building, glass doors reflected his image and he saw himself glittering like some luminous creature. The fabric of his suit caught and transformed the sunlight into a thousand colors so that he seemed to be walking in a circle of radiance—and the image recalled Lillian . . . and he felt a twinge of pain.

He passed through the door into an open hall, and as he entered a woman rose from a seat near the door. She advanced toward him with an anxious expression. She was tall and thin and in her late fifties. Layer upon layer of flimsy but expensive cloths had been draped about her body giving her the semblance of a shimmering bird with wings partially opened for flight. Shannon recognized her as the replica of

Janet Brood on this planet—the same Janet who still served as Zen Richelem's council chair back in the Kibbutz world.

"Ra-ra," cried this replica of Janet, and Shannon now knew who Ra-ra was. Himself. "Oh, Ra-ra, at last. My dear."

She came to him and embraced him lightly. He smelled her exquisite perfume.

"Is it true?" she asked, drawing back and looking at him as her fingers lightly touched his arm. "You don't remember anything?"

"I'm afraid it is," Shannon said. "I have a vague memory of you. Are you Janet?" Her face revealed that he had caught her name at least. "Well, that's something," he said. "But I'm afraid I don't know how we are related—or even *if* we are. Are you my mother?"

Janet laughed. "Oh, dear," she said. "It's quite bad, isn't it. I'm your aunt, my dear. But I'm almost your mother. You've always lived with me—not counting those years in Paris." She looked at him. She shook her head. "What did they do to you? That lip. And even your hair . . . it seems . . ."

"I'm wearing a wig," Shannon said. "They shaved my head in the Raddies. You're not looking at my real hair. As for the lip—"

Janet shook her head, cutting him off.

"Let's talk in the car," she said. She looked about her with evident unease. "I always feel so nervous outside the city. Harvey!" she called, turning toward three men who stood by a bar, "we're ready."

The men at the bar moved as one. Two went ahead, out through a swinging door. The third one, presumably Harvey, stayed behind to hold the door open for Janet and Shannon. Then he followed behind them. They were making for a sleek, silvery sedan parked in front of the terminal building, its back doors open to receive them.

"Well," Janet said as the car surged forward. "You must

tell me everything. I want to know exactly what has happened to you, dear boy.''

Shannon collected his wits. ''It's not a very long story,'' he began, still wondering how much to tell his 'aunt,' ''but it feels like a long one. Perhpas I'd better start from the point when I . . . when I came to again.''

He went on to tell the woman—so familiar and yet also so strange—essentially everything that he had experienced. He omitted one or two events. He did not speak of Lilly Waterburg and he did not speak about PD's. Neither subject seemed to him too safe—not until he knew a lot more about the BP world.

Staring at Shannon, Janet listened to his story without expression. She stared so intensely that Shannon grew uncomfortable. At last she shook her head slowly.

''Poor, dear Ra-ra,'' she said. ''What revolting experiences. And to think that we were searching for you in New York, in Paris . . . and all the while you were right here, under our noses, so to speak . . . '' She shook her head again. ''And you have no idea who those men were? The ones who took you from the church?''

''None,'' Shannon said.

''Extraordinary,'' Janet said. ''Really extraordinary. As I'm always telling Tubby, God only knows what this world is coming to. To think that someone of our class can be abducted, treated like that . . . ''

Meanwhile the car had stopped at a gate leading into the city. Attached to a high concrete wall curving away into the distance on either side, the bubble over Phoenix rose up high, reddish in sheen, a network of hexagons. The driver showed some kind of card to a uniformed official who had approached the vehicle. The official nodded and the car surged forward into a dark tunnel piercing the concrete wall.

''I wonder if you could help me a little,'' Shannon said as they entered the tunnel.

''Why of course, my dear.''

''Could you tell me a little about myself? I know how

strange it must sound to you—but I don't even know who I really am.''

''My dear Ra-ra,'' Janet said. ''Of course, my dear . . . Where shall I start? Let's see . . . Well, I suppose I might as well start at the beginning.''

She moved in her seat. Her hands fluttered as they adjusted a layer of scarves covering her upper body. Then she began.

Shannon learned that his parents had separated soon after his birth. His mother lived in California these days. His father directed Desirium's European operations from Geneva. ''You've never gotten along with him,'' Janet said. ''You're too much like your mother, and Banks cannot abide her, alas.'' Shannon grew up in Janet's household. He had lived with her until just eight years ago. ''Then you went off to Paris,'' Janet said. ''I did not approve, you know, but you were always headstrong. You had just come back.'' she said, ''less than a month ago, when you suddenly disappeared on a Thursday night after a party. We were sure that you had gone back to Europe—or east again. You always liked New York. We didn't even start to look for you until a week had passed. You'll pardon my saying so, Ra-ra,'' she concluded, ''but you were always a little erratic.''

The car had reached Phoenix proper and moved briskly up toward the center of the city by one of the spiralling skyways. The traffic was light this afternoon. Most of the pendulating bubble-cars Shannon glimpsed moving on cable-tracks between huge buildings rode empty.

Ra-ra's history was unusually sparse, devoid of meaningful content. Janet had said nothing about Ra-ra's education, profession, or ambitions. He almost asked her to elaborate, but then it came to him that it was right and fitting that Ra-ra's history was sparse. For reasons Shannon couldn't find just now, he was sure that Ra-ra had never existed. Damned if he knew why he thought so—but he did. He did—despite Janet's presence and her solicitous words.

''It'll all come back to you,'' Janet said after a moment. ''A little rest, proper care . . . I'm arranging a big party for you the day after tomorrow. I'm inviting all your friends. It can't possibly harm you, and it might help you remember. Don't you agree?''

"That would be very nice," Shannon said. "It's very kind of you."

Janet—and Shannon—lived in Hazienda Tower, one of those marvels of architecture in the heart of Phoenix. Two entire floors of the apartment house, floors high up in the structure, belonged to the Shannons. An elevator whisked them up to Shannon's floor.

"I hope you don't mind terribly being left alone," Janet said as the elevator stopped. One of the bodyguards—the man called Harvey—held a button to keep the elevator door from closing. "I am meeting with some friends in an hour, and I can't get out of it. But I'll see you again for dinner." She pecked a kiss on Shannon's cheek. "Just ring the bell," she said. "Ludwig will take care of you."

"Thank you," Shannon said. And he stepped into a hall.

He looked around as the elevator closed and Janet disappeared. The hall was not terribly large—not more than a vestibule with the elevator at one end and a heavy door opposite. On the door stood his name—Ravi Shannon—in large, raised letters painted gold. The door opened as he rang the bell and he saw a man in black. Some distance behind him stood two women side by side, an elderly matron and a young, pale creature; both wore white aprons over black dresses. Like the man in black, they had anxious expressions.

"Mr. Shannon," the man said, "I—I'm Ludwig, your butler. I understand that you . . . "

"That's right," Shannon said. "I don't remember." In a vague sort of way he understood the nervousness of these servants of his. They feared for their jobs . . . ?

"A—and this is Fritzie, your cook and Jenny, the maid."

The two women made curious movements. It took Shannon a moment to find the name for their actions. They had just curtseyed.

"I am pleased to meet you—again," Shannon said. He

smiled at them reassuringly. "I am very glad that I am back," he said after an awkward pause. "I'm so glad that you are here to welcome me back. But . . . I am very tired and would like to be alone for a while. If you would just, uh, point me toward my quarters, Ludwig . . ."

"Certainly, sir," Ludwig said. He nodded toward the two women briskly; they curtseyed again and disappeared to Shannon's right. "Would you like me to give you a tour?"

"Thank you," Shannon said, "but that won't be necessary. If you'll just point me in the right direction . . ."

"This way, Sir," Ludwig said. He opened and held a door to Shannon's left. "Just ring if you wish something."

"Thank you," Shannon said and went through the door. Ludwig closed it behind him.

His quarters were immense. From a huge living room richly furnished and equipped with what looked like a place for burning logs of wood, he moved through a succession of rooms that, in the aggregate, provided more space for his personal activities then Zen Richelem put at the disposal of fifty people.

He passed through an enormous study lined with books. A nearby entertainment center boasted a wall-sized glass screen and an electronic control panel more intricate than that of many an airplane. Next door stood pool tables and electronic game machines. Then came a spacious area with a high wooden counter, a brass railing, and a great assortment of bottles filled with a bewildering variety of alcoholic beverages. He inspected an entire complex dedicated to sports—a swimming pool, an exercise room with numerous machines, a long narrow hall used evidently for archery, fencing, and target practice with pistols and rifles. Adjacent to the complex was something labelled a "sauna" and several other rooms whose functions he couldn't even guess. He found a "wine room," "a smoking room" (judging by a collection of pipes in racks along a wall), an immense eating room, several other rooms with tables, and finally a gigantic bedroom with a large round bed. Adjacent to the bedroom were toilet facilities including a steam room, another "sauna," showers, and a very deep tub-like basin filled with circulating hot water.

Shannon sat down on the bed at last; then he laid himself flat, gazing up at the ceiling. Up there he noticed a painting showing the sky, clouds, and little creatures—fat children, really—with tiny wings sprouting from their shoulders. The winged children held a long chain woven of flowers and seemed to be engaged in some kind of dance.

Shannon took a deep breath and exhaled it. It was very still in the room and in his "quarters."

He lay on the bed and mused. Too many things had happened to him lately—too fast. His mind and his emotions could not keep up. He found it almost impossible to react. At this time yesterday, he had been an oyster in a cramped shell subject to unmentionable tortures. Now he lay on a soft bed in an apartment with more room than that of his entire dormitory in the Kibbutz Zone.

A week ago he had been unsure, frightened, confused, and angry. Now he felt an odd sort of certainty. He was certain about *something* but did not know exactly what. His feelings had improved, but he was still confused. But he no longer worried about his confusion. He no longer worried, but he was very curious. *What is it?* he asked himself. *Something bugs me about this world, but I'll be damned if I can lay my hands on it.*

He meant to get to the bottom of the feeling. He was determined to understand the Purgatory Zone—and his oddly changed feelings.

He stood up and began to walk around the room. He touched the walls, he fingered the curtains. He stopped before a chest of drawers and touched the drawer's knobs. He pulled open a drawer and looked at tidily stacked underwear. He touched a pair of underpants and rubbed the textile between his fingertips. Then he closed the drawer and returned to the bed again.

Everything around him was soberly solid, rigidly real.

Then why did it seem to him that the world he now inhabited was a vision, was a dream?

He thought about that.

It's not the things that are unreal; it's all the things that've happened—and are still happening.

He pondered the events of his brief time in the Purgatory Zone. Bad fortune had dogged him from the moment that he had arrived. Bums beneath that skyway had attacked him. As a consequence of his ignorance about money, a man named George had died. He'd found himself mistaken for a dope-fiend named Raver—and after that he'd undergone one humiliation after the other. He reached up to touch the scar across his lips, recalling Lilly Waterburg. Least comprehensible of all had been that PD trip, that out-of-body experience. His dealings with John St. John had convinced him that someone still watched him from the Kibbutz Zone. He found that difficult to understand.

Then, suddenly, and just like *that*! His fortunes had changed when he had least expected it. After refusing to carry out Donaldson's orders, he'd been sure that he'd be killed—somehow. Yet the opposite had happened. Here he was enclosed by luxury, living at the top of Phoenix. It was plausible, sort of, provided that some character named Ravi Shannon had really existed as a BP in the Purgatory Zone, provided that Ravi Shannon had gone into the slums of Phoenix calling himself Raver Shanty, provided that Raver Shanty had died just before Shannon's arrival . . . Plausible, sort of, Shannon concluded, but he found it difficult to believe that sequence of events.

He sat on that huge round bed and stared at walls of white-and-brown finished to look like a tiger's skin.

He compared his days in the Purgatory Zone to his years back home in Kibbutz. He compared the "feel" of that life with the "feel" of this one and wondered whether or not the strangeness he felt here might not be culture shock after all, nothing but culture shock.

Irritatingly, he heard in the silence around him the hum-

ming of a defective neon bulb. He looked at the edges of the
ceiling from whence milky light shone, illuminating both the
room and those winged children holding a garland of flowers. The humming sound was not coming from there. It came
from nowhere in particular.

Suddenly he rose. He had remembered something. He had
remembered wondering what the word "purgatory"
meant—back in the Time Van and then again in the helicopter on his way to Camp Bridges. He still lacked an answer to
his question. Perhaps he could find the answer here.

He went off to find that handsome study again, that study
so richly stocked with books. As he began to walk, the
humming sound that he'd just heard faded way.

He found the study after one or two false starts. His place
was so sizeable that he could get lost in it. He made light in
the study and surveyed three walls covered with shelves from
floor to ceiling. He began to search the shelves for a dictionary. Most of the books he saw dealt with history. Among
them he recognized some of his own favorites, his treasured
books, the same books he had thrown to the floor and kicked
about in that last fit of rage back home, with Benny looking
on. The books puzzled him, but now he was searching for a
dictionary. Didn't "Ra-ra" use those things. Ah, here they
were. He squatted down and pulled a thick volume from one
of the bottom shelves. His fingers ran over the pages looking
for the letter P, PU, PUR. Here was the word. Purgatory.

"An intermediate state after death," he read, "for expiatory purification. A place or state of punishment wherein
according to Roman Catholic doctrine the sins of those who
die in God's grace may make satisfaction for past sins and so
become fit for heaven."

Shivers of apprehension passed over Shannon's body.
Beads of sweat moistened his pores. His scalp itched fierce-
ly, and he removed his wig. He scratched his scalp absently,
still staring at the words.

"An intermediate state *after death* . . . "

I'm dead, he thought. *That son of a bitch Schuster killed me!*

A swarm of thoughts rushed across his mind, but he stopped himself. He did not fully understand the definition he had read. He wanted to know what "Roman Catholic doctrine" meant, for instance. And what exactly did they mean by "expiatory purification?"

He straightened up and went to the desk, carrying the dictionary. He meant to look up every word before he drew his final conclusion.

26

Shannon studied until evening, until Ludwig suddenly appeared to tell him that he was wanted for dinner "upstairs." Shannon looked up. Ra-ra's desk was piled with dictionaries and with books on religious subjects, and Shannon was so immersed in his investigations that he stared at Ludwig for a moment before he understood that Janet had called to summon him. He rose from his desk, picked up and fitted the wig over his head again, and followed Ludwig out.

He went up one floor to Janet's apartment in a distracted frame of mind and barely noticed the luxury in which his 'aunt' lived—a luxury far more glittering even than that surrounding Ra-ra. A tall, severe, and frosty butler clothed in a long coat with winged tails led him over marble floors and sinking carpet to a dining room where Janet and two others waited. Janet fluttered forward to greet and to introduce him to "Tubby," a young man she described as her "companion," and to Cecilia, a young woman whom Janet tagged as "my secretary." Then they sat down to eat.

Janet seemed unnaturally lively. Her eyes shone so brightly that Shannon guessed she was on drugs. After some preliminaries, she turned the talk to terrorism. Less than an hour after she and Ra-ra had arrived that afternoon, she said, five Kamikazis hiding out in the garage had attacked Jody Hollman as she was driving in. "Five, mind you," she said. "How *ever* did they get in!" Hazienda Towers was supposed to have security second to none. Jody escaped, thank God, she said, but one of her guards was killed while trying to save her, and Jody was in the hospital for tear-gas inhalation. What was the world coming to!

She went on in more general terms talking of anarchists and saboteurs and death squads from the slums. Nobody was safe these days, no matter where you lived she said. If "they" could assault you inside Hazienda Towers, they could just as well come into this apartment with their guns and bombs. Janet was agitated and paused frequently to empty her wine glass; the frosty butler hovering at her left shoulder kept filling up her glass.

Shannon was surprised by his own lack of interest in what she said. She was visibly upset despite the drugs that made her eyes blaze and the wine that flushed her cheeks. She spoke of the world's collapse and of the plight of the Beautiful People, but ever since he'd read that definition of "purgatory," Shannon could no longer believe in this world. What if, indeed, it was just illusion—and Janet as much as her tall butler, young Tubby, shy Cecilia were all, like Shannon, made of some ghostly, unreal stuff . . . ?

Course followed course—soup, salad, bits of fish fried in batter and eaten with a spicy sauce, rare beef, roast duck . . . The food was real. The smell of it was pleasant. Nonetheless, Shannon wondered. He wanted to go back to reading.

Janet's monologue about the state of the society ran out at last. Seeming to remember Shannon, she began to speak about his "cure." She had asked Cecilia to schedule Ra-ra for a medical examination the following morning. "That's all set, isn't it?" she asked. Cecilia nodded shyly. "Tubby will take you," Janet told Shannon, and Tubby smiled and nodded.

"Of course," Janet said, "the doctors . . . I don't believe

they *know* anything, you know. Still. It won't hurt to go. But as far as I'm concerned, I think the party will do you a lot more good."

Then she spoke about the party that she had already mentioned to Shannon in the car. All of Shannon's closest friends had been invited for the evening after next. Seeing them, Janet hoped, might help Ra-ra remember.

"But I do so wish that we had time to fix that lip of yours, my dear," she said, peering anxiously at Shannon. "I hope you don't mind my saying so, but it gives you a . . . a sneering look. But I'm afraid that we can't help that. The party is all arranged, and plastic surgery takes frightfully long. The best people are booked for months ahead."

Tubby and Cecilia took only a token part in the dinner conversation. Neither wore the exquisite clothing of BP's, and Shannon guessed that they were servants of high rank but nevertheless servants. Lesser servitors, supervised by the tall and frosty butler, waited on the table beneath a glittering chandelier whose lights were reflected in dozens of dishes covered by silver domes.

Shannon excused himself after the meal, pleading fatigue, but when he arrived in his own apartment again, he returned to his study, and went on reading the book he had left open in the center of the desk. Very late that night, he stumbled off to the bedroom with the tiger-skin walls and the round bed. His head was full of all manner of strange matters about heaven and hell, sin and forgiveness, the soul's immortality, the end of time, the resurrection of the body, and the final judgement.

The next morning passed swiftly. Shannon spent most of his time in a clinic under the probing fingers, instruments, and eyes of two doctors. He was alert and careful. The doctors were puzzled; they could not explain Shannon's amnesia, and in efforts to penetrate the case, they administered test after test and subjected Shannon to lengthy interrogation. They gave up at last and asked that Shannon return within a week for another check. Meanwhile the results of his physical examination would be evaluated by laboratories and computers.

On the way back to Hazienda Towers, Shannon learned that Tubby—who had brought him to the clinic—was Janet's lover. The young man was richly rewarded for the job, at least in his own estimation. Shannon gathered that a good many young men 'specialized' in what Tubby called 'intimate services.' ''What with the new aphrodisiacs,'' Tubby said, ''the job's really a snap—unless the client goes in for S&M.''

''S&M?'' Shannon asked.

''Sadism-masochism,'' Tubby said.

''Oh,'' Shannon said. He had two new words to look up when he finished with his own investigation.

Alone in his study again, he went on reading.

Ludwig brought him a tray of food after a while and set it down on a narrow table next to one of the leather armchairs in Ra-ra's comfortable study. Shannon did not touch the meal. Food did not attract him now. He was as puzzled as the doctors had been—but about a different matter. He read everything that Roman Catholic doctrine had to say about purgation, redemption, death, and resurrection. He moved from book to book; he looked up articles in encyclopediae, he made notes to himself; he stared into the relative gloom of the room, thinking. Toward evening, at last, he pushed the books aside and laid a writing tablet before him.

He had reached a conclusion. Everything that he had read convinced him that a ''purgatory'' was a place where dead men dwelled. If this was *really* Purgatory—rather than just a time zone fancifully called by that name—then Ravi Shannon had died in the Time Van; he was nothing but a disembodied soul; and the solid world around him was not really a solid world at all.

Yet, as Shannon now recalled, James P. Schuster had said that people could return to Kibbutz. Shannon recalled the words distinctly. He had been surprised by that. But Schuster had said it clearly enough—Shannon could come back—at some risk—provided that he went back to the same spot where he had entered the Purgatory Zone. And provided that the Kibbutz Zone was still monitoring that spot.

Two weeks or so, Schuster had said. They'd monitor the spot for fourteen days or so. The question was—how long had Shannon spent in this zone? Had he already missed his chance to slip back to the Kibbutz Zone . . . in order to see if it really existed . . . in order to check whether he was alive or dead . . . ?

He took an exquisitely sharpened pencil from a tray and began to reconstruct his time in Purgatory.

He had arrived late one night, on a Wednesday night. His first full day in Purgatory had been the day when Benny and his "animals" had scrubbed the Neo-Catholic Catharsis Church in anticipation of Parents' Day. And Parents' Day was Day Number Two.

Then had come the day when Benny had threatened him with death unless he agreed to leave the city by a tunnel and settle in the Squattings with a hundred "bucks." That had been a Saturday.

The next day, Sunday, had come the mass, his violent abduction, Murphy, police, and his arrival in Dalton's stinking jail. He had swallowed the PD pill that night and tripped out to Paradise. Roman Catholic doctrine called it heaven, the Church Triumphant.

Then came five days in a dark cell, but Shannon wasn't sure of that. It might have been a longer or a shorter time. He had lost count of the days in darkness. He'd spent those many hours sleeping at odd times of day and night.

Then had come a day that seemed like two in retrospect— his trial before Judge Noland, his trip to Camp Bridges, and his oystering. The next day he had trained. The day after that the train had moved them out into the country. And in the afternoon he had refused to shoot those women and those children.

Here was another murky point. Had he spent one or two

days in front of those caves? He could not remember. It seemed like two. But if two, and if his extraction and return to Phoenix had taken place on the third day, then altogether fifteen days had passed. Or one too many.

Shannon scratched his head. Fifteen days. Under the best of circumstances, assuming that he had spent four days in solitary confinement and only one before the caves, he had spent thirteen days on this side of that skin of time. One day would be left, only one. If he acted at all, he'd have to act tomorrow at the latest.

He did more scratching on a pad. If fifteen days had passed, today would be Thursday. But what day was it. He hadn't the faintest idea.

Shannon had noticed a panel with buttons on the left side of his desk. He pushed one of the buttons now hoping that Ludwig would come. Within a minute, Ludwig entered the study.

"You rang, sir?"

"Yes. Yes, I did. I wanted to ask you a question, Ludwig. I got so disoriented these last few days, I don't even know what day it is."

"Today is the twenty-third," the butler said.

"The twenty-third? And what day of the week is it?"

"Friday, sir."

"Friday?" Shannon cried, dismayed. "Are you sure of that?"

"I am, sir. It is Jenny's day off, and Jenny is off on Fridays. But I will check it just to make certain."

"No, no," Shannon said. "Don't do that. I'm sure that you are right."

Ludwig walked to the narrow table next to one of the leather armchairs and lifted the silvery lid from a dish that Shannon hadn't touched. He lifted the tray.

"You did not eat your lunch, sir. Was there something wrong with it? Could I fetch you something else?"

"It's all right," Shannon said. "I wasn't very hungry. I—I have been studying. I have a lot of catching up to do."

"I understand, sir. Is there anything else you wish?"

"No, Ludwig. Thanks very much."

"Very good, sir," Ludwig said. He disappeared as silently as he had come.

Shannon walked around his desk and threw himself into an armchair. The room was dark. One lamp burned on the desk. He had never bothered peering behind the curtains that covered one of the walls.

So it was Friday, the twenty-third, or the sixteenth day of his sojourn in the Purgatory Zone. During the first fourteen days of his stay, he had been more or less a prisoner and unable even to try to make a get-away. Now that he had achieved a modicum of freedom, his chance to return was past. It seemed so fateful. And so sad.

Sad? Why should he feel sad?

He mulled about that for a minute and concluded that he viewed the Kibbutz Zone through different eyes these days. Kibbutz had a friendly aspect. Mysterious? Yes. But no more so than Purgatory. The mystery of Kibbutz came from his retrogression. The people there saw things he didn't see. They knew things he didn't know. The Kibbutz Zone radiated kindness. It was a kindness wrapped in toughness, it occurred to him. Kibbutz folk did not believe in coddling you, exactly. But that pervasive sense of violence was absent from the air of Kibbutz whereas the atmosphere was full of it here.

He found it difficult to believe that James P. Schuster had really killed him in that Time Van—much less could he believe that all the Time Vans existed for one purpose only: to eradicate the retrogrades.

But how could he make sure of that unless he returned?

And how could he return unless they still monitored the spot where he had landed.

I'll just have to try. Trying can't harm me. They may still be monitoring. You can never know for sure.

He made a mental note to ask Ludwig about the availability of a car. Could he even operate one of those fast cars they used in this zone? And he would need maps of Phoenix and its vicinity. He needed something to guide him to that spot beneath the speedway where he had materialized suddenly sixteen days and a night ago.

Shannon felt good about that decision. He rose and stretched, thinking that he might be nothing more than a disembodied spirit, but his body was still stiff from sitting at a desk too long. Why live in the lap of luxury unless you made use of it? So thinking, he went off to the exercise area of his spacious quarters to take a swim in the marvellously azure pool.

27

Three hundred young men and women assembled the next evening for Shannon's "return party," as Janet had dubbed the elaborate affair. As the evening began to swing, most of these "close friends" of Shannon were in the ballroom of Janet's sumptuous domain. Seated on a comfortable armchair against a wall, Shannon watched the color and the glitter and listened to the roar and hiss of people talking. The sound recalled an ocean surf, but Shannon was not calm. Tension was building in his body as he waited for his chance to slip away.

Magnificent chandeliers illuminated the hall, their lights reflected from a ceiling made of mirrors. Behind walls made of some sort of soft yet translucent material coils and swirls of rich color moved in ever-changing and never-repeated patterns.

The young people drank and talked and moved about. Waiters and maids, in black and white respectively, walked among them carrying trays with glasses and with little snacks. The room was getting hot despite the ventilation.

Red was rising to the cheeks of the ladies, and the men were dabbing beads of sweat from their tanned foreheads. The drinking was getting serious. Here and there laughter roared and shrieked beyond control.

Shannon glimpsed Janet at last. She came toward him dressed in a bright, red gown. Her eyes gleamed from a drug.

"Are you enjoying yourself, Ra-ra, my dear," she asked.

"Very much so," Shannon said. He gestured toward the couch where he had been sitting. "I was just taking a little rest."

"You should," she said. "Don't overexert yourself. The doctors thought that you were in excellent condition, but I'm not sure that I agree." She patted his arm maternally. "Is the party helping?" she asked. "Is anything coming back?"

"I think it's helping," Shannon said. He did not want to disappoint her. She was a nice, well-meaning woman. "Here and there, as I talk to people, I'm getting a glimmer or two."

"Really?" she cried, evidently pleased. "That's very nice. Isn't it nice to see how many friends you have?"

"Yes," Shannon said. "It's reassuring."

"Well, my dear," she said, patting him on the arm again, "enjoy yourself. I came by to say good-night. I'm going out to dinner. It's your party, after all, and I don't want to be in the way."

"Thank you again," Shannon said. "And have a nice evening. And really," he added, "thanks for everything."

Janet's drug-bright eyes gleamed up at the warmth of his tone. She stepped up to him and pecked a kiss on his cheek.

"Dear boy," she said, "don't mention it."

Shannon watched her walk away across the room, a splash of bright red. She stopped to exchange a word with people here and there. Then she was gone.

Shannon checked his watch. He had a lovely time-piece now, a glittering, narrow object. A pure, black oval formed its center. Silvery digits pulsed in its depths indicating the time, the day, the date. He had found the watch in a drawer. The time was a shade after eight. He decided to give her twenty minutes or so to get away from Hazienda Towers before he acted in his turn.

He sat down again.

If he could believe his aunt, he had a lot of friends, but most of the people in the room had not even bothered to say hello. They were strange and tortured by boredom—or so it had seemed when he had mingled with the guests a little earlier. They had asked him one or two questions, had clicked their tongue, had uttered phrases of commiseration. Then after an awkward silence, the talk had returned to the concerns of Beautiful People again in cluster after cluster. What did these people talk about? They talked about other parties, about trips around the world, about the scandalous vices of people not immediately present. They suggested strongly that Shannon might really be in purgatory—a place where everyone was always under pain or pressure or bored to tears, even the Beautiful People at the top of the hierarchial heap.

He glanced at his watch again, but no time had passed. Restlessness gnawed him, and he stood up.

Encircling Janet's apartment was a glass-enclosed space she called The Gardens and Shannon thought of as a balcony. The space was subdivided into secluded areas by trelliswork supporting a thick growth of vines. Wicker chairs and tables stood out there amidst flower beds and miniature trees and gigantic potted plants. The Gardens could be entered from various points, including the ballroom where Shannon now found himself. He headed for the glass doors to his right nodding to people vaguely. He was the guest of honor, but he wasn't really needed. Out there he could sit by himself and brood away the twenty minutes left him before his departure.

A few of his three hundred friends had come out on the balcony. They stood in two's and three's and watched the magnificent view of Phoenix from the top down—a hundred lovely buildings bathed in light, slender towers,

spiralling constructs, glittering cable-ways carrying pendulating transport-gondolas; and far down beneath them a
carpet of lights where lesser mortals lived. It was dark in The
Gardens and the view through the enormous, concave panes
of glass was clear.

Shannon moved to his left, away from the clustering of
guests. He was about to slip into another subdivision of the
balcony when he felt a hand on his arm.

"Here you are, Ravi. I knew that I would bump into you
sooner or later. I put myself here, in the shadows. I guessed
that you'd soon tire of the rabble and seek sweet solitude."

The speaker was a man in his forties, and one glance
sufficed to show that he was not one of the Beautiful
People—or at least he wasn't dressed like one. He wore a
white sweater with a round collar and over that a woolen
jacket with leather patches at the elbows. He held a pipe in
one hand. He had a long, narrow face and eyes that seemed
to be on fire with some kind of zeal.

"Janet did not invite me, by the way," the man said. "But
when I heard that all of your friends were coming, I decided
that I must come too. Presumptuous of me, I suppose, but
there you are. By the way," he said, gesturing with the stem
of his pipe, "your security people are quite lax. I just
marched in. 'Professor Siegel,' I said. I gave them one of my
famous stares. They didn't dare to question me. I might have
been a kamikaze for all they knew. It must be my eyes. I
intimidate people, don't you think?"

The man's eyes did have a certain power. Among the
guests Shannon had met this evening, Professor Siegel stood
out. He had something—a quality of personality rather than
just glitter. Nevertheless, Shannon had no yen for conversation at the moment.

"I'm glad that you could come," he said, moving on, but
the man stopped him again.

"Not so fast, my dear Ravi," the professor said. "Don't
give me the brush-off. It's not polite, for one thing. And I
was your mentor, after all. I don't believe that you have
really lost your memory. That's a convenient story, but

patently untrue. Are you angry with me? Do you resent my sending you into the trenches? Is that it? You should be grateful. The experience must have been . . . enlarging, shall we say?''

Shannon felt a stir of curiosity.

"I don't know what you're talking about," he said. "My loss of memory is genuine. I don't remember you."

"Fascinating," the professor cried, eyes flashing. "Simply fascinating. You know," he said, "I could hardly wait to see you. I've been wondering for weeks what you'd be like when you came back. This was the acid test, my friend. When I heard that story about your amnesia, I guessed that you had failed—but I wanted to see for myself. 'Perhaps it's just a ruse,' I told myself. 'He is using that as camouflage,' I said. I waited for you to call. But you didn't call."

"I wonder if you could do me a favor," Shannon said.

"A favor? What favor? To get out of your precious life?"

"No," Shannon said. "Just as a favor, take me at my word. Pretend that you believe me—even if you can't. And tell me what this is all about."

The fiery eyes looked at him for a moment.

"You really don't know?" Siegel asked.

"I do not," Shannon said. "But there is no way that I can prove that. If I knew something, I could prove that. But I can't possibly prove my own ignorance."

Professor Siegel regarded him for a silent moment. From the ballroom now came the sound of music. The band had arrived and dancing had begun. Siegel's face mirrored a process of thought. He seemed to be debating the truth or falsehood of Shannon's statement; his bright eyes sought for clues in Shannon's face.

"I am the one who sent you off," Siegel said at last. "I'm the one who urged you to find out what life was all about— the life of the exploited masses down in the trenches, down on the battlefields of the real world."

"Why?" Shannon asked. "Why did you urge me to do that?"

"I had hopes for you."

"What kind of hopes?"

"You are a wealthy man," Siegel said. "You are fabulously wealthy. And I always thought that you had the talent and the will to dominate this society some day—and once in power, you might transform it. You've always had the talent and the will—not to mention the means. What you've always lacked is fire, revolutionary fervor. I hoped to ignite you. That's why I urged you to find out how people lived. On the other side."

"Revolutionary fervor?" Shannon asked.

"That's right. Nothing will ever change in this wretched country until a leader rises from the BP class and puts himself in the vanguard of the revolution."

"And you thought that *I* would be that man?" Shannon was genuinely surprised.

"Perhaps I still do," Siegel said. "You really don't remember, do you? It's too bad, in a way. You had become enlightened under my tutelage. Now we will have to start all over again. Otherwise nothing has changed. You still have the makings of the iron man—he with the iron broom."

"The iron broom?"

"A broom to sweep across this land, a broom to sweep away the filth, the scum, the decadence."

Siegel's eyes burned in the semi-darkness of The Gardens. Shannon felt contrary emotions. Ra-ra was more than he had seemed to Shannon. The man of power? All those books of history in Ra-ra's study now had an explanation. *Perhaps this is what I was meant to do. Lead a revolution . . .* Echoes of his own readings of history sounded in his mind: great battles, cracking banners, and the movements of great men on the stage of the world. It was tempting to imagine himself the master of this society, transforming it, molding it . . . If he had the power, he could remake the Purgatory Zone in the Kibbutz model.

The thought amused him. Had he left the Kibbutz Zone only to create it elsewhere? By the use of power? How?

"How would I go about it?" he asked.

"In ten years or so," Siegel said, "you'll control Desirium. Did anybody tell you that? The Shannon family is extensive, but you're next in line. You will control the drugs. And drugs are the real hinge of power. Nobody knows that yet. You might be the first; you could exploit that vast potential, you could rule by drugs alone, you could—"

"Ra-ra," cried a voice. "I found you at last." A woman wearing a flowing flimsy, silky gown rushed toward them from the glass doors leading to the ballroom. She came in a cloud of perfume. "You must excuse me," she said to the professor, "but I simply have to talk to Ra-ra. Come along, darling," she said. Taking Shannon by an arm, she half-led, half-dragged him away into another part of The Gardens.

Shannon followed her without protesting, overcome by surprise. She was Lilly Waterburg. She moved with purpose, one arm slung into his. They traversed several subdivisions of The Gardens, brushing against miniature trees and the leaves of giant potted plants. Then she turned and made for a door. She pulled Shannon into a room. The door closed. Mild light shone along the edges of the ceiling. It was a bedroom with a huge round bed—another huge round bed.

"Ra-ra, darling," Lillian said huskily. Then she embraced Shannon. Her parted lips sought his. Her body pressed against his body, and he could feel the outlines of her figure beneath the flowing robes.

Suddenly and debilitatingly, almost like that pulse of pain that he had felt inside the little tank, Shannon experienced sexual desire. Blood rushed up and made a veil behind his eyes. She sensed his mood and pressed herself against him, she pressed her midriff in little pulses, imitating copulation. Still kissing him with a fierce, passionate tongue, she reached down, placed a hand over each of his buttocks, and pressed him against herself. Meanwhile she moaned, she growled. Then, as her passion grew, she opened her mouth wider; her growling took on a threatening intonation, and her teeth began to grope.

Shannon disengaged himself forcibly. He retreated from her, breathing hard. He felt an unreasoning terror. She had ignited him to lust; his body was a single, searing flame. The erotic wafts of her perfume surrounded him like a cloud. The very possibility of intercourse, right here, right now, without delay or waiting or ceremonies of any kind whatever except to bare himself from the waist down—that possibility alone knocked his breath away. She was Lillian—and unlike the Lillian back home, this woman heaved with a fervor as intense as his own. Yet he was afraid, afraid to lose his life. Why? He did not understand his own emotions.

Halfway across the room, Lillian was disrobing. She worked matter-of-factly, as if she could set her passion aside momentarily the better to satisfy it, the sooner to enjoy it. Swiftly she removed layers of silky stuff until she stood in bra and panties. She reached behind her back. The bra came off, her breasts spilled out—long, pointed breasts with stiff dark nipples. She wiggled out of her panties. They dropped to her ankles. She stepped out of them. They lay on the dark carpet, a patch of wrinkled white next to her heaped gown. She ran to the bed and laid herself down, knees up but wide apart. She placed her hands over the dark pelting of pubic hair. She rocked her buttocks; she thrust her pelvis.

"Come *on*," she cried when Shannon still did not move. "Rape me again, sweet Ra-ra. I knew it was you all along."

Shannon stared at her. She moved her body seductively. She spread her knees wider apart. "Come *on*," she called again. "Come on you brutish raper. Tear me apart."

Shannon made a move toward her, yielding to her command, but then he stopped himself.

"You were going to let them execute me," he said huskily. "In the electric chair."

"So what?" she said, still rocking and still thrusting. "If the others hadn't heard me scream, you would've strangled me, you beast. Come on, come *on*, I want to *do* it."

What harm could it do? Shannon was more than willing and nerves twitched madly in his loins. He reached for his belt. He slipped off his luminous pants and shorts, brushing them down in a single movement. Lillian moaned again with expectation or from the pleasure she caused herself with her pressing hands. He advanced toward her, roused beyond endurance, and looked down on her body spread out before him, breasts flattened, nipples like tiny towers.

For a second he looked at her. Then with a shudder he turned away. He slipped into his pants again.

No, he said to Raver. *No,* he told himself, as forcefully as he was able. *No, no, and no again!*

Lillian was unaware of his decision. She sat up just as he reached the door. "Hey," she cried, and her voice was sharp with anger and disappointment. "Hey! Come back here you son of a bitch. Come *back*!" But Shannon was already gone.

THE TRAVELLER

28

By ramps and spiralling skyways, Shannon drove toward
the western gates of Phoenix. He guided a long-slung, mus-
tard-colored, glistening, and powerful roadster rolling on
huge, wide tires, their tops even with the level of his hood.
The sports car made a low, rumbling noise—the purring of
a giant cat.

Shivers still ran across his skin, but Shannon was calmer
now. A dissident voice inside his head still bitched and
moaned and told him what a fool he'd been. Having tasted
sharp arousal, his body urged him to recall that vision of Lilly
Waterburg spread naked on the bed, a fruit trembling to be
picked. He silenced the voice and put aside the image time
and time again.

Why had he refused a pleasure freely offered in the Purgatory Zone—a pleasure that his Lillian back home had
steadfastly refused him. He was not entirely sure. In that last
moment, his knees already touching the bed, ready to yield to
her urgent calls, a feeling of disgust had caught him, a touch

of nausea, a whiff of James P. Schuster's soap. Her face had made him bolt—her wanton expression, the roll of her eyes beneath closed lids, her lips parted in sensuous greed. He had seen a stranger's face, not Lillian's. And in that strangeness he had sensed the threat of destruction.

What destruction? he now asked himself, but try as he might, he found no answer.

After a drive of twenty minutes, he reached the western gate and passed from the city by a way of a tunnel. The sky was overcast but bright this evening. Low-lying clouds reflected the light of the Phoenix dome. Many cars were moving toward the city; Shannon's was one of a few heading out. Cars passed him because he drove very slowly; he was looking for a turn-off ramp. The ramp would lead him down into the Squattings and then out along the same highway that had brought him into Phoenix as a prisoner of Benny Franks.

Then the turn-off loomed up ahead, a green sign with white letters. He went down and soon drove between miserable shacks and shanties. Smoke curling low across the road, like fog, reflected his headlight beams. He saw glints of lights here and there and guessed that they were candles.

Then he found the road and headed out.

As the road began to sing beneath his tires, he felt the onset of doubt. Phoenix's reddish dome fell farther and farther back. Ahead lay darkness and uncertainty. Would he even find the spot where he had landed? And if he did, would those bums still be there? And even if the bums had moved, would the Kibbutz Zone still be watching the spot. If they didn't see him, they couldn't fetch him back.

I really don't know why I am doing this, he thought. *I've got it made now, finally. Or at least I had it made.* He was thinking of Professor Siegel whose words had promised future greatness and the exercise of power . . . and of Lilly Waterburg who had offered him the pleasures of her body.

It's not too late yet. I could always give her some kind of explanation . . .

Despite such thought, he went on driving. He was afraid and he was gambling—but he simply had to try to reach the Kibbutz Zone again . . . if for no other reason than to look back at the Purgatory Zone from that perspective. Was he alive or dead? And he longed to look at Lillian—not the one he had just left but the other one. Her radiance and pool-like eyes now seemed almost beyond belief—like a remembered dream.

As he moved from the city, the darkness grew around him, and when the lights of the late George's eatery and filling station appeared in the distance, they seemed unusually bright, threatening. Shannon increased his speed. He zoomed by the place without even looking at it, fearful in an irrational way that if he looked he might be seen. Peek-a-boo. The car sped away into darkness.

Two kilometers farther on, he slowed the car down. A wooden fence now paralleled the road at his right hand; he recognized the fence. He pulled the car to the side of the road, turned off the engine, put out the lights.

Silence. The engine crackled. The palms of his hands were sweaty.

Love you, intelligent hand.

A shudder passed over him; a fierce hunger and longing for order and meaning and plain decency rose in him. He wanted to get away from here. The air sweated with fear and violence and lust above this planet. Better to be a retrograde in Kibbutz than a BP in the Purgatory Zone!

He got out of the car, climbed over the fence, and headed off across the field toward the distantly moving lights of the skyway.

If only they're still monitoring. If only they're still watching . . .

Little by little, step by step, he approached the highway. The flimsy BP shoes he wore were soon soaked with the dew of night. He had begun to sweat. Pausing from time to time to catch his breath, he smelled the sweetness of soil.

Nature was nature regardless of the zone of time. But in the distance glowed Phoenix, and in the sky stretched invisible cables filled with tension.

At last he reached the highway and paused to observe. It ran high above him, a triple-decker monstrosity held up by concrete trunks. Was this the spot where he had landed? He didn't know. Schuster had urged him to fix in mind the *exact* spot. But how could he have done that under the circumstances, with those bums attacking.

He peered into the shadows beneath the highway looking for figures, for movement. He saw nothing. Either he had missed the spot or the bums had moved. No. He was further from the city than he had been that night. He took a deep breath for courage and moved forward. He walked toward the city, the highway to his left.

Five minutes later, still walking along, very slowly and carefully, he was suddenly startled by a harsh, raspy voice. It issued from the darkness of that forest of concrete pillars.

"Hey, you," the voice called.

Shannon stopped in his tracks. A sharp itching under his arms marked the emission of fear-sweat. He recognized the voice—and now he recognized the spot as well. *Damnation*, he thought, *I'm not going to make it*. He glanced in the direction where he had fled the last time, eighteen nights ago. Should he run? And then what? Would it start all over again?

Then Shannon saw the skinny figure of a man, the same man: loose trousers and an open jacket; saggy cheeks, whitish stubble, washed out eyes. The man approached and stopped. His body bent into a crouch, he peered at Shannon in the semi-darkness.

"You again," he rasped. "Didn't I tell you to clear out of here?"

"I don't want anything that's yours," Shannon said. His voice trembled with fear. "I just want to wait here for a while. I'm supposed to meet someone here."

His feet itched to run. He didn't think that he could stand here very long. The skinny man exuded hatred. Crouching near Shannon with something in his hand, he symbolized the Purgatory Zone.

"Meet him somewhere else," the skinny man said. "You heard me. Zoom off. My turf is not a waiting room."

"It's not going to take long," Shannon said. "Really," he added. And he hoped despite all evidence that he would be right.

Surprisingly, the little man retreated into the shadows. He walked backwards. His feet disturbed an accumulation of cans and paper litter so that his every step rattled. Then he disappeared in darkness.

Shannon scratched his armpits. He was both hot and cold. Sweat stood on his forehead, yet his teeth tried to rattle; he bit down on them. He listened. He found it difficult to believe that the skinny man would yield so readily. The last time . . . *Maybe he is alone this time*. The thought reassured him.

A minute or two passed, one or two very long minutes, a painfully long time, time enough to sharpen Shannon's doubts. How long could he stand here, waiting? Waiting for what? If they had really killed him in that Time Van and if this was really purgatory rather than the Purgatory Zone; if, as he had read somewhere the day before, everything he saw and heard was nothing but the play of mind, his soul's imagination running riot—then he might stand on this spot forever or until those other bums returned from their scavenging expedition. What foolishness. Nevertheless he waited. Deep down, far deeper and far more obscured than it had been in that little tank some days ago, he felt a kind of certainty and reassurance. He tried to reach that point of stability. He groped about in the darkness of his own feelings, but then events burst all around him and he was swept back up to the surface of the immediate, the here and now.

He heard a ragged cry from many throats and saw shadows leaping from the ground all around him. Objects flew through the air, glittering as they caught the light. Something struck him on the side of the head with such force that a thousand fireflies exploded. Something drove against his

knees. He pitched forward. He pitched forward with his arms
flung out toward a figure wielding a broken bottle. Pain
stabbed at his neck. Blood filled his mouth as he tried to
scream. He choked. Blackness rushed toward his head. His
eyes rolled. He floated very slowly now, sideways, toward
the ground, crumbling, dying.

29

He lay in darkness for a long time, not daring to move. He
was on his back, his hands by his side, and it seemed that he
was naked. The air reeked of James P. Schuster's shaving
soap, but the smell was clear and sharp now, not merely the
echo of a smell. He noticed other changes in his awareness as
well—a sharpness and a focus. As he explored the feeling, he
sensed a nearby presence. It was a body in another room, a
body in a bent position, peering at an instrument. He couldn't
see the body but felt it as a clustering of heat and as a play of
millions of impulses, traceries of electrical messages that, in
the aggregate, sketched a figure, leaning, peering. Then the
figure moved. A door opened and sharp light fell into the
room. Shannon blinked involuntarily.

"Welcome back," James P. Schuster said.

He was the same ratty-looking fellow Shannon had seen
here better than two weeks ago and, more recently, at Camp
Bridges somewhere near Phoenix—over there, across a skin
of time. Schuster was "opaque." Shannon did not know
what he meant by that observation, but he was certain that he
soon would. He sat up and noticed that he was not attached to
any wires now. The metal construct hung above him.

"You got me back in the nick of time," he said to
Schuster. "A bunch of bums were just about to kill me."

James P. Schuster smiled. "We aim to please," he said.

Shannon swung off the cot. There stood the barber chair,

the mug, the brush. The room was still as grimy as on the day that he had left, but he didn't mind dirt now. He had seen real filth—over there.

"I wonder if I might borrow some clothes," he said. "And I'll need some transportation to Zen Richelem. Could you give them a call?"

"You've come back to stay?" Schuster asked. "I could send you to some other zone if you'd prefer that."

Shannon laughed and shook his head. "I might venture out again," he said, "but not until I have a lot more answers. I'd like to know a lot more about this spook machine of yours before I let you shoot me out again."

"I take it that you had a pretty rough trip?"

"Not one I'd want to repeat so soon," Shannon said and laughed again. He felt like laughing. He was so *damn* glad to be back.

"It just so happens," Schuster said, "that we still have your old clothes. And there is a jeep out there that you could use. If you don't mind driving yourself. You might not feel like driving after what you've been through."

"I feel fine," Shannon said. And he did. His body tingled with well-being and he did not even mind the stink of Schuster's soap. "I feel fine—but would you mind? I'd like to get some clothes on."

"Oh, sure," Schuster said hastily, remembering the clothes. He left the room and came back in an instant. He laid a pile of folded clothing on the coat and dropped a pair of boots on the floor.

"Would you mind answering some questions?" Shannon asked, beginning to dress.

"Probably," Schuster said. "You know as well as I do that this is a protected technology. I'm not at liberty to talk about it."

"I don't want to ask technical questions," Shannon said. He unzipped the one-piece jump-suit and, leaning against the cot, slipped into the leg portions of the garment. "How come that you were still monitoring the spot where I entered the

. . . the other zone.'' He did not want to call it 'purgatory.'
"You said two weeks when I left.''

"You were just lucky,'' Schuster said. "Soon after you
left, they lengthened the monitoring period.''

"All right,'' Shannon said, struggling into the upper portion of his suit. "Next question. When I left the other side, I
had a scar across my lip. It was quite a scar. Here.'' He
touched his lip to indicate the spot. "Now there is no scar.
How do you explain that?''

"That question starts to border on the technical,'' Schuster
said. "But I guess it's all right. In this time zone you don't
have a scar. It's as simple as that. In this zone you're subject
only to the laws of this zone. You can't carry things across.''

Shannon laughed. "You're not telling me the truth,'' he
said. "Don't ask me how I know, but I do.'' He wormed his
feet into his boots. They felt comfortably sturdy after those
slippers he had just worn.

Schuster shrugged. "I'm telling you what I am authorized
to tell you,'' he said. "And if you're so sure that I am lying,
you'll soon have it all figured out anyway.''

"What do you mean by that?'' Shannon asked.

"I meant what I said,'' Schuster replied. "Nothing more
and nothing less.''

"One more question,'' Shannon said. "What kind of soap
did you use when you shaved my head?''

"Just ordinary soap.''

"No, it's not,'' Shannon said. "It contains some kind of
drug. Doesn't it?''

"You said it,'' Schuster said. "I didn't.''

"You're very careful, aren't you,'' Shannon said, smiling.

"I have to be,'' Schuster said. "It's my job. Your trip isn't
officially over until you leave this van. While you're on the
premises, I have to follow regulations . . . Are you ready? I
have to get you out of here. Another traveller is coming.''

"Just a minute,'' Shannon said. He finished lacing his
boot.

Schuster was leading him toward the narrow laboratory that led to the lobby when they heard the opening of a door. Schuster stopped.

"She is already here," he said. "We can't go that way. It's another of our regulations. Travellers are not allowed to meet. Here. You can leave this way." He walked past the barber-chair and opened a door next to a dark corner of the room. Shannon hadn't noticed a door there. "Down that hall and out the other end," Schuster said. "And once again, good luck."

"You too," Shannon said. "And by the way—thanks a lot."

"Don't mention it," Schuster said.

Two jeeps stood side by side next to the van. The yellow one belonged to Richelem, the green one came from elsewhere. Shannon drove away, out of Gatosward. The Time Van's circling beam against the sky fell behind him.

Shannon was sure and yet unsure. Vague feelings and intimations moved beneath the level of his awareness, a feeling he had experienced before, in the Purgatory Zone. Something was very right about this night, something still deceived him, something tried to surface; laughter stirred somewhere.

The jeep he drove puzzled him, for one thing. It seemed to be the same vehicle that he had brought to Gatosward eighteen nights ago. The seat had a loose spring. It pressed his left buttock now in the same way as it had then. But what about the cap? A cap lay on the front seat next to him, a simple round cap with a bill of the sort he always wore on very sunny or rainy days. He did not remember bringing a cap. Driving along, he reached for the cap and put it over his recently shaved skull—the skull that Lieutenant Schuster had shaved. Which also cried for an explanation, somehow. The cap fit him perfectly. He took it off and looked at it. The cap was stiff and new. No one's forehead had ever moistened its band. He put the cap on again, sure that it was meant for him, unsure still about the how or why—but also uncaring. Home.

What a wondrously cool and starry night it was. The clock on the jeep's dash indicated twenty minutes after three in greenish, phosphorescent numerals. A great deal of time had passed since his last spèll of consciousness in the Purgatory Zone, since those last moments of murderous tension, a memory already vague, receding, fading . . . Why receding, why fading?

He was still puzzling over them when he noticed an oddity in the sky. He knew immediately that he was seeing Teilhardian phantasmas, and a gladness sprang into his throat. He understood his trip, more or less, even if its details still refused to lock into sharp focus.

The night was velvety and black and wealthy with the diamonds of distant stars. Shannon saw all this clearly and distinctly behind and through the psychic ether stretching like a band across the horizon above the agricultural settlements of which Zen Richelem was one.

The phantasmas resembled a light or shining and yet were also shapes and figures. They were patterns of energies meeting and merging, linking and then separating, now dense and now subtle, now like phosphorescent ocean waves crashing in moonlight against a rocky shore, now like meadows with millions of identically swaying golden flowers, then again like lava flowing over hundreds of dark valleys, then like a hundred-thousand snow-white birds wheeling, dropping and rising against a continent of dark and stately pines.

Shannon sat and stared at the phenomenon. He had let his jeep coast to a halt. The engine idled. The headlights rested on the road piercing a short distance into the darkness. Oddly enought, Shannon was aware of his surrounding. The etherial events did not interfere with his perceptions. He saw the world with his ordinary senses and the phantasmas with an extra sense that he hadn't known he had.

Curious. Very curious.

The images he saw were not so much 'there,' to be seen, as pictures that his own mind formed out of an elemental dance of a new and infinitely maleable world of waves or particles or both. His mind tried to lock this vision into comprehensibility, but nothing could 'freeze' that dance—mountain vistas turned into herds of flaming horses galloping over milky beaches; the horses became forests running across an arctic waste; then again, briefly, he saw merely a sparkling, a flowing, a shimmer and, inexplicably, behind all this ceaseless motion he could still clearly see the night-sky and the stars.

The vision enthralled and fascinated him. He understood now why normal people watched the sky so much, especially by night, never tiring of the spectacle. It was lovely, more lovely than anything he had seen.

Then, slowly, he felt rising up within him an understanding of that energetic process. He felt himself expanding, exploding, and scattering. In another sense it was as if thick, powerful, solid walls were falling with a crash and as if, for the first time in his life, he was truly free.

The experience transcended description, but Shannon knew with sudden certainty that he could never die or lose or fear or suffer pain again as he had in the past. The lose spring in the seat of the jeep still pressed his left buttock irritatingly. The idling jeep exuded an unpleasant, oily reek. He knew that he would still have disappointments, fevers, angers, and struggles, but none of these things would touch him the same way again. The world was still the same—but it had been turned about.

The oceanic feeling faded very slowly, lingering. Shannon sighed deeply. His joy was pain. He noticed that tears had streamed over his face. His nose was running. He didn't have a handkerchief. He never carried a handkerchief. He wiped his eyes with the back of his fingers and sniffed his nose. Then he drove on.

In another kilometer or so, he began to feel the presence of

Zen Richelem. He felt a number of other communities as well, but as he grew stronger or more skilled in the use of this new ability—if it was an ability—he could distinguish Richelem from all the others.

Several things came to his awareness right away. He felt an immense exhaustion in the people of the station, a bone-cracking weariness. His people had been tested to the utmost, and now they were sprawled out and resting. Particles of vision entered Shannon's head, and when he put those slivers together, he formed a view of Richelem's auditorium where all the people were. They were sprawled out on benches or lay on the floor, many with eyes closed. Only a few were circulating through this weary throng; they carried coffee containers and baskets filled with sandwiches, but only a handful had the energy to partake of these refreshments.

The people were exhausted, but they were also glad. A sense of joy pervaded the assembly. They had saved him, Ravi Shannon. They had helped a retrograde to save himself.

How had they saved him—and what had caused their weariness? Shannon was still too far away or too clumsy to glean that information from the tired yet joyous flow of their stream of consciousness, but he understood enough to know that somehow they had shared his trip. Somehow they had watched his doings across that skin of time. He had been right to think that he'd been watched. That recurring dream of his, in Dalton's stinking jail, had been a vision of reality. The people of Zen Richelem had really filled the auditorium during his absence. And somehow they had helped him.

I'll understand it in a minute, in just a minute.

It was strange to think that he was home in Kibbutz once again and no longer a retrograde—stranger still to be so filled, surrounded. He felt himself afloat in an ocean of minds, those of Zen Richelem and those of all the other stations in the valley. They were all awake, despite the lateness of the hour. He would have a lot to learn, Shannon thought; he had catching up to do. He had yet to learn to sail this supple, human sea.

Above him in the night the phantasmas still shimmered, but now he concentrated on the ''voices'' of the people. The ocean of mind he couldn't help perceiving manifested as a thousand voices, a thousand shades of changing feelings—as if the phantasmas in the sky had an internal counterpart. He concentrated on the voices, trying to understand his trip at last. He still did not fully grasp what he had experienced— even as he felt the meaning of this zone.

Yes, he was in Paradise at last, and not just *in* but of it. Like a yawning chasm beneath him he sensed the depths from which humanity had risen to this new plateau, the place of spirit, peace, creativeness where the darkness had been vanquished once and for all. The nature of the universe, he felt, was still occluded, but he saw its meaning better now; he experienced the joy of creation as it unfolded, hid, unfolded . . .

He drove along, moving slowly, distracted by a world of new, subtle sensations, trying all the while to sort through the voices to focus his new powers of perception. Little by little he learned a new way to concentrate. He began to localize, to isolate individual minds, and as he scanned the flow across their surfaces, he picked up a surprising thought.

The people of Zen Richelem sat or lay about exhausted from a ''long night's work.'' A long night's work? Shannon found the thought in several minds, but when he probed deeper to catch the meaning of the phrase, the people shied and laughed as if they had been tickled; they chuckled at his puzzlement; they laughed goodnaturedly then slipped from his mental grasp adroitly and let him search still other minds.

A night of work? Had he been gone no longer than that?

Then, hearing more laughter and catching a few glimpses of thought that people tried to hide from him in a teasing, playful manner, he had a flash of understanding.

Good God, he thought, *I can't believe it.* But even as he thought this, the facts eluded him. *What* couldn't he believe?

Then it seemed as if a spell were breaking. The ocean of

minds began to laugh as one; the ocean danced with hundreds
of joyful waves. Then a single mind rose up from that sea of
minds. It came forth and seemed to take shape, to solidify by
an effort of will. Shannon recognized Benny Franks.

"*Hello Ravi,*" Benny said. "*Welcome to the community.*"

With these unspoken words came a surge of warm emotion
from the people of the station—and not from them alone.
Shannon perceived the echoing of feelings from thousands of
other minds as well; they took part in this event all over the
valley and perhaps even from points beyond. The entire
Kibbutz Zone reached out to him, embraced him, welcomed
him—and it seemed now as if the sky-girding Teilhardian
phantasmas were bursting into ten thousand exquisite flowers of alluring color and exotic shape.

"*Do you understand what happened?*" Benny asked.

"*Yes,*" Shannon said. "*I mean, no, not quite.*"

"*Then listen,*" Benny said. "*Stand by and listen.*"

Shannon then felt—although he did not know how—that a
"committee" was gathering, people with unusual skill in
mind-to-mind communications. They ranged themselves
with Benny in some space that was no specific space. Shannon 'watched' as they too solidified into entities inside his
head, and he recognized Janet Brood, and Clancy Roberts,
and Malcolm Dalton, and James P. Schuster. But where in
that group was Lillian?

Then came a moment—as of waiting. And then, in a single
pulse, Shannon received and absorbed a message.

It took a moment before he conquered his surprise. The
committee had just told him that he had never been away.
There was no Purgatory Zone. There were no zones of time.
The place where he had been was a creation—the creation of
his own mind and that of the minds gathered at the station.
Together they had formed a world in all its intricacies and
had maintained it for approximately six hours. "*You saw the
insides of your mind displayed,*" the committee told him.

"You lived your thoughts and memories and the books that you had read. You saw your fears and your wishes. You played your part and we played ours—in person or disguised. You had a very difficult trip, more difficult than most—but now you're back at last and welcome."

Along with the message came information about the manner in which that world across that non-existent skin of time had been created. In his dreams in Dalton's jail, in solitary confinement, he had seen the people of Zen Richelem sitting about with headsets staring at a stage. The headsets had picked up, meshed, and projected the thoughts of the community. Scenes of the Purgatory Zone had been projected on a screen so that the people could behold the world that they and Shannon were creating. When Shannon had dreamed that he stood on the stage, he had been close to the truth. The people of Zen Richelem had seen his image on a screen.

Shannon was still astonished. No time zones. No Purgatory world. It made sense, of course, now that he knew the solution. Not a few things about his trip had seemed a little strange. He had had trouble thinking, 'over there,' and the story of his sojourn had had some flaws in plot. But if there was no Purgatory Zone . . .

Shannon formed the question that still bothered him: If there were no skins in time, no Purgatory Zone, could his trip have ended any other way than it had? With his return?

In answer he beheld a darkness, a point of darkness in the heart of Kibbutz, and the members of the committee showed him a vision of himself, lying in the Time Van, his body stiff, then arcing, stiff, then arcing. High-voltage currents had pulsed over his body for a number of hours. With each pulse he had been on the point of death.

He had really had an out-of-body experience, the committee told him. His spirit had been driven from his body, had been detached, and in that intermediate state between life and death his mind had been free to live in a world of his own making.

"We could only detach you," Benny said. *"We couldn't*

*bring you back. Only you could make that decision. Had you
not chosen to return, you would have died, within the hour.
And you would never have chosen to return until you had
passed the test.''*

The test. The test. So his trip had been a test—with death
the penalty for failure. It had been a cruel trick, and he
realized that every brightness, even the brightness of the
Kibbutz, had its point of darkness. The past had had its wars
and slaveries, disease and exploitation. And the Kibbutz had
its Time Vans tempting retrogrades to trips into the void. It
seemed an acceptable price to pay for Paradise, Shannon
reflected, but he thought so only because he had succeeded.
But what test had he passed?

The committee gave no answer to his unvoiced query, but
Shannon knew the answer nevertheless . . .

*Hurry home, Benny said. There is someone here longing
to see you.*

She waited for him outside the entrance to Zen Richelem
station. Dark behind her, cutting off the light of stars and the
shimmer of Teilhardian phantasmas, rose the dome.

She radiated with excitement and anticipation, a silvery,
sparkling, and shining in the dark. Her hair, moving in the
breeze, twinkled with ten thousand shiny sparks. Her dark
eyes glowed like jewels hiding fire. Her skin had an irridescent sheen.

He stopped the jeep, got out, and walked toward her. And
noticed that now, like her, he too was aglow.

She reached out for him and he for her; their fingers
touched and sparked. They stood thus for a moment, gazing
at each other. And when they embraced, the light of their
bodies mingled.

FRED SABERHAGEN

☐ 49548	**LOVE CONQUERS ALL**	$1.95
☐ 52077	**THE MASK OF THE SUN**	$1.95
☐ 86064	**THE VEILS OF AZLAROC**	$2.25
☐ 20563	**EMPIRE OF THE EAST**	$2.95
☐ 77766	**A SPADEFUL OF SPACETIME**	$2.50

BERSERKER SERIES

Humanity struggles against inhuman death machines whose mission is to destroy life wherever they find it:

☐ 05462	**BERSERKER**	$2.25
☐ 05407	**BERSERKER MAN**	$1.95
☐ 05408	**BERSERKER'S PLANET**	$2.25
☐ 08215	**BROTHER ASSASSIN**	$1.95
☐ 84315	**THE ULTIMATE ENEMY**	$1.95

THE NEW DRACULA

The *real* story—as told by the dread Count himself!

☐ 34245	**THE HOLMES DRACULA FILE**	$1.95
☐ 16600	**THE DRACULA TAPE**	$1.95
☐ 62160	**AN OLD FRIEND OF THE FAMILY**	$1.95
☐ 80744	**THORN**	$2.75

H. BEAM PIPER

ANDRE NORTON

Classic stories by America's most distinguished and successful author of science fiction and fantasy.

☐ 12314	**CROSSROADS OF TIME**	$1.95
☐ 33704	**HIGH SORCERY**	$1.95
☐ 37292	**IRON CAGE**	$2.25
☐ 45001	**KNAVE OF DREAMS**	$1.95
☐ 47441	**LAVENDER GREEN MAGIC**	$1.95
☐ 43675	**KEY OUT OF TIME**	$2.25
☐ 67556	**POSTMARKED THE STARS**	$1.25
☐ 69684	**QUEST CROSSTIME**	$2.50
☐ 71100	**RED HART MAGIC**	$1.95
☐ 78015	**STAR BORN**	$1.95

ANDRE NORTON

MORE TRADE SCIENCE FICTION

Ace Books is proud to publish these latest works by major SF authors in deluxe large format collectors' editions. Many are illustrated by top artists such as Alicia Austin, Esteban Maroto and Fernando.

Gordon R. Dickson

☐	16015	Dorsai!	1.95
☐	34256	Home From The Shore	2.25
☐	56010	Naked To The Stars	1.95
☐	63160	On The Run	1.95
☐	68023	Pro	1.95
☐	77417	Soldier, Ask Not	1.95
☐	77765	The Space Swimmers	1.95
☐	77749	Spacial Deliver	1.95
☐	77803	The Spirit Of Dorsai	2.50

Available wherever paperbacks are sold or use this coupon.

ACE SCIENCE FICTION
P.O. Box 400, Kirkwood, N.Y. 13795

Please send me the titles checked above. I enclose _____.
Include 75¢ for postage and handling if one book is ordered; 50¢ per book for two to five. If six or more are ordered, postage is free. California, Illinois, New York and Tennessee residents please add sales tax.

NAME_____

ADDRESS_____

CITY_____ STATE_____ ZIP_____

Andre Norton

☐ 12314	Crossroads Of Time	$1.95
☐ 16664	Dragon Magic	1.95
☐ 33704	High Sorcery	1.95
☐ 37291	Iron Cage	1.95
☐ 45001	Knave Of Dreams	1.95
☐ 47441	Lavender Green Magic	1.95
☐ 67556	Postmarked The Stars	1.25
☐ 71100	Red Hart Magic	1.95
☐ 78015	Star Born	1.75

Available wherever paperbacks are sold or use this coupon.

▲ ACE SCIENCE FICTION
P.O. Box 400, Kirkwood, N.Y. 13795

Please send me the titles checked above. I enclose _____ .
Include 75¢ for postage and handling if one book is ordered; 50¢ per
book for two to five. If six or more are ordered, postage is free. California, Illinois, New York and Tennessee residents please add sales tax.

NAME_____

ADDRESS_____

CITY_____STATE_____ZIP_____

Fred
Saberhagen

☐ 05404　Berserker　$1.75

☐ 05407　Berserker Man　1.95

☐ 05408　Berserker's Planet　2.25

☐ 08215　Brother Assassin　1.95

☐ 16600　The Dracula Tape　1.95

☐ 49548　Love Conquers All　1.95

☐ 84315　The Ultimate Enemy　1.95

☐ 52077　The Mask Of The Sun　1.95

☐ 62160　An Old Friend Of The Family　1.95

☐ 86064　The Veils of Azlaroc　1.95

Available wherever paperbacks are sold or use this coupon.

FRITZ LEIBER

FAFHRD AND THE GRAY MOUSER SAGA